Praise for Into E

Rosalind Brackenbury ... is a natural writer who combines fineness of perception with a professional horror of unnecessary verbal encumbrance.
Anthony Quinton, Sunday Telegraph

This is a complex novel ... it contains valuable imaginative insights into the psyche of its heroine and into various aspects of the Israeli character.
Anne Frankel, Jewish Chronicle

Imagination and respect are needed to make such personal use of a country and its actual turmoil ... Rosalind Brackenbury has plenty of both, and goes delicately over dangerous ground.
The Times Literary Supplement

INTO EGYPT

fiction by the same author

A Day to Remember to Forget (1971)
A Virtual Image (1971)
Into Egypt (1973)
No Such Thing as a Free Lunch (1975)
A Superstitious Age (1977)
The Coelacanth (1979)
The Woman in the Tower (1982)
Sense and Sensuality (1985)
Crossing the Water (1986)
The Circus at the End of the World (1998)
Seas Outside the Reef (2000)
Between Man and Woman Keys (2002)
The House in Morocco (2003)
Windstorm and Flood (2007)
Becoming George Sand (2009)
The Third Swimmer (2016)
Paris Still Life (2018)
The Lost Love Letters of Henri Fournier (2018)
Without Her (2019)

INTO EGYPT

by

ROSALIND BRACKENBURY

introduced by

RUTH FAINLIGHT

and with a prefatory note by the author

SANDNESS
MICHAEL WALMER
2021

Into Egypt first published 1973
© Rosalind Brackenbury 1973

Introduction first published in this edition
© Ruth Fainlight 2021

Prefatory note first published in this edition
© Rosalind Brackenbury 2021

This edition published 2021 by

Michael Walmer
North House
Melby
Sandness
Shetland, ZE2 9PL

ISBN 978-0-6489204-9-6 paperback

ERRATA
This edition has been created utilizing a previous edition; thus errors have been reproduced. On page 74, line 15, for *honey white* please read *honey to white*; on page 110, line 37, for *Judao-Christian* please read *Judeo-Christian*; on page 142, line 16/17, for *packets cigarettes* please read *packets of cigarettes*; and on page 160, line 12, for *carpenter's workship* please read *carpenter's workshop*.

INTRODUCTION

In the 1960s, young men and women from what was called the developed world would travel to places with totally different customs and cultures in order to 'find themselves'. At that time, the newly formed state of Israel attracted many such seekers. Inspired by the recent victory of fighters drawn not only from the local Jewish population but also from other countries, and impressed by the socialist idealism of the Kibbutz movement, they were prepared to spend months of their lives working in agricultural settlements to help build the new society. But that was another era. Attitudes to Israel changed completely. One reads this book (first published in 1973) with rueful nostalgia.

It is September 1962 when we meet Jo Catterall, the protagonist of Rosalind Brackenbury's third novel, on a Turkish cargo boat sailing from Barcelona to Haifa. A nineteen-year-old middle class English girl with no apparent connection to Judaism, something impels her to visit Israel. She is attracted to a fellow passenger, Gilbert, a young Israeli of Algerian origin returning home from a trip to Europe, who invites her to visit his kibbutz near the Egyptian border, and she accepts. He begins to teach her Hebrew and educate her about recent history: not only local, but also what has been happening in the larger region, such as the defeat of French colonialism in North Africa. He is impressed by how serious she is about learning these things, and by how hard she is prepared to work in the fruit groves. One of the young kibbutzniks gives birth, and there is a general assumption that Jo and Gilbert will become a couple, but she does not want their relationship to develop further. She is only at the start of her own voyage of self-discovery which covers the next ten years and makes this novel into a *bildungsroman*. She tells him that she wants to see more of the country, but half-promises to return. Her first destination is Jerusalem, but before arriving there she decides to investigate the artist colony of Safed. At a guitar performance she meets Rowan Rattigan, a young Australian woman at the start of her hippie world pilgrimage, and Zvi Mosseri, a professor from the Hebrew University whose name had been given to her in London by friends of her parents.

Zvi has the reputation of a radical and a trouble-maker. But by comparison to the people at the kibbutz and the Safed bohemians, he and his wife represent a familiar stability, and Jo is glad to accept their invitation to stay with them in Jerusalem. His questions about her view of the world and motive for coming to Israel make her realise:

> "I stand apart, I listen, I judge, I am looking for right and wrong, black and white, the absolutes which I must have come here to find."

He labels her an idealist, she calls him a cynic. Through Zvi she discovers an entirely different aspect of Israeli society. He tells her that he works with a group of Palestinians and Israelis trying to improve relations between the communities. One evening he takes her to a concert and, after a message is delivered to him in the interval, explains that he must meet someone afterwards and hopes she won't mind waiting. In fact, she finds the whiff of conspiracy exciting. By the time he has promised to return the place is almost empty, but through the glass doors she sees Zvi still standing on the theatre steps. Then suddenly a large car mounts the pavement, knocks him down and speeds away without stopping, leaving him with a broken leg. She rushes outside and waits with him for an ambulance, quite sure that this was not the accident he insists it must be.

The incident has rattled her; with no explanation to Zvi (nor to the reader), Jo returns to the kibbutz. She soon makes Gilbert understand that she has no interest in marriage, even though she still agrees with the communal ethos of this society and is glad to be accepted by it. But it is not clear how much time passes before she leaves Israel, nor what else she does before integrating back into London life. She qualifies as an infant teacher and for a few years lives with Francis, an interesting but difficult medical student, the sort of man her parents might well expect her to marry. She broods:

> "At some point in my life I found that I wanted to rid myself of the split vision, the good on one side, the bad on the other; ever since childhood I have searched for a way out of causality".

Then Francis disappears; she learns that he went back to his parents' house and killed himself. She contacts his analyst, Dr. Vidler, and they each absolve the other of responsibility for the suicide. "I am alone and in the present," she thinks. "That is the reality now."

It is ten years since Jo's previous, and only, visit to Israel, and she is on her way to Jerusalem, being given a ride from Eilat to Beersheba by an Israeli soldier, his Russian wife, and their two children. Jo and he talk for the entire journey; he explains that his English is so good because he had been imprisoned twice by the British when they governed Palestine. Ten years ago he was a member of the Irgun Zvai Leumi, an organization that later transitioned from a terrorist group to a political party. He managed to leave it, but still wanted to protect his country, and had fought with the army in the past three wars. Jo admires and abhors him: he shares many of the qualities of the kibbutzniks who had so impressed her a decade ago, but she cannot tolerate his opinions about the Arab population and Islam. For a time there is tension between them, as his wife and children lie asleep in his van, but before reaching Beersheba where they will part and go their different ways – he to his settlement, she to the bus-station and on to Jerusalem - he is smiling again.

Gilbert, Zvi, Francis, Dr. Vidler and even the Israeli soldier, are all significant influences on Jo's life. The fact that she is the only important female character in the story might be a sign of the period when this fascinating book first appeared. But it well displays the fine psychological perception, and the literary sensitivity and skill, which Rosalind Brackenbury has continued to demonstrate in her subsequent work.

RUTH FAINLIGHT

London, March 2021.

PREFATORY NOTE

It's a strange time to be re-publishing a novel I wrote in the early 1970s about Israel/Palestine. I've changed, and the world has changed, and yet, re-reading what I somewhat naïvely wrote all that time ago, I don't discount some of the insights I had at the time, though I now think that the theme of a privileged English person setting out to discover 'the world' and therefore herself, has to be an outmoded one. It struggled on through the idea of the 'gap year' in which students went to third world countries, so-called, to build houses, dig fields and so on, probably not very usefully. It does seem to me now an extension of the colonialist past, in a watered-down form. My own father commented rather caustically, when I told him I was working on a kibbutz, that I hadn't seemed very keen on digging the garden at home, so why did I have to go to another country to do it? He had a point. (I wasn't so keen on doing housework, even in a kibbutz, and my only remaining sentence in Hebrew fifty years later is "I don't want to wash the floor...")

But I—and my protagonist, Jo Catterall—needed to discover a different world by working in it, immersing ourselves in it and on the way absorbing its values. My friend Helen and I, in real life, were enthusiastic Zionists when we reached Israel, as is Jo in my book. Buoyed up by the theme from *Exodus* and enchanted by the bronzed kibbutzniks we met—all those wonderful tanned legs—we were ripe for indoctrination.

Israel, when I first went there in 1961, only thirteen years after the end of the war, was still trying to be 'the good place' that it had set out to be. But the contradictions were all in place. You couldn't help wondering, why all those empty stone houses, falling into ruin? In the novel, Jo asks the question about the abandoned houses of Safed. She watches the Arab man who is captured by the kibbutzniks and kept locked in a room. She asks the questions—naïve, yes, but probably essential—and receives varied answers from the people she meets.

Any insights I learned at the time about history, the War of Independence, the Nakba, the events that created the problems Israel/Palestine experiences today, came from a meeting with the peace activist, journalist and one-time Knesset member, a friend of my cousins in London — Uri Avnery. On a hot afternoon in a café in Tel Aviv he sat us down, my friend and me, and told us the truth as he saw it. It changed our minds, then and forever, and if my unwitting foray into Israel that year had any value, it was to have met him, and paid attention. Maybe he liked having two eager young women listening to him. Maybe he had nothing else to do that afternoon. I'll never know. But he changed my mind, and so changed the course of the book I eventually wrote, telling me the inside story of the absent house-owners of Safed as well as of the Arab man locked into the kibbutz house, the scene with which my novel opens.

ROSALIND BRACKENBURY

June 2021

Time past and time future
What might have been and what has been
Point to one end, which is always present.
>T. S. Eliot, 'Burnt Norton'

Fear not to go into Egypt
>Exodus

1

Where the different patterns of plough curl back to back a man stands at the parting place and hesitates. Against the dark red earth and the evening sky that is like the dark dust upon a plum, he is white, an easily picked target. He huddles upon the earth, moving quickly yet imperceptibly, he scuttles, his head ducked. From the smallest shrub and stick long shadows pour across the earth. On the western horizon the sun lies in a stripe of fire, blinding whoever might look in that direction; there is no target from the east, no seeing a man moving fast as a swallow against that blazing sky, no choosing cloth from dust nor hands and face from the brown earth. The sentry at his hut door turns against the wind to light a cigarette, lifts his head briefly to suck smoke and see glass on a far window burn with the sun and go out; his head in the sunset light is a shining blond cap, touched with red. He goes into the hut to check the time and tune in to the news. In spite of deodorants, toothpaste and after-shave brought from home, he knows himself to sweat and stink like an animal. He has come to hate this place, this indefinable border stuck between field and bare field, in which he must interminably wait. His friend gets a little melon out of a paper bag and slices it neatly in half, and they eat, smiling silently with fatigue, using little plastic spoons. The news comes in, first from Kol Israel, then in Arabic from Cairo. Thesis, antithesis, and then the burst of irrelevant music; they have heard it so many times before. Outside the evening darkens suddenly, without warning. The sun has dropped behind the land, the western sky is suddenly green. Outside, the furrows run like ink lines. It is hard running on plough on the Israeli side, for the plough has gone deeper, tilling more than the surface. He feels the difference beneath his feet; but it is only a short stretch, seconds later there is the shelter of a small orchard, the trees just tall enough to hide him; beyond there is the blunt stump of the water tower, blue white in concrete; beyond that an open field, then the black line of eucalyptus trees, then the road. A yellow light goes down the road, switched on and off and on again by the passing trees. There is no other traffic. At the centre of the kibbutz whiter light pours from the windows of the dining-room, where they are all eating. He stands beside a little tree and feels its hard fruit like a small grenade in his hand. There is none ripe enough to eat, nor even to quench his thirst with a few drops of juice. He rubs his eyes that are sore and gritty from sun and dust. His skin feels like the dried skin of a fruit that has been thrown away. From the field beyond the water tower he hears the sudden noise of a goat disturbed, a harsh agitated bray, and he crouches, preparing to run. There seems to be a near crunching of little hoofs, a breathing somewhere close; goats patrolling like guard dogs. And as he moves, everything changes. There is a sudden light, noise, braying, a voice, he is facing into the muzzle of a gun, a boy stands behind it with others at his side, his eyes wide and staring in his face. There is a nightmare of faces, furred and human, a painful searching of light. The barrel of the submachine-gun lifts. It is hard to believe that he will be killed. The man under the orange tree begins to mumble prayers where he is; and the prayers go on, repeated and repeated even as they pick him out and push him along in front of them, a ragged bird blinking in the light. They do not ask him, but pat him carefully with their hands, all down his sides; and he tells them over and over, between the prayers, that he has nothing, knows nothing; but they simply peer at him and seem not to understand. Their language spans him like an arch he cannot reach. When they leave him alone, it is at last a relief.

Water dries, land hardens, the line of horizon at morning and evening remains the same. Where swimmers have stood the falling drops have forged rivers in the dust, patterned the red earth, dried and gone. As I move my foot a lizard runs out, is choked with dust, turns and darts back towards the trenches, and beneath my foot the new place scorches the flesh. There are little red spiders struggling up the lumps of dried earth, buried in a crumbling fall as my weight shifts. From a new hole, ants begin to pour upward and out until the place overflows, a jug into which insect life is poured; they fight upwards and fall and are engulfed and begin to struggle again. And the silence is numb, dizzying. A solitary tractor crawls in its cloud of dust. Egypt, marked off only by the white United Nations huts at every five hundred metres, is smooth and tawny as Israel, and empty. I sit at the centre of this landscape of raw earth and whirling hot air, arbitrarily placed. Events have taken place here that I have not seen; I have seen nothing. Behind me, paces away across the burned hillocks, a transistor radio will be whining somewhere, couples will be whispering and drinking coffee behind blinds, the wind will move fragments from the blistered walls. Behind the doors there will be people spread out lax and flat, hands hanging down, waking to this Shabbat afternoon, waking to this stillness. They lie everywhere with the wary relaxation of cats ready to open an eye, the young men on their narrow beds wound in a sheet. Gilbert is asleep down there, his blind drawn down so that only a slit lights the room, a hint of the outside heat; his body spread face downwards, naked except for a pair of shorts, his cheek sideways, flat against the bottom sheet, his hand near it curled, his black lashes sweeping the curve of his cheekbone that were matted with water as he rose from swimming, that sparkled like a hedge under dew, hiding his glance; so that I see him now rising before me like a seal, the smooth black rounded head and pursed mouth spitting water; like an impervious water animal, playing, asleep. I am alone here, I have walked out into the bite of the sun with the nausea of afternoon sleep in my throat, skin caked dry, bones jolted by the thud of steps upon the baked earth, a ringing in the head; once again it is a first excursion out into the afternoon, first cigarette almost stifling, aloneness necessary; it is a first opening of still gummy eyes on a world whose beauty may be relied upon. I am alone, and where he lies asleep, cigarette pack and ashtray at his elbow, sandals kicked aside at the foot of the bed and belt hanging across a chair, there lies a gun. The far tractor turns in the sun, gleams a touch of blue, begins to plough back again, its dustcloud following like a steamer's wake in a bay; beyond it the United Nations flags flutter against a dark sky, and I think that in those little huts I see the uniformed men sigh and open another can of Coca Cola and light another menthol cigarette, check their clocks, feel perhaps some guilt, some lack; look towards Egypt and then back towards me, push back their caps and sigh with helplessness and long for Sweden, Denmark, home. Blond men they are, tall and long-boned, fine gold hairs upon their wrists; they wear beautiful watches with metal straps and their finger nails are cut and clean. Nothing is their fault. But I am going, I am leaving. Today, 20 September 1962, is the last day. The hours move to darker shades of blue, to purple, to twilight again, to the long moonlit windy evening, and will at last be all used up. In the cycle of things there is no other way, only a return; to a safer known world where decisions are no more than the gradual erosions of habit, where reality does not wear the face of a stranger, an old captured cattle-thief of an Arab, in his separate unknown life as real as my thoughts and movements homeward; where I must go, not having found a place in the order of others. The next day is different from the one before. The edges of identity one day blur, the hard separate core of being gone, experience coming unasked to distort the certainties already found; out of the past and out of the future another life approaches, impinges, augurs alarm and change. But the day after that, all will harden, clear and separate again; I will be gone. I lean to trail one arm in the water now and feel the anaesthetic cold fade, the water grow warmer, the arm at last mine again to feel, so that I have to move, immerse the other one, start again; the water is never so cold that one may not eventually feel, the air never so hot that one will not eventually welcome its touch again.

The voices clamour, so that they are indistinguishable. One, two, three more join in. The centre is a solid mass of bodies, voices rising.
    'What's happened?'
    'How did you bring him in? Where is he?'
    'I got him covered with the Uzi and shouted and luckily Dov and Bernard were around and they came over.'
    'And we got him down and locked him in the empty hut.'
    'Where the children used to be, you know, before we built the children's house. He wasn't armed.'
    'Or if he was, he'd thrown it away by the time I got to him. He's still in there.'
    'What's happening? Did you ring the police?'
    'Yes they're coming out from Beersheva.'
    'When?'
    'Tomorrow first thing. There's some special check. I don't know.'
    'What is he, a spy?'

'Are you sure he had no grenades on him, nothing like that?'

'Not when we searched him. I suppose he could have dumped them on the border, or come on reconnaissance. Dov and I held him and Bernard searched. There wasn't anything.'

'What's happened?'

'An Arab.'

'Pesach was on guard and caught him creeping in. In the field beyond the water tower, wasn't it?'

'Could have been planning to blow up the water tower.'

'Or simply rustling a few sheep or goats. They aren't all desperadoes.'

'But one can't take a chance on it.'

'You never know.'

'Of course they'd send one who looked harmless, wouldn't they?'

'I mean, he'd hardly come across with plans for an air raid on Tel Aviv in his pocket.'

'Gilbert!'

'I should think he's probably harmless enough. But then the police will find out. You have to tell them, after all.'

'Where did you say he was?'

'In the empty hut.'

'Let's have a look.'

'Come on, then.'

'Can't he get out through the window?'

'No, we nailed some wood.'

'Aren't you coming? He can't hurt you.'

'No, I'm going to bed early. No thanks.'

'Gilbert?'

'Are you going?'

'Why not? Leila tov. Sleep well.'

'Good night.'

Aren't you coming, where are you going, why will

you not come with us; why will you make me go with you, why must you tell me this. The voices are a perfect chorus, there is none that rises above the rest. It is dark; only teeth and eyes really show. We face the same way and are all of us found wanting.

The ships go out of port, sailing in all directions. In the port of Marseilles, a small old cargo boat called the *Adana*, under a Turkish flag, has put in from Barcelona and is preparing to set out again, bound for Naples, Genoa, Haifa, moving slowly round among ships, cranes, smoky little tugs pulling liners out of harbour. Everywhere against the sky there are cranes dipping, rising, their great black skeletal claws, their hard outlines blurring the line of hills beyond. I am still watching them as we move out into the open sea. The coastline of southern France passes, rocks red in the sunset, the baroque lines of cliffs stage furniture behind the sea. For the sea is quickly all that is real, as dusk falls and the wind grows cooler. This small moving world isolates itself so fast, cutting forward through water; the vague dark bulk still visible, Nice, Menton, Monte Carlo, is the land mass of a world already left behind. We move eastward now. High on the starboard the moon has risen; otherwise there is only dark thick water meeting the night sky. There are perhaps warships, patrol boats; they have been here. I sit about among the lifeboats and numbered crates and coils of rope, thinking of them. Near to midnight our course changes and we turn south, by morning we will be close to Italy. Till then, the lighthouses of France are the only link with an anchored world; immediately, the black sea rolls up against the port holes and away again, tipping the horizon this way and that. The ship moves on in the path of a thousand, ten thousand others, under the moon's eye.

'Vous allez à Haifa, mademoiselle?' On this first night, exchanges are still tentative. Not knowing what to say to the others I stand beneath the railing and see the sea grow purple, then black, dotted with passing lights. Our solid wake of silver is a constant surprise. Silence and the movement of the ship contain me; when there is a movement, a small cough of introduction, I am shocked out of thought. It is an old man who has come to lean on the rail to smoke a cigarette, the man who sat opposite me at supper, blushed and turned away as an aubergine skin stuck inside his tooth. To save his dignity, at supper, he asked me my opinion of Dostoevsky, seeing *Crime and Punishment* beside my plate.

'Vous allez à Haifa, mademoiselle?' We talked a little of literature; I watched the movement of his wrinkled face, the lips drawing back precisely to emit the French language; thought of his generation in Europe; and we talked of Raskolnikov.

'Oui, monsieur.' The existential act; his eyes were moist and grey, his false teeth clicked up and down as he spoke; we spoke of dreams. Now his profile is of a cardinal, a medieval churchman on a medallion.

'You know Israel? You are on holiday? Or have you family there?'

It is hard to say; I tell him that I am on holiday, that it is a long visit, that I know nobody.

'Ah, you will love it. It is the most beautiful country in the world. People are alive there, idealistic, brave. You will see.'

'Do you live there, monsieur?'

'No, not live. I have family there, my son, my sister, cousins. It is my first visit. You see, until recently I had so much work, I am a geologist you understand, it was hard to find the time. Now I am thinking of retiring, of doing less work anyway. Besides, I am an old man. I must see my country before I die, you understand?'

A country of the mind, promised throughout generations, seen between sleep and waking at the beginnings and endings of ordinary days. 'You are Jewish, mademoiselle?'

'No, no, I'm not.'

'Ah, a Christian.'

'Not exactly, either.'

One does not forgive and will therefore not be forgiven. The summer sun streams through the long windows making haloes for bent heads, the smallest girls sob, the staff sit to listen to the sermon, their heads slightly tilted back the better to drink in the words; the whole ferment of feeling stirred and stirred again by each word from the resonant young masculine voice from the dais, so that even the headmistress has deep patches of pink mottling her neck as she stands to announce the last hymn. 'Jerusalem the golden, with milk and honey blest.' Jerusalem; forever entangled, gold, milky, with the specks of dust from those dim windows in the sinking evening sun; and as the music dies away and the voices mournfully shout the last verse, the longing is not for abstract things, not for this religion, but for hands, knees, a beard, a tongue, a solid body, the abandonment to the other which must be there. 'Have you been received by Christ?' And in and out of the mind, quick as a fish escaping, goes the picture of Christ in his long robes and sandals, holding out a tray of sherry and biscuits, like a don's drinks party at home.

'I am sorry I thought—'

'Please don't be sorry.' Over the ship's rail the black waves are always the same, as if time means nothing. And they are all here, packed below deck, the students, mothers, businessmen, children, who have a reason for their journey, something tangible, to justify them in the eyes of the world. 'I only meant—' I doubt if my inarticulate French has conveyed my meaning, I am left with sudden shame. He smokes and stares out ahead of him, an old buzzard wrapped in a scarf, and after minutes, as if I have not spoken, he says, 'You will like it, I am sure of that. It is the finest place in the world.' And I know that he is thinking only of his arrival; that what I say or mean or do not say does not matter at all.

'I'm sure I will.'

'Yes, yes. Ah well, good night, mademoiselle. A demain.' A solitary, old, dreaming man, with Raskolnikov in the back of his mind, unable now to remember before this journey's beginning, or to imagine beyond its end

The first day is still the clearest, for the routine of greeting, comment and conversation has not yet established itself, the sleepwalking from breakfast to lunch to dinner, the stunning weight of the sun and the rocking of the ship and the hot oiled smells below deck and the thirst that sends one back to the bar again, the alcohol that makes each evening hard to remember. The faces are not yet well known, the characters only potential people, presenting a single facet, hurrying past in the passage; eyes still meet each other hesitatingly, waiting for a third meeting, a fourth time of holding a door open, the next chance proximity at the bar. We withhold recognition yet wonder who, by the end of the week, will recognise us. Once Naples and Genoa are past we may see each other as passengers to Israel, at least, but until then there is this reserve, in case he or she may be going ashore tomorrow, never to return, having chosen a holiday in Italy rather than a pilgrimage east. 'You are going to Haifa, mademoiselle?' None of us will waste time upon anybody who is not.

'Would you like a cigarette?' Hours of silence have passed now, or perhaps minutes. The voice that breaks into my thoughts this time finds the English language almost impossible, for each word comes out with a ring of effort.

'Thank you.' I take a French cigarette from the blue packet offered, draw up the flame from a match that is held turned inward, cupped in one hand, as if the bearer is used to lighting matches in a strong wind and keeping them alight.

'May I join you?'

'If you like'

'Do you speak French, Hebrew?'

'French, yes. Not Hebrew.'

'Ah good,' and he laughs, showing a very wide mouth. 'Then I need not break my teeth to speak English. We speak French, yes?'

'Yes.' We sort and choose them carefully, the words, the forms we will use, laying them out in advance like weapons.

'You like it here better than in the bar? I saw you standing out here for a long time.'

'Yes. I like looking at the sea. I saw the moon come up, the first time for years.'

'I too prefer it outside. But you are not depressed? I thought you looked a little nervous.' The French is pronounced with a strange twang, even more noticeable than that of the people of Marseilles the vowels all dropped into the throat. The muscles of language struggle with meaning.

'I was feeling – well, not nervous or depressed, but rather confused, I suppose. I was wondering why I was going to Israel. If there was any point.'

'Why are you going to Israel?' His head moves up abruptly, his face is clear of doubt for a moment, as if he will speak out of impulse; then he lights another match, sees it burn, drops it flaming over the edge and laughs. 'Why do you need a reason?'

'I don't know. Everybody else seems to have one. What's yours? Simply being Jewish?'

'Me? Oh, no, I live there. For me it's the other way round. I have to find a reason to go to Europe. But,' he purses his lips, looks at me with amusement, 'no reason. I just wanted to have a look. So I did. Simple for me, you see.'

'And now you're going home?'

'Yes.'

'Where? Whereabouts in Israel?'

'In a kibbutz. Near Gaza, do you know where that is?'

'No.'

'Near Egypt. Near the border.' He smokes and throws matches and is so laconic that I relax into his contentment with the bare bones of conversation, feeling the silences, the unsaid things carry us on.

'What is it like?' Minutes have passed.

'Questions, questions.' He smiles, again that surprised, mocking smile, 'I think now that everywhere is a little like everywhere else. But it's a good place.'

'In spite of Egypt?'

'In spite of Egypt. It's the same earth, you know. Same land, same farmers. Only we can never go into Egypt, and they can never come over to us.'

He saw her stand at the rail, her arms taut, hands gripping wide apart to support her body, the sway and movement of her skirt as the ship ploughed; noticed a tension in her stance, and her head thrown back once as if in anger or frustration, and heard her sigh. At supper she had sat across the room elbow to elbow with an old man sucking up food, his face close to his plate in case with the ship's roll anything should escape, and then he had seen her aloofness, as the old man turned and smiled and asked about the book that lay wedged between their plates. The dining-room was cramped, hot, the air heavy with cooking smells, the food too greasy for his taste; and he came in late and could only find a seat close to the door, where the Turkish waiter slopped a little meat juice from the tipped tray each time he passed; Gilbert sat with his elbows on the table and his shirt sleeves rolled up, hunching his shoulders to accommodate himself beside the door jamb, and watched the other diners as he ate his stuffed eggplant quickly and mopped a little at the juice. At last he sat smoking and picking at the dessert, and she passed him on her way out, and he saw that the book she carried (against loneliness, against importunate conversation?) was *Crime and Punishment* and that she was tall and rather bony, with a straight cut of hair that swung against her jaw, eyebrows set high and supercilious in the face that turned slightly to acknowledge him, for he had to squash himself even more to allow her to open the door; that same nervousness would not let her give more than a brief nod in his direction. And then, as he sat upon a coil of rope outside and looked up to count the stars, there was the old man again, pottering up to the ship's rail, asking her, interrupting her, talking about Israel, Israel, Israel, as if he knew. Gilbert sat and heard a few words as the wind blew them to him, and dismissed the dream and began to think with relief of the reality. Three months was too long to be away. They would have finished the children's house by now, that he had begun, the plumbing would be in and the new showers, the concrete would be down round the edge of the swimming-pool, Gaston might even have finished painting the new huts for married couples. People could have got married, could have died. The new fruit trees could be bearing fruit, they might have bought the new tractor this month. But who would have changed? Enough, he said, turning to the sea (and there was the old man, the old Jew, 'the most beautiful country in the world', sucking his teeth), enough, I have not changed that much. There had been a letter from Gaston, when he was in London, a letter from a stranger with a stranger's news. Then he had walked in the green parkland at Greenwich and gone into the observatory and stood aloft and looked through that telescope and then – read Gaston's letter. The soft blue-green of grass, rolling down to the Queen's House. London, grey and warm and somehow muted in the early summer light. Young men in their brilliant shirts prone upon the grass, striding with girls, pulling

down flowers. And he sat alone and saw the green
grass stains upon his crumpled trousers and the black
hairiness of his legs above the short pale nylon socks,
and got out Gaston's letter again and read of agricultural implements and irrigation sprays. Somewhere
people worked, sweated, were real; and meanwhile
London passed before him, an insubstantial charade,
yet teasing him and somehow proving him inadequate.
There had been one time, though; when he went to
Stratford-on-Avon and got on the wrong bus and had to
get off to stand at a roadside under vast dark green trees,
amid clouds of gnats, and there was nobody there until
a man came down the road from a turning higher up,
wearing a sacking apron around his waist and driving
before him a lazy herd of cows. He had been at the roadside, his small bag at his feet, his hair brushed, his
trousers and shirt clean and pressed, somewhere in the
middle of England where no tourists came; and there
was this man, switching away flies with a long twig,
heavy-footed in his turned-down boots, wearing a sacking apron tied with string and a dirty striped shirt open
on his chest and a peaked cap perched on the back
of his head, pushed back for a good scratch, swearing
softly at his cows as they went, slap, slap, their bony
rumps rocking down the lane, into the dark and out
into the light, their fragile feet splayed, the mottled
green sunlight making them strange. The man stopped,
or paused in mid-stride, and said something in a soft
voice that needed no answer, that could have been a
greeting, a curse, anything; and on he went, the flap of
his rubber boots, the following swarms of flies and the
splat of runny cows' droppings hitting the tarmac, and
was gone. He, Gilbert thought, was real as Gaston was
real (and the old Frenchman was leaving the girl's side,
creeping away, an old turtle wrapped in a scarf); it was
so everywhere; each place, each English lane and hidden French village that he had passed in the tourist

buses and cross-country trains, contained people to whom it was home. It was true, work was the universal reality. The rest, the monuments, the caravan of exotic people spread across the parks, the glittering Thames, Greenwich, that carpet of culture and luxury across which he was invited to step with bated breath, that was the sham. 'Europe', he would say, to Gaston, to Pesach, 'is like everywhere else. Europe is another man with another cow, going down another lane.' And yet there was something that worried him, making him dissatisfied; possibly it was to do with that girl's aloof little nod and the way she had walked out, an unconscious flaunting, fine cloth, fine bones; and the way she stood alone now at the rail, her head flung back as if she did not care what anyone thought.

'What is it like?' Minutes had passed. Should he tell her, you are ridiculous, should he say, you are asking me to describe my life? A red line of horizon, flimsy little box-houses put together so laboriously, plumbing pipes set into holes, drainage dug, water pipes set underground, their way marked now by the slow greening, the line of life? Machinery, tools, wood, steel, concrete, sand, earth? A small place near the border which has been fought over, where men have died, where there was nothing at all but thirst? Where now there is eucalyptus and fig and water-melon, where we have forced up peaches, oranges, grapes? In England once a lady asked him, politely, in a quiet drawing-room somewhere, and said, 'It must be lovely to have green fingers.' Which was why, now, he almost laughed.

She was not laughing, though, not smiling; but stood apparently thinking hard, a severity in her face softened by unselfconciousness. 'It's so different in England, isn't it. I mean, we can go out anywhere we like. Yet nobody bothers to.'

'You are not afraid of being eaten by Scotsmen.'

'Not any more. I suppose we were once. People are

still afraid of things, other things. But there aren't any borders, nothing definite any more.'

'There is always the sea. To keep out foreigners.'

And she turned her face to him, suddenly animated, and asked, 'What on earth did you think of it? It must have seemed extraordinary to you.'

'England?' One could not explain, there was Greenwich, there were all those monuments; such age, such dirt, such irrelevance. One could not say, I only felt that I was a stranger, but in that lane, in that hidden country place— He said, 'It was nice. Very comfortable, very kind people. Too much rain, though. I am glad to be going home.' And to soften this, he added, 'You see, everybody can only live where he has work to do.' And because she was still frowning, uncertain of being mocked, he laid a hand on her arm where it lay along the rail, found it cold, smiled at her when she did not draw it away. Her bones felt close under the flesh, long and delicate like those of a fine-bred young dog that shivers out of apprehension; and then she moved and shook her head and said lightly, 'How peculiar it is meeting people on ships. It's as if we were meeting nowhere. It has no identity.'

'Would you like to come down and have a cognac before the bar closes? I think it will still be open. I think you are cold. It is not hot at night, not at sea.' In London there were all those girls striding down the streets in their flowery blowing skirts, at once lost and aggressive, or so he thought; and now there remained a sense of sadness, of regret, as he stood by her, that he could not identify. Yet why identify feelings? Why persist in the useless analysis, risk one's self in the endless round of narcissism that was living in the west? There were things to be done, always; there were tasks in his life that were not completed, that had been absorbing. And yet before returning to them he must satisfy some curiosity, assuage some restlessness that his journey had only intensified. He was relieved when she said, 'No, if you don't mind, I think I must go to bed.'

Gilbert Bouknine, born in Oran, Algeria, 4 April 1941. Co-founder of the kibbutz Gan Hagar on the Gaza strip. Fought in the Sinai campaign, 1956, in which he stole a horse from the Arabs. 1963 admitted to the Hebrew University in Jerusalem; 1965 married; 1967 killed at Rafah in Gaza, before Israeli armoured units took the town; buried with military honours in Sinai.

'In the morning we will be in Naples. Would you like to walk round it with me perhaps? We could take a bus, I think, and go out to Pompeii.'
    'And see how a civilisation can be buried in a moment, choked and buried in dust?'

Naples in the early morning is empty, and then suddenly filled with traffic as if all the cars are let out at once, greyhounds screaming upon a clockwork track. Mist still lies above the harbour, veiling Vesuvius, but we climb the steep cobbled streets to meet a sun already strong and clear. There is no time to see Pompeii, as we must be on board again by eleven, and I am relieved that this obligation has been removed.
    Gilbert says, 'I suppose I will not see it ever, now.'
    And I reply, 'They are all dead, in Pompeii. It's in Naples that things are happening.'
    Up a silent back street, away from the lines of traffic, we walk in the cold shadow of long eaves until we come to a monastery, a place of refuge made from a decaying fortress where there is singing behind closed doors and garbage rots in the sun and bright purple flowers grow in clefts above a crumbling statue of the Virgin Mary. The cracked paintwork flakes in the sun, I press my face to the door, strain to hear the singing inside; later I remember the touch of the cold shadow that cuts

across the little square outside, the silence around that singing, behind the far-down traffic noise; I can feel upon my hand the warmed curve of the stone virgin's side, pocked and rough with lichen, grained by the constant wind; something harder to re-create is the presence of Gilbert himself as he appears at that moment, the smell of his sweat after his walk uphill, the bluish shine of his cropped hair in the sun, the moving muscle of his arm beneath the rolled white shirt sleeve as he cups his hands and bends from the wind again to light my cigarette; and how we walk back, carelessly back down the steep stones, tripping over the rise and fall, from light into shade and he tells me of Algeria, where he was born. I know that we sit in the gutter to eat peaches, till an old man comes out of his house to offer us each a rickety chair that hardly balances upon the cobbles; that in the post office where we stand to write our postcards home I watch his hand running the biro marks from right to left, and slip off my sandals to feel the cold of the marble floor a shock to my hot feet. I have diaries to tell me of the time, the place, the exact hour on the exact day. There is a map of Naples to tell me where to walk to find that hidden monastery upon the hill. But these years later, after all that has come between that stone statue, those purple flowers and me, there seems no point in trying. I see later that its point, its worth, was this; our innocence, having not yet arrived.

'Jo?' He pronounces my name like a small explosion, wants to call me 'Joséphine, comme l'Empresse.'
 'Yes?' I sit opposite him, after Naples, at a little table in the bar where we are drinking Cinzano before supper. All around us are books and filled ashtrays.
 'Can you say them now?'
 'Ahat, shtaim, shalosh, arba, khamesh, shesh, sheva—'
 'Shmone.'

'Shmone, tesha, eser.'

'Très bien. You are learning fast.'

'But I can hardly go round Israel just counting things.

'It's a beginning. The rest will come quite quickly. Tomorrow we'll do some basic words and then sentences. You'll be able to speak in no time.'

'But tomorrow we'll be there. And all I'll know will be ahat, shtaim, shalosh.'

He bends to print the letters of the Hebrew alphabet carefully down the side of my page, matches them with cursive, his hand moving slowly and firmly as if he is unused to writing, his mouth compressed in a line of concentration. It is at moments like this that I am struck with unease, seeing a labourer struggling to wield the point of a pen, a yokel, a handsome yokel, a man entirely alien to me, in whom I am interested only because he is a foreigner. From across the bar we are watched by the Turkish barman, his eyes small and hostile, used to watching the uneasy beginnings of affairs. From a side entrance three musicians come in and they tuck their violins under their chins and begin a wailing tune which quickens at last into a tango; they glare at us, as if our absorption is insulting them.

'Dance tonight,' the barman says, washing up glasses, banging them down on the bar top where they skid to and fro in the wet.

'Where?' One of us has to answer, and Gilbert, writing, is impervious.

'In the second-class lounge. You want to dance tonight?'

'Well, maybe.' The musicians move nearer, bend threateningly, like men playing for coins.

'I am studying. Learning Hebrew. Later, perhaps, we will dance.' They screw up their eyes and pout their disbelief, put an end to the tango and begin again their Turkish wail, the untuned violins rising separately.

'Could I have another drink? The same again, please.

Two Cinzanos, with ice.'

The drinks slide across, their pale liquid rocking. 'This money you give me is no good. Only Turkish money now.'

'But I haven't got any Turkish money. Is Italian any good?'

'Turkish money.'

'But we never landed in Turkey, I haven't any.' Angry, I leave the francs and lire in a heap and begin to pick up the drinks and nuts on a little tray.

'Francs this time. Next time, only Turkish money.'

To Gilbert I say, 'It looks as though these are our last drinks.'

'It looks as if we'd better dance. Did you buy him a drink?'

'No, should I have?'

He crosses to the bar, speaks to the barman in a language that is not Hebrew, slips more money across the counter; the barman lets his cheek muscles relax into a small smile and pours some spirit into a tiny glass.

Gilbert says, 'Come on.'

'I didn't know you spoke Turkish.'

'Not really. A few words from a sailor on the trip out, that's all. Do you want a drink, and good health, you know. Come on, we'll dance.'

The three men in the little band lift their chins with a proud jerk, one after the other, tuck their violins more firmly under their cheeks, the leader only apparent from the violent movements of his eyeballs as he urges the others on. I move into the circle of Gilbert's stiff arms like a débutante at a ball who does not know what to do otherwise; sandalled, in our shorts, we begin to dance an absurd tango round the deck, knees bumping frequently, heads held rigid, I think of old films, legs striding from black satin and passionate heads thrown back; our limbs ache from the strange positions, but the music goes on and on.

'Do you think a tango's the only one they know?'

'I don't know. Keep going, you're doing well.'

We hiss to each other from the corners of our mouths as we posture and stamp a travesty of any conventional dance, but the musicians smile, the music grows faster, I feel that we are absurd. At last they draw their instruments from their shoulders, bow and turn towards the bar. The deck tips beneath our feet, chairs scutter across the floor into the fixed tables. 'We don't have to buy them another drink, do we?'

'I think they only wanted somebody to appreciate their music.'

We fall against each other in our laughter, in the confusion of the ship's sudden heave; and then he lets me go as if this were all a mistake, and we walk quite soberly back to our tables and the books.

That clear voice calling out so plainly, 'We don't have to buy them another drink, do we?' He saw the musicians at the bar, the closed faces, controlled after all that wild music; and caught her as she fell across, tripping over a chair leg perhaps, collapsing with exhaustion, into his arms. She was all loose and relaxed after that dance, as if she had wanted to make some absurd public exhibition, flaunting herself and making him look clumsy. There was this extraordinary eagerness to please; she was really trying to learn Hebrew; and then there was the apparently unconscious flouting of all manners or conventions, the blindness and deafness to what anybody might be feeling, the lack of understanding that made him feel at once furious and protective. And it was familiar, this feeling, it was all at once well known and far more intense than it had ever been; it was how he had felt in England. The English had made him feel clumsy, ill-fitting; and had yet appalled him with being able to do this to him without a qualm. He put her away from him quite firmly, but after smelling her breath, her skin, feeling the weight sink against him for a moment in complete relaxation; and led her back to the table. All morning and afternoon they had lain a foot apart on the deck, half naked, their bodies turning a darker shade of brown, their tongues dry with so much talk and smoking, and his head had buzzed with the reception of her thoughts; but their hands had not stretched out to feel, their eyes had hardly glanced at each other's bodies. They had lain with dark glasses on, masked against the sun. And now, he thought, we sit, showered, dressed, in the bar with our drinks, and dance a tango to please some Turkish musicians whom she does not realise she has insulted, and we clutch at each other, and I pretend to laugh, and we draw away again. Disliking the complications, he shook himself involuntarily, and saw her glance. With composed lips she began again, 'Ahat, shtaim, shalosh. . . .'

'Even after tomorrow,' he said, 'I can be there to teach you.' And her look, direct, inquiring was so brilliant – grey-green light eyes, those peculiarly arched brows – that he blushed and felt a recurrence of heat, dizziness, a nausea of excitement in the pit of his stomach that made him afraid.

'What?' It has not occurred that we can make plans that last beyond tomorrow, that we can have the same destination. But I catch sight of the edges of his very full lips trembling, I think, ah, that is it, there is something after all; and it is not simply that he is alone, and a foreigner, and beautiful; he is not used to it, he has not planned to say this, or said it a hundred times before.

'Well, where are you going, in Israel?'

'I don't know. I mean, I've got a lot of addresses, but I hadn't thought where first.'

'You could come and see where I live.'

'Well, I could, yes.'

'I'm going down there in a week or two. I've got two

weeks of my holiday left. I'm going to see a cousin of mine in the Emek, then I'm going south. Come with me, you'll see the country.'

'All right. Thank you.'

'All right, tov, beseder. You will come.' The sounds of the words are new currency, the harsh consonants and simple vowels are as unlike French or English as I imagine the rocks of Israel, the dry mountain sides where the prophets waited, to be unlike the valleys of western Europe. We begin to repeat an ancient language; and I turn my face with resolution towards total change, a whole new order, a new way to say things now.

'Say something to me in Hebrew, something long.' Wanting to hear the flow of language from his lips, not the staccato phrases of casual conversation but something measured, archaic. And he, sitting upright, his open shirt falling away from his chest, his cigarette laid down to burn itself out in the ashtray, his head raised slightly as if he is listening for a cue, beginning to speak. I watch his mouth move, the animation of tongue and throat; and the words come out fast and fluent yet with a rhythmic intensity, like a poem. I catch a repetition of phrases, a regular pattern of pauses, and am lulled by it as if it were familiar.

'It's the Old Testament. The very beginning.'

'You had to learn it?'

'Of course.'

From far back the words come to me in English, the faint echo of the Hebrew original, for a moment drawing all together, earth, sea, light, dark, pleasure, pain; the passage of a dark ship upon brilliant waters. 'And the earth was without form and void, and darkness was upon the face of the deep. And the spirit of God moved upon the face of the waters. And God said, let there be light, and there was light. And God saw the light, that it was good, and God divided the light from the darkness. And God called the light Day and the darkness he called Night. And the evening and morning were the first day.'

The sea, the land, the sky, layers of horizontal calm through which mist is rising. The day pauses in mid-afternoon, bullfinches hop upon wires, a pair of pied birds fly in a line down the estuary. Two children stranded on the white sand sit still for a moment, brown arms caked with drying sand and mud, dangling upon crooked knees. The little girl with the round face and round light eyes and a straight fringe of hair says, 'It was all I had.'

Her brother, older, fidgets his toes through the sand with his annoyance at the stupidity of it and says, 'All your money. How much was in it? You are stupid, Jo.'

'More than a pound. One pound, five shillings and tuppence.' She looks out to sea, where small pale figures splash in the waves, far across the sand. She has half forgotten, half ceased to care; if it is gone, it is gone. But he cannot bear it, that she should be so careless; he frowns and begins to draw large squares upon the sand with a stick, telling her, 'You begin with this one, dig right through it, see, and I'll do this one. Then you move on to this, and I'll do the next. It must be somewhere, after all.'

And so they begin to move again, crouching, sifting the dry sand through their fingers. He builds pyramids, flattens their sides geometrically for a moment in the pleasure of building, destroys them remembering what he is about. She flops down every now and again, drives her arms to the elbow through the cooling sand, feeling its silkiness upon her skin, she dawdles, the thought of the lost money only sometimes falling like a shadow upon her mind. There is so much else, the bright afternoon, the sea like jewels, the little shells that lie upon the palm of the hand, the strange bulk of adults going into the sea to bathe. But he has it, his fingers close upon the flat sides of her tin, he pulls it out and blows the sand from its shining familiar red surface.

'Here it is,' he says laconically. 'Now, put it away in your pocket, Jo, and don't bury it again.' His words clip at her spreading mind, he will always be there, telling her. She puts the tin calmly away in the pocket of her dress, sits back on her heels while her hands pat away at the sand, making a smooth heap patterned with fingers. After a bit she says, her hands still again, 'Something bad always turns out good in the end.'

His head comes up, large dark eyes flash sudden antagonism. 'No, it doesn't.'

'Yes, it does.'

'No it *doesn't.*'

She does not move. She says, 'For me it does.'

He says, 'I know what happens to you, and it *doesn't.*' But now he is muttering only to himself, his attention is caught elsewhere, he jumps up and seizes his spade and runs away up into the sandhills to where a smooth white slope awaits him and begins to dig hard, throwing up spadefuls of sand with all his energy. When he is gone, she simply says to herself 'It *does*' with a calm conviction that nobody may hear; and begins to walk towards the sea, taking her bucket with her so that she may catch a share of its immensity and watch the water pool and sink into her wells of sand.

Once they are back at the house, differences fade as familiarity greets them. The house stands open and the wind blows through, banging the front door, swinging the french windows upon their hinges. The kitchen leads into the garden, bare feet carry sand in upon the worn brick floor, out again over the flags into the grass. Children, coming and going, are hardly noticed, yet assimilated. Ghosts walk through the rooms, pause upon the stairs where the oak treads are smooth; Chopin is playing the piano in the garden, garlanded his bust smiles down from the top of a wardrobe in one of the upstairs rooms; in the garden a tall thin man stretched out in a wicker chair is talking of Proust. The children enter and move about and pick up scents and associations and hear words fly across rooms, the tail-ends of conversations, jokes that do not seem to be funny and yet can set a whole company laughing. The words will recur, the associations will come back to mystify and exhilarate, much later on; the jokes will be heard again and again until they are plain; the conversations murmured between grown-up people across a table will assume a heaviness as they are questioned and then understood. Chopin will always smile from the top of a wardrobe, Proust always recline in the shaded garden in a wicker chair. They come into the centre of it all; the little girl feels through the thin cotton of her dress pocket the square flat outline of her money tin.

There is activity at the centre of the kitchen where hands knead bread, chop rhubarb, open beer bottles, a dozen different pairs of hands, practical each in their own way; and the activity slopes off, out into the trellised back garden where heads only turn inquiringly and hands lift to feel the passage of wind and pages flick over of their own accord and a smaller child follows a blackbird after crumbs; until far at the bottom of the garden, among nettles and bindweed and syringa, somebody stands entirely still, staring out towards the sea. The movement is of a dance, the beat changes, the role changes, a glance meets another in the chain of passing.

They heard him say, 'It depends what you mean by kill.' And knew that a year ago when they sat down nineteen at table and opened bottles as they were opened today, there was one here who plummeted white one night into the dark binding weeds of the river Cam, never to be released. It was a first knowledge of death, this knowledge of a gap. At dinner as the talk flows and then becomes staccato, three dead men come in and sit down, then rise, bow and go out again. A girl jumps to her feet and cries after them once they are gone, 'What are you doing here?' Among the live, the eating, the new children. To the rest they are familiar, hardly noticed. The second is a brown man who ran barefoot through the streets of London carrying hot bread to his friends. The third, a person shot instead of another, nameless and faceless across the world. To a child the memory is of warmth and particularity; they were there as easily as are the rest, and only the words by which they are introduced are strange. She thinks that they are welcome here. Secretly under the table she stretches her limbs and feels the flexibility of toes, the nearing heat of another's living hand.

He said, 'It depends what you mean by kill.' To kill can never be intransitive. There must be a subject; subject-object. Children sleep soundly, wrapped in their own and private dreams, with only a word from the adult world to impinge. Their thumbs in their mouths are their own. The doors open and a wind comes up the garden from the sea in the growing darkness, and a small fear that gathered about the table indoors is dissipated in the freshness. Late at night the house closes again and the sleepers are enclosed. Boards creak, a tree bends beneath a gust, a sea bird screams. But the house contains the stirring of limbs in sleep and love, and the dim cries from the bedrooms. We wake, sit up, wonder if this is it, the place that we were searching for. An obscure longing is briefly appeased; is it this, we ask, is it here, is it now, is it and must it be evanescent, a passing dream? In dreams, brick rises upon brick, mortar closes the gaps, a roof is found and fits like a cap where it was wanted, eternity is found and pinned between the walls like a dead butterfly; and then there is the awakening.

The boy with the bright dark eyes and restless movements flies up a ladder, hardly touching it with his feet, his hands gripping fast upon the banister. 'Gosh! But we could live here!' There is the staircase ladder, like a ship's, the wooden floor, the rickety red roof, tar-black walls, ships through the window panes, birds visiting, a sea wind from strange places rattling the beams; there is the kitchen, packed as a galley, the Elsan tucked away, the tea-kettle blackened, the bottles for a smuggler's feast of long ago. Here, all that is unnecessary is pruned away. The bed sags under the vagrant changing forms that rest there, the tables may be spread with maps, X marking the spot. It is all he has been waiting for. He flies from window to window, beating his wings, his heart lightened. He cries out, 'But we could live here!' This is somewhere his sister has not been; and later in the day, perched in the wind that ruffles his blackbird feathers on a speeding open car, the beauty of the thought possesses him, 'Just wait till I tell Jo about this! And won't she be jealous!'

A pair of pied birds fly in a line down the estuary, a line of walkers spans out against bracken and gorse and the mad yellow broom, barefoot pilgrims carrying clothes, following the point of a church's tower. They walk behind their father, in his long shadow, feeling the immediacy of hot earth. It is another point in an infinite summer day, in which they are small in the congregation.

One says, 'Will it be here?'

Another, 'Sometimes it is here, sometimes not.' The treasure may be buried, the map lost. One day the way will be found again, quite simply, so that they will forget to exclaim that once it was lost. 'There was a man on the hill buried upside down, an eccentric resident of Dorking.' Sometimes, somebody says, his grave was there, and sometimes not. The boy at my side, his dark head bent and toes scuffing, is talking about the end of the world. And suddenly I want photographs, I want proofs; I am seven years old here, and yet suddenly much older; I cannot turn my head and breathing four times the breath of the sea wind forget the beauty of a single person standing waist high among ferns. I hardly know the girl I am looking at; she is a cousin of my parents, she is moody as she chews a long stem of grass, she is much older than I, she is beautiful, she is in love. I want to pull at her pale flowing skirt and ask her. But the path goes on, deeper into silence, and feet step into footprints, twigs swing back to flick and flick against the passing faces; the curved shadow falls upon us all. We chew leaves like deer and lie among prickling grass to share a feast of prawns and beer and lemonade, the warbling of church music in our heads from where the Sunday organ plays. High upon the church roof the green man crouches and lifts his paws to the sky. Sir Gervase, Sir Edmund, Sir Ralph and his wife lie brittle beneath the softness of our feet on grass; and in the corner among long weeds, the bright brief curve of the scythe rises and falls, the old man bends and smiles and turns back to work after showing us; the same curved shadow falls upon us all. Lying moments later in the soft underbelly of the young oak, we are acorns, we are young tight leaves, the sky above us is the all-possible, the path with its dust is there for our return, we know we will follow each other, children and adults, like Indians and hardly talk; here a thought flashes like sun between leaves, here and then not-here; now I could sit and let it all fall like the dry sand between my fingers, saying as I did much earlier, long ago in childhood, 'It was all I had.'

At night as they lie in their narrow beds their whispers bridge the darkness of the upstairs room.

'I saw the hermit's house. The one on stilts by the river.'

'Did you?'

'The black one with the red roof. He's got everything inside. It's like a ship. He wasn't there.'

'Oh. Should you have gone in?'

'Yes, of course. We all did, we were invited, me and Dad and the Crowthers.'

She will be outside it always now, the direct experience of the hermit's house, the first flying up those stairs. She stands among the marsh grasses still and sees the mysterious figure of Gemma, who is in love. There are the gargoyles on the church and the hot pine smell of the earth. 'Did Matt Ferguson just die? Or did he do it on purpose? Or was he killed?'

'I don't know. He drowned.'

'I know. In Cambridge.' But she has swum in the Cam herself, they have picnicked and there are punts and canoes and the harmless ducks and sunshine. 'It isn't very deep, though.'

'Up at Grantchester meadows it is.'

'But how could he drown? Couldn't he swim?'

'You can drown in a bath if you try.'

'I liked him. He was terribly nice.' He is still there, surely, he will come in tomorrow with his heavy tweed jacket smelling of dogs, his pipe, his lifting black eyebrows. They will hear the noise of his motorbike outside and nobody will be surprised; they will all go to the pub and lie about on the grass again and hear the story about the nuns that he told last year, when somebody said, 'Frances, your children will grow up delinquent,' and their mother, drinking shandy, only laughed and kissed Matt Ferguson on the cheek, as if he were a child too; and she and Tom will eat crisps and drink their bottles of fizzy orange and pretend not to be listening. It will begin again tomorrow, exactly the same, and there will not be that shudder, that sudden cold there was at supper on the first night, when they all remembered. Sir Edmund, Sir Gervase, Sir Ralph; the dead knights rise up from their grassy tombs to walk through her dreams, smiling their stone smiles towards something that remains forever out of sight.

And the boy at the bottom of the street, who crouches in a patch of shade hardly bigger than himself, watches and wonders if he can bear to see it all. First, there was just himself, alone for hours of the morning, squatting still while others came and went, feet passing in the dust, worn brown feet in sandals, a hem flapping, other feet in those particular brown polished boots, walking fast. Now there is a group, only yards away, clear in the sunlight that strikes the white earth like metal, and every now and then they turn their faces towards him, daring him to move; he sees their faces contorted, the faces of devils. They are hardly bigger than he is, they are boys like himself, but there are many of them, four or five, and he is alone. The piebald scrap of fur and flesh at the centre of their circle writhes on the ground, smaller than any of them.

There are always stray animals dumped in the street here, litters of kittens sometimes tied in a bag, wandering with sores, licking up garbage. The man who left the puppy simply opened the door of a battered car and set it down. It was fat, not like the starving dogs that lay about panting and raided the open kitchen doors for scraps. Some dog, some pet bitch from one of the houses gave birth to this one; the man who put it here was a Frenchman, with rights over more than the lives of dogs. And when the car was gone, only yesterday, the boy crept out from his place where he sat playing with marbles, drawing in the dust with his finger to make alleys and runnels for them, and held out a hand, and saw the little dog quiver and move towards him. There was no food for it; so he saved a scrap of meat from his dinner and gave it a bowl of water in the shade. All night he heard it cry outside his window, locked out upon the street. In the morning it lay inert and its excrement was a yellow mess all around it, for it was too weak to move away. Yet it lived, and wagged the stump of a tail, and moved its paws against the flies; and he felt his heart like an engine, filling his body, as he thought of how small it was, how young and helpless. And then the gang of boys come down the street, following an old man with a donkey, with shouts of abuse; and when the old man shuffles away up a side turning and they are bored with him, they notice the Jewish boy and his dog and in a minute the dog is gone.

'Gilbert? Qu'est-ce-que tu fais? Gilbert, viens ici!' His mother is screaming from inside the house as she always does, pulling him back into the dark interior. But today he does not move. He sits, held, appalled by what is happening; by his ability to sit there, and watch and not move. They are killing the little dog, up the street. The muscular older boys, with their mops of hair and their thin quick fingers are putting it to death. Yelps sound in the street, and nobody cares. A European walks past, and a squeak sounds from his shoes as he goes. The old women with their baskets are going home laden for the midday meal, and they turn up their eyes and click their teeth, but move on. And then at last the boys rise, as one, and the leader calls out to him carelessly, 'Well, do you want your doggy back?'

And the small brown and white patch far away is stamped into the dust with blood and does not move again. He goes indoors without another look and fights down the rage and sickness that threaten to destroy him and eats his dinner without a word. No look, no word. Everything goes on as before. First there is life, movement, and then nothing. 'That is how it is,' is what he says to himself inside, over and over, 'That is how it is.'

The evening and the morning were the first day.

2

THE last miles of sea between our bows and the land shrink, become yards, are at last feet easily spanned by a narrow gangplank, a far-down churn of soiled harbour water beneath our feet as we follow one another ashore. As the moment for landing draws closer, the crowd on the foredeck spreads; people come up from below, blinking, the seasick young wives who have not appeared during the whole voyage, the grandmothers who sat playing patience in the lounge, the Spanish children whose parents would not let them out into the sun; the greetings become more casual, less embarrassed, the longing to see Israel is out in the open, the men at the rail carelessly let their arms touch as they lean and stare out landward, as if they are brothers. The mauve stripe along the horizon, that could have been cloud, thickens and solidifies. The Swiss geologist is on deck with field glasses, erect as an old soldier. A child escapes from a hatchway and runs screaming down the deck, the mother staggers scolding after, plump on her thin white legs, but stops in mid-stride, forgetting, following the pointing fingers, looking towards land. The stripe darkens and has outlines, the mass of hills, the long-strung-out port buildings, the inland darkness of vegetation. Something flashes, caught in light as we turn. The young Frenchman, his arm around his wife, crooks up his wrist to examine his waterproof watch, check the mysterious accuracies that seemed somehow pointless while the ship was far out at sea. Now he can determine the exact moment of landing; he fingers the winder in anticipation. His wife, her blond chignon coming apart in the wind, drums her fingers to a dance tune on the white painted rail; she it was who joined the wild dancing in the bar last night, charging round with the others as the music for the hora began, her hair and dress loose, her feet clattering in beach sandals, while he sat smoking, dark glasses pushed up on his forehead, ordering more cognac. This afternoon he is pale, exhausted; but I see his own excitement as he checks that chronometer, moves his feet in their plaited white shoes impatiently on the deck.

'Six-thirty we land.' The geologist announces it, as if he were asked a question.

Six-thirty, after a week afloat; after seven days of heat and light, nights with those stars in the water like peonies. The blond Frenchwoman blinks with surprise as if she, no more than I, can take this prediction seriously. We have been adrift, all of us; mealtimes the only fixed points of the day, as in a child's routine. We have been looked after, assembled, dispersed again, carried along. The only decisions have been to buy another drink to start a conversation, to sit in the sun or find the shade. Only now, with the landing, will we be set loose to find our own way about, make sense of situations that will appear quite foreign to us, make decisions that may have some consequence. Gilbert stands apart, I see him by the coil of rope as I come up, leaning against a peeling white door. He alone appears relaxed, he is smoking as usual and watching through half-closed lids. He is like somebody standing carelessly on the running-board of a bus, knowing so exactly where he is going that all he has to do is swing, jump, regain his balance and disappear into the crowd before the bus has even stopped.

'Aren't you excited?'

'Of course.'

'I can't believe it, in an hour we'll actually be in Haifa. Have you packed?'

He thumbs towards a stained blue duffel bag at his feet.

'Oh. I suppose I'd better go and get my things together. I've got rather more than that.'

But, 'No, no,' he says. 'You can't go down now. Look, there's the Carmel, and that glittering thing's the Ba'hai temple, and look, now you can see the whole waterfront.' He seizes my arm, I can feel his separate fingers gripping the elbow. From the deck below a sudden shout goes up and the singing starts again, a circle forms, the hands clap out a steady rhythm, faster, faster, and the dancers go on where they ended at three in the morning; as if they cannot bear to stop, bare feet and sneakers scampering, a loud 'Ho! Ho!' of effort, a rising cry of 'Encore, encore!' which might be from dancers or watchers or both; a burst of noise that seems to carry the ship right up into the harbour. Gilbert smiles a little tolerantly and does not move. The Frenchman has taken off his glasses and is staring, drawn at last out of himself. His wife, barefoot, hums to herself and dances a little hora all alone where she stands, her painted toes curling. The geologist puts down his binoculars and rubs his eyes as if they are filmed and sighs like a man sunk in melancholy. And I am gripped in that tension of expectation that makes men cry, dance or stare stock-still; and yet it is vicarious, not mine. The realisation comes a minute later that it is nausea that rises in me; that I have been feeling sick all morning, that the Turkish breakfast of eggs, jam, cheese, olives, fish and coffee is heaving to the surface. This is my own experience, this vomiting below deck as the ship docks and people embrace and cry, and the town of Haifa spreads its white arms to us. I do not know what Gilbert is doing at the time.

A country of the mind: one enters it as one enters a dream, uncertain of sleeping or waking, only knowing that a threshold has been crossed. It happens once, the landscape is there, the people are there, events unfold with a charming and familiar certainty. And surely the entrance was once here, surely a tree grew there, to the left, and a stick lay across the path, and surely that cluster of bushes seems familiar? And surely it was on just such a day, with just such a pattern of clouds, that I first came to this place and slipped so easily into the other life? And the entrance eludes and eludes, until the search wears me out, I am miserable with the doubt that I may ever return; and then in another place, another way, I am suddenly there, in another part of the place, but there. There is that walk, up a road, down a path to the left through some clusters of trees, past a small lake and a hollow tree in which I have placed a twig. I am six or seven years old, we go on the walk again, and yet it has gone. There is the road, the path, there are the trees; and yet never again do we arrive at that little muddy lake, and the hollow tree with its twig so deliberately placed. I have been there, and seen the lake and the hollow tree. Somebody was with me as I went. The tactile memory, that tree with its hollowed trunk, the dark, the damp loamy interior, the hole in which I place my twig, all remain. And yet it is never there again. A year or two, and I give up trying to go for that walk; or nobody will come with me now.

And now I have stepped ashore in Haifa and felt the jolt of hard land beneath my feet after the uncertainty of water; as the customs man has opened up my suitcase and written in Hebrew on my passport I have waited, a shell to hold the pain in my head, a packet of cargo, a thing left upon the shore. I have shrunk from the light, bandaged my head with a silk scarf, seen the crowds pass in long lines, in a delirium. The ships are still steaming down towards this port, carrying refugees from all points in Europe, all going in this direction. The water is alive with people swimming to reach the shore, is the graveyard of those shot from the decks of ships, thrown back into the water as their hands grope for dry land. There are babies falling like bundles of discarded clothes to spread upon the surface of the sea, there are the long streamers bleeding red into the green, there are people leaping to drown, their eyes turned up in relief. There are still the cries, echoing to the sky. Only the outline of the land has changed, has become an illusion of safety; the prosperous housefronts, the white hotels, the spiked plants growing in tubs, the streets full of cars and people. I stand confused, I have been afloat a week on that same sea and am caught up in a hope that is not now, is not mine, yet that makes nothing of the anaesthetic passage of time.

'Jo!'

'I'm coming. I'll be all right in a minute.'

'We'll find a hotel, and I'll try and get you something from the chemist. You'll be all right in an hour or so, it's the sun. It happens when you are not used to it. I should have realised.'

Lying in bed in the Hotel Eden, the curtains drawn, a pattern of shade all that shows, as if I am going blind, I hear the noises of the street and wait only for his face to reappear, now that I am sick and he is the only one in a strange land. When he comes back I swallow a large khaki pill without asking what it is, and lie back upon the pillow without considering. The blind swings open now that the wind is rising, showing just a crack of the still brilliant harsh light outside. The memory of that light is terrifying, I shut my eyes and yet feel it still; outside there is still the quay, the crowd, the noise, the questions, the heat that searches for a weak spot in the skull, the land tipping this way and that, the sky a sideways wedge of violet. The customs man going through everything, looking for spies. Shoes, sponge, notebooks, suntan oil tumble out on to the counter.

They are all recognisable but I am unable to pick them up and put them back. Gilbert packs them away angrily and says something sarcastic to the man, who purses his lips and jerks his head upward, who, like officials the world over, does not answer but writes laboriously across my passport that I do not have a work permit.

'We'll find a hotel. You'll be better after a rest.' I sense a certain impatience with illness; in Israel, he is telling me, one must be able to stand beneath that blistering sun. 'Tomorrow we will buy you a hat and get the bus to Afula. You can come, if you are better?'

'Perhaps. I expect so.'

He will never press, never ask, and I will never make him ask me; this much is established already. When he buys me a drink he simply sets it down in front of me and when my glass is empty he waits for me to buy the next. Offering a cigarette, he throws down the packet on the table and expects me to help myself. Finding a room free, he books it, throws my suitcase down on the bed and goes to find a cheaper room for himself elsewhere. 'The bus goes at nine. I'll come and collect you.' And he leaves the room quietly and I lie and imagine him walking down the street below in the short late twilight, hands in the pockets of his trousers, the duffel bag swinging, holding all his belongings; stopping to buy something to eat, munching quickly, his broad hands delicately picking up a tiny cup of Turkish coffee, his elbows on the table; lighting a cigarette and taking great puffs at it to keep it alight, holding it till it burns low, covering his fingers with nicotine; pushing through a swing door out into the evening, into Haifa, into this country in which he is so easily at home. Once, I raise the blind a little, just to see what is outside. The light is mauve, dusty, it is after nine o'clock. I see a curly rooftop, a palm tree growing oddly high up a house, purple shadows upon a white wall. Far down in the canyon immediately below me is the street. A big yellow Chevrolet starts and draws away, a gangster's car, full of shouting people. A man left in the street bends to pick something up, waves it after them, but I cannot see what it is. The smell is of metal, petrol, the baked bricked walls; a hot city late on a summer evening, in which I am a stranger.

The fiction continues, strands come from all directions to be wound together. The storyteller produces a wood, of beech trees I imagine, their smooth grey elephant skins stretched tight to burst higher up into that peculiar beech paleness of green. I – we – the heroine – is waiting. In this story she is called Caroline. She knows what she is waiting for, for she has been here before; and yet there is always the uncertainty, of the rhythm that may break, the repetition that may come no more, the laws of expectancy that may be broken. She has to be there at exactly the right place at exactly the right time. Listening, I catch her anxiety, that she may have forgotten, that last time was the last time ever. But no, she thinks she hears something, yes, it is, it must be, the distant rattle of a train coming closer, its rhythm shaking the wood, its rumble closer upon the rails; it will stop, it stops for her, she gets into a carriage that appears to be empty. The listening children laugh and poke each other with relief, knowing what will come, the anxiety falling away pleasurably. And suddenly Caroline sees that she is not alone but that there is a very old lady sitting in the corner of the carriage, knitting. Her face, her clicking needles, are familiar, as is the Edwardian upholstery of the carriage, and the beech leaf green at the windows and her voice, always the same, punctuating her words, 'my dee-ah'; but most of all she is a sign that all is well, that one is really on the way, that all the familiar attributes of the story will be waiting around the next corner, and the next. The adventure will unroll, different to the last one yet predictable because in some part of the listeners already known. For a few minutes, for half an hour, I am Caroline; all around me is familiar as the clocks that toll across the river in the city where I live. I have walked through that wood, waited in it, hunted at the right time for the right place, a conjunction of trees, a knot on a trunk, a low bending branch, a parting of fallen leaves on the soft ground to reveal railway lines, not rusted over but bright with use; a far rumble which would be only the wind of a rising storm, yet which might be, which is, the noise of an approaching train.

'There was a group of us in Oran, when I was at school. We were Zionists, of course, we were brought up with the idea. We knew that it would happen and that we'd have to get out. But there was no life for us there. We did not want to exist like that, unemployed. Ghetto children, what else could we be? Israel was our chance. To be people at least, however hard the work might be. There were twenty of us at the beginning. Of course, the government help, give you money. There was really nothing there, when we began. But now we've got houses, a swimming-pool, we have trees coming up and some good crops already. Do you know, when the Sinai affair happened we had only begun to settle, we were living in two huts, with tents. That was something. I was only sixteen, I didn't know what was happening. Suddenly, war. For us it was a question of waiting, for something outside to decide what will happen to us. I thought, who is going to decide what will happen to it, this little piece of land where we have done so much digging? The English, the French? That is when I get out of my hiding-place and remember I know how to use a gun.'

'Right on the Egyptian border?'
'In Gaza. That is where I live.'

And to me it is still geography, a tiny patch drawn on a map. I am drawn after his words as seagulls follow a ship for food, flying miles from their starting-place in the belief that crumbs will always drop from a moving boat.

'There were agents provocateurs in Algeria. You know what that is? Zionists too. To make it worse, so that more of us would move out.'

'I didn't know that.' Ignorance, a culpable innocence.

'It is the marxist law of dialectic, it is what the true revolutionary believes. What is the point of making things appear better when they are rotten to the core?'

The bus to Afula carries us on along the empty burning tarmac road, the miles of red-brown rocky land, cabbages growing in dust, the brief blue eucalyptus shade. The old metal carcass, bull-nosed, left from the Mandate, shudders at last in the square where the benches are empty, the shops pulling down blinds against the sun. We stroll about and buy melon pips to crack with our back teeth while picking out the sweet kernel with our tongues; and spit the husks sideways, still talking. And buy grapefruit juice from a stall and feel that ache of sourness at the backs of our throats and smoke, waiting for the next bus.

'And so Algeria is independent. Did you not know that?'

'But I thought the French were winning. I thought de Gaulle would never let it go.'

He only raises an eyebrow at me, at such ignorance. 'There was independence in June. Finished, end of de Gaulle. What could he do? The French were foreigners, colonialists, the Arabs were fighting for their lives. Every individual in Algeria was a fighter, even the children. They could burn the whole place down, the French,' he pauses to suck a stray pip from his back teeth. 'But they couldn't win. All they could do was pull everything out, medical facilities, power, equipment, everything they had controlled. But it isn't enough.' The man behind the grapefruit stall slaps his used halves away like plastic imitations. There is the bitter, fresh smell; flies; petrol engines running; an urban half-quiet. 'That is one thing you in Europe cannot understand,' Gilbert says.

'What?'

'That it's not always strength of arms that wins.' He taps his forehead, leaning forward. 'It is what is in here. The morale. De Gaulle, the imperialists, they are helpless. One could see this coming for a long time. The F.L.N. and the French, it was two different qualities of fighting. The régime was so corrupt, how could it have any energy, any effect, when the time came?'

'But the war went on for so long.' Korea, Algeria, the vague backgrounds of the time.

'True, but in the end one cannot subdue a people like that. Colonialism, it carries the seeds of its own destruction. That is how it seems to me. Tell me, you know those insects, what do you call them? That eat their way through houses?'

'Death-watch beetles?'

'*Nahon*. Well, there have been death-watch beetles eating at the French régime in Algeria. I saw it, even when I was young. Until now. What happens is that the French army comes home from Indo-China. Here they have learned terrible things. How to degrade the human being. And they bring this to North Africa.'

'Do you mean the French are torturing the Arabs?'

'Of course. And they are bringing corruption. And the Arabs, the Algerians, learn it. Who can tell where it will end?'

'You must be glad to have left.'

'Of course. But I must carry it with me. One cannot forget what one knows.'

He sits beside me on the gangway, looks past me to see the countryside pass, as the bus draws out of Afula and into the valley of Gilboa; upright, alive with energy, his hands moving up and down and shaping things as he talks, his eyes fixed on the passing scenery but seeing other things beyond. A boy in a ghetto in an African town, a French colony, standing about on a street corner, bored, with nothing to do. Cleaning shoes, running errands. Catching a coin as it falls down the steps of a big hotel, where men in polished brown shoes sit about drinking anis and playing cards. The empty expanse of street when nobody comes near, only old men who shuffle to smoke in the shade; glances from the Arab boys, their curly reddened hair, glances from the sons of colonials. The provincial decayed hierarchies smashed sideways by revolution once he is no longer there; as if, going out through a door, one made a draught that knocked the card-packs flat.

In the Kalahari desert the bushmen each have a story, a private myth, which is entirely their own. For a man to tell his story is for him to lay himself open, make himself entirely vulnerable, put all defences down. If his story is forced out of him, then he will die.

'One day,' Gilbert says to me on the bus travelling to Gilboa, 'perhaps I will tell you more.'

At five, before the sun is up, the hills of the Emek are grey. There is a chill blue dawn of terrible beauty. In the first week we go out to the grapefruit orchards and loosen the earth around the roots of the young trees so that they can breathe. The mosquitoes hang in clouds before daybreak, thickest in the hour before the sun is hauled up the sky. Our flesh is eaten by them, we cover each exposed inch with an oily insect-repellent that mixes with sweat and dust to make a mud coating for the skin. The spades strike the earth and send shocks up our arms. After an hour it is impossible to straighten our backs. We fling ourselves down, sip water from a tin mug in turns; sometimes a boy comes down with water melons in a basket, throws a couple from his tractor so that the juices spurt out; we grab them and suck whole melons dry, till the red juices and black seeds stain the earth. We begin to work again.

I am a girl from England, I am nineteen, I still have thin white arms. I have sixty-five mosquito bites on one leg. The horizon is familiar now, the far blue hill-line. Gilboa rises up behind us and is our protection. There is never a cloud in the sky. The olive trees stoop like old men. The yoghourt might all be finished at breakfast before the trolley reaches me and I have forgotten the word. Yitzhak is taking the last of the jam. The brown speck in the distance, moving towards me, is Gilbert. The brown bitten flesh is common, the sweat runs from us all. Nobody speaks. The heat at midday clubs the back of the head. The metal of the trailer is burning my thighs. The valley fills like a bowl with heat and drains slowly towards evening. Darkness comes, and sleep, I eat, I work, I sleep, I eat, I work—

He saw her easily assimilated, watching from a slight distance rather as a mother cat might watch her kitten grow. 'Yes, I did tell her she didn't have to work, but she wanted to, so I thought, all right. I've never seen anything like it. It's not good to work so in the full sun when you're not used to it. I've told her. But she won't listen.' He waited for her outside her hut and walked with her across the grass to the dining-room, where others to him were still strangers, apart from his cousin and his cousin's wife. 'There's Amnon and the fair Yolande.'

'Who?'

'She's new. She's French. She fancies him.'

'How do you know all this?'

'Oh, I listen to gossip.'

He frowned, taking her arm lightly as they went up

the steps, letting it go again at the top, retaining that fragility at his fingertips. There was something that had changed.

'I have to go, in a day or two. Do you want to stay here? Reuven says it's quite all right, if you want to stay.'

'No, no, I'd like to come with you.'

It would be different, perhaps, once he was at home. Here, he saw only the mocking, envious glances of strangers, felt the curiosity of Reuven and Naomi – 'Is she Jewish? Well, of course, she's very attractive. But Gilbert, have you thought . . . ?' – as irritation. At home he would be among friends, true friends. Yet the anxiety persisted; that he had begun something which he could not finish, that something important remained unsaid; that somewhere, during the past week, he had been guilty of deception. He saw her in his mind's eye, her wide searching look, the raised eyebrows, the down-drawn pursed mouth as she glanced about her, giving nothing away. There were those fleeting London girls, legs like scissors above the pavements, there was that defensive, inscrutable stare between the parted curtains of hair; on buses, at railway stations, in shops, outside cinemas: passing him in a group as he sat on the grass at Greenwich; girls like wan virgins, and yet with a steely hardness. He thought of arriving home, of how she would glance around her. There was something unsettling here, and his stomach moved uncomfortably inside him, as if by going to Europe he had contracted some disease.

'Gilbert! Aren't you coming to swim? Come on, I said we'd meet them up there.' She passed, taunted him, flicking her bathing towel, her limbs dry and brown already with sun and dust. She was arrogant, too sure of herself; and then, as soon as he had seen this, told himself of it, found something reassuring in the thought, he saw her droop in his presence, cast inward upon herself by his unfeeling ignorance. 'What's the matter, Jo?'

'Nothing. Nothing. I was just thinking.'

'What about?' He smiled, put out a hand; some trivial female thing, it would be, some lack of attention on his part.

'Algeria. About what you told me. It's odd, until now I haven't had time to think at all. Working like this makes one sort of numb. Numb, numb; are you numb?' And her hand moved to his, pinching the flesh white, making him gasp; she was here, there, like some butterfly or humming-bird, sucking deep at the flower and flying on, reassuring him and making him restless, irritating him with her flippancy, in the next moment deeply serious, as if he were not serious at all.

'That hurts.' And with a bound he was away, freeing himself, suddenly moving into a series of cartwheels and handsprings across the grass, an aimless animal energy possessing him, an inner anger driving at his heart. She sat and watched him, and when at last he collapsed at her feet, tired but unassuaged, what he saw in her face was more intense than admiration.

That week is out and the next begins. The grapefruit trees breathe more easily and are left to grow towards their harvest. In the olive groves the hard green fruit hangs waiting, and we go out with our apron bags of sacking at our waists to milk the olives from the stalk. The aluminium ladders spring against the branches and we mount them, leaning our weight into the trees to keep the ladders upright. The tall old olive trees creak with the weight of the pickers. Through the fringe of grey leaves I see the valley again, its blue edges rising to the sky; ridged hillsides, the flash of metal as a tractor rides a slope; sharp spurts of light as a water spray turns in the sun. Faces appear, high up, in other trees, brown faces, blue faded denim hats, stained check workshirts, hands moving like monkeys'. The wind changes quarter and blows different snatches of conversation, Hebrew, French, English, Arabic: the voices grunt as the hands work. After an hour my hands move automatically, stripping the thin branches; the weight at my waist grows like a pregnancy. At the foot of the tree the boxes fill slowly, wooden crates already marked for sale, and children sort through the olives, pick out stray leaves or twigs, throw out any fruit that is rotten. We come down, we take off our hats, wipe our faces, crouch beside the water barrel again to drink and smoke. The work is different, the ritual the same. Rest times are by common accord, the tractor's arrival is marked by a shout from the white track, meals are eaten and digested and we grow hungry again. I am a child, deep in an exhausting and necessary routine. Something is silenced, satisfied. Lunch is ready for us and we sit and eat the platefuls of meat stew, fish, beans, eggplant, and leave our plates clean. At noon the sun is a familiar, fills the sky like a furnace; we run from it, the afternoon is for sleep, swimming, breathing lightly in the shade; it is in the twilight that we meet again, Gilbert and I, to eat supper, drink coffee outside the guest huts, see the long patterns of moonlight grow, the falling drops of the turning sprays upon the grass.

'I have to go, in a day or two. Do you want to stay here?'

'No, no, I'd like to come with you.'

We have worked side by side, scratching and hacking at the red earth. The closeness is almost more intense than a sexual relationship, there being no abandon and no relief; only the exhausted flinging down of the hoe, the emptying of the olive bags, the falling to gasp for air upon the stony ground. I know his labour and his tiredness, and he knows mine. We have glanced at each other with the sweat in our eyes. Now I feel that I know what it is like to be him, to rub my black hair from my eyes with a large dirty hand, sighing and stretching and lighting a cigarette and leaning back, closing my eyes. Yet there is something subdued, kept out of sight. I am waiting. When he turns away something makes me bite my lip, makes me sit watching the moon, reluctant to sleep, makes me hold my hands tight in my lap in case one of them, unguarded, should reach out suddenly to touch, stroke, claim, draw him down, break the bond that is between us, shock him into seeing me anew. And here nothing comes that is not willed; existence itself is a conscious creation; the vegetables and fruit we eat are forced out of the ground, the huts in which we sleep sit unshaded on the earth. The watering sprays turn and turn and each circling brings another blade of grass to life. The land itself undergoes vast surgery, cut and quarried and planted by remorseless instruments. I sit beside Gilbert and see his hands spread, the square blunt-fingered hands of a man who has made his life only with their help; who may not understand that a life can be accidental, vague, even pointless. . . .

'Typical Jo.' She hears the words ring behind her down the corridor; she is in the garden outside the back door at school and it is the last morning of term; she is wearing summer clothes and carrying a shoebag with her initials embroidered and they have been told to take everything out of their lockers and take it home because it is the end of the school year and in the autumn everything will be changed. Down the corridor, blocking the light from the window behind, comes one of the teachers who lives there when the others have gone home. 'Typical Jo.' She shudders, wondering what she has done to deserve that sarcasm, that thrust of the outstretched hand that dangles something in the indoor gloom.

'I thought I told you that everything had to be taken

out of the shoe lockers. Everybody else seems to be able to manage it. But, of course, not Jo.'

She sees the alien dangling gym shoe and rejects it at once. For a moment, it might have been hers; but as soon as she sees it close, its green grass stains where her own shoes are clean, its grubby laces and unfamiliar shape, she knows it cannot be hers. There are some things about oneself which are certain.

'It's not mine.'

'Don't be silly, child, it was in your locker and it's got your name in it.'

She stares in fear and embarrassment, for everybody is listening now. The things which are not hers – carelessness, untidiness, falsehood, that dirty shoe – will be forever assigned to her. She begins to feel around in her shoe bag, for in a moment there is an element of doubt. Unreal, her mind says, untrue, unreal. And yet the inventions of adults take precedence over the realities of children. Her fingers pass over the smooth toes of two bronze dancing-shoes, the leather of a too-small pair of sandals, find one gym shoe and then the other.

'Mine are here,' she says.

'Oh, well, that's funny. Must be someone else's, then. J.C., now, who can that be? Oh Janet, that's it. Janet, come here a minute, will you?'

And so the accusation moves on and comes to rest on somebody else; but the anger does not, for it is she who has been accredited with Janet's shoe, Janet who is fat and pink with hair like cotton grass, who smells sour, cries easily from watery blue eyes, has fingers like sausages. Janet has a friend, Anne, who lives next door to her. They come on the bus together, all the way from the terminus, choosing their seats. Anne is distinctive, bright, malicious, so that Janet at her side seems dangerous. They stand together and swing their shoebags and stare, accusing her of nearly having stolen Janet's shoe; suggesting that she is a person who might possibly want Janet's shoe, which is too big, too squashed, too dirty. Tense with the anger that may not be expressed, she sits down on the step, bending away from them; opens her satchel, gets out her pencil-box, begins to sort through her new coloured crayons, laying them out in the order of the colours of the spectrum, ostentatiously so that Janet Cole may see. Real Conte crayons, sharpened to points, their glossy backs to the sun; she lays them slowly beside each other in the right order; but when the arrangement is finished there are two pencils left, the white and the black, which are not colours of the rainbow. To put one at each end seems to mock the gradations of subtle colour within, for they are too extreme, too absolute; they are not a part of the rainbow but something exterior and hard to place; perhaps they are not even colours. To avoid the decision she puts them separately in her satchel. And looks up from her task to see that her mother, with Tom, is walking towards her up the drive, shrinking the little girls around, that therefore term is over, school is closed, the house behind her will be locked away until the autumn, when everything will have changed.

There are some things about oneself that are certain, that do not change. The child on the step spreads her feet upon the gravel, counts the treasure in her lap, '... blue, indigo, violet.' I stretch a hand back across the years to greet her; a decision is made, I am this, I am that; no other, pulling in the tide towards me, has a right to change this picture. The place becomes the edge of the desert, the time another, the outrage at misapprehension remains the same. At this time everything seems clear, like a mirage. At this time I am still young.

'I don't understand.' I want him to explain himself, lay himself out in pieces to be seen.

The answer is a cough of embarrassment, his profile

turned.

'What is it, what's the matter?'

He walks restlessly a yard or two away and stands facing the darkness, his hands in the back pockets of his shorts. The oil lamp burns on the step of the hut, lighting a small semicircle of grass where I lie on the hard cropped patch he calls a lawn. In the bushes, among the dark clumps, grasshoppers scrape their legs in their endless tune; further away a jackal screams. We are here, we have arrived. I watch for a movement as he stands there turned away from me; I am hot and angry with my question. He turns at last, just as I think that he has forgotten me and is watching something move across the horizon, he comes slowly back and squats beside me on his heels, hands hanging over his knees, black eyebrows drawn down. I wait, hard and angry, for him to admit his mistake; for I will not say that it was mine.

'It's not right, like this.'

'Don't people do it here, then?'

'Not like this.'

'What do you mean? I don't understand. What do you mean?'

I am so tired all at once of our strange mixture of French and Hebrew, long to relapse into English, that known, worn tongue of many subtleties in which I can move. The words evade and mock us and we lumber after them with our nets.

'Not to make love unless we love somebody.'

'Oh. I see.' The word 'love' darts away, changing colour. I hear the hardness of my voice, hard under insult, disappointment, misunderstanding.

'Do you do differently in England?'

'Well, yes. I suppose so. I mean, of course one does if one loves somebody. But we don't spend so much time talking about it. I mean, deciding exactly what we do or don't feel.' I mean, I mean.... 'You kill everything,'

I tell him, deliberately, 'You want to pin it down.'

'I did not mean to make you angry.' His voice grunts, he finds it hard to apologise.

'No, well, forget it.' Kissing on a patch of grass near the swimming-pool, on the rocky orange soil beside the trenches, holding each other while the water spray circles and soaks our legs; an experimental softness, always like a farewell. I want his black head bowed in a profane love.

'You see, I like you very much. But it is not the sort of thing for which one marries. I don't want to marry yet.'

'Oh, God, I wasn't thinking of marriage. Do you always marry the people you sleep with, here? Or perhaps you only do it after you're married. I'm sorry, Gilbert.' But for a moment I dislike him, for his culture so alien to mine, for a puritanism which still perhaps lies buried in myself. There are feet of stunted grass between us; his fingers pluck it up and scatter it. In between his squared fingers, there is whiter skin. His lips, when they even touched mine, drew away quickly I remember, with caution or with fear. In my dreams he enters quietly and afterwards the face he turns to me is not his own; there is something darker, wilder, an abandonment of reason which both of us have come to fear.

'I'll go tomorrow. I'll start off on my tour of Israel. I must see the country. There are lots of people I want to look up. And, anyway, it's time I went.'

'But you will come back here?'

'I don't know.'

'Please come back. I would like it if you'd come back.'

'Well, maybe I will.' The tenderness I have felt, that strong bond of admiration, begins to return; a feeling grown out of vanity, based on his ability to find the extraordinary in me. It soothes me, so that I see now how I have outraged him. 'Yes, all right, I will.'

'Now, I'll make an itinerary for you.' He is easily cheered, relieved, diverted; like a boy he turns at once to route-planning and map-making. His long face lifts into animation, and I am once again depressed. Blue, indigo, violet. But white? Black?

'You want to go north first? It's best that you should go north first and see the Negev last, I think.' The gradations of feeling never reach an absolute. The absolute is inaccessible. Gloomily I say, 'I don't mind. Perhaps.'

'No, listen, it is best that you should do it this way.'

'Well, I don't know that I'd stick to an itinerary. I'm not all that good at plans. Look at me now.'

'Tveria, Tsfat, then you could go to Kiryat Schmoneh, to the north, back by the coast, Akko, Haifa you have seen, Tel Aviv, then Jerusalem; you can get a bus from Jerusalem to Beersheva, then here, then we can perhaps go together to see the Negev, I don't know. Sdom, Eilat, there is much to see in the Negev but the roads are lonely.' He has forgotten, his mind moves on with relief along the roads and set paths, planning things for me. He is a stranger. The thought drums in my head, urging me to admit a mistake; but no, not yet, I will not yet allow that I have been mistaken. The purple flowers growing by the monastery door, the hidden chant, the worn stone madonna, the peach stones red in the dust of the gutter, it is all still there, in the time before we arrived; but our time of innocence it was, ignorance, the immunity of the traveller who has not yet opened his eyes.

Tveria. Tsfat. Kiryat Schmoneh. Akko. He marked the points on the map in his mind, fumbled in his back pockets for a pencil but found none. The towns were spots on the grass, twigs, stones. The Mediterranean and the Dead Sea were shadows in the hollows of his hands. Something could be imagined, planned, executed; there was no need to flounder in the vagaries of feelings, to know oneself at such a loss and to suffer for it. There had been a mistake, and it had not been his; he was stifled still by his anger that she should have humiliated him. The girls of London, striding by on their thin legs like birds, watched him with scorn as they passed. And he was at home, in the place that he had made, insulted even here. The known landscape, shallows of red earth black in moonlight, gentle horizon, spikes of trees moved by the wind, had made no difference. Gaston in passing said, 'I hope you know what you are doing. She won't stay here, you know that.' And he only grunted and looked away, not knowing what to say. 'You aren't in Europe now.' Nobody had yet said it, yet it was in the air as they watched him, watched her, with friendly and uncomprehending curiosity. They found him changed, and he did not want to have changed. Things which had been simple were to become complex. The pale processions through the green parks of London mocked him, the faces turning in the tube trains mocked him, suggesting that there was no point; that the world ended at nightfall, that one met and coupled and parted without a word.

She told him, 'There are some other people I must go and see,' and reduced him to another name in an address book to be vaguely remembered; so neat, so self-assured she was, sitting there now as if nothing had happened, as if his home were not already subtly changed before his eyes, as if it were not her fault that a new dissatisfaction with himself made him pull up blades of grass angrily by the root and long for movement, violence, change. He squatted upon the balls of his feet, longing to spring up and move away.

'I've got an address of somebody in Tel Aviv. A friend of an aunt of mine. And another in Jerusalem. Wait a minute, what was that name? Friends of friends of mine in London.' The pages flipped, her finger moved down. 'Jerusalem 2304, Zvi Mosseri, that's it.' Her long legs, smooth kneebones, white in moonlight. In Algeria there had been no time, at Gan Hagar neither time nor inclination; the land demanded everything. In London the girls had passed him by and he had not known their language. He lit another cigarette, curbing that restlessness. 'She won't stay here,' they said. 'You know that.' There was no point in any of it; involvement, the intricacy of feeling, the ruins she would leave in her path.

He said, 'Zvi Mosseri. I shouldn't bother to go and see him. He's no good.'

'Why not? D'you know him?'

'I know of him.' There had been a newspaper article, students shouting in the streets, a scandal somewhere, far away. A long dark face, he remembered, bearded, the lips drawn back to speak aloud to crowds.

'Well, why do you say he's no good?'

'He is a trouble-maker.' Rabble-rouser, demagogue, those had been the words. 'He's an anti-Zionist, an anti-patriot. You will hear stupid things if you see him, that is all.' To break, to deflect that will that stared back at him out of her wide light eyes, that was all he wanted. Any plan but his would not do.

'Well, surely I can decide for myself what's stupid and what is not.'

'No, that's just it, I do not think you can. What do you know of life here? You have only just arrived. What can you know of the dangers that surround us? You live on a safe little island. I have heard the things that are said in Europe, against Zionism, against this government. But what can you know? You have no conception of it, you in Europe.'

It was done, he saw her droop and her eyes flicker and look away. It hardly mattered what he had said; what was politics, what belief, beside that challenging stare of hers, the unconscious arrogance; beside the uncurling of that body that had pressed itself with such insistence against his own.

'Anyway,' he said, uncomfortable in a moment at her defeat, 'there are other things. He is not a good man.'

'What other things? Sex? Well, I can look after myself quite well, thank you very much.' And the dart returned, his poisoned arrow, swift as he had sent it out. 'That'll be a nice change,' she said. All that seemed certain was their ability to hurt one another. He thought of his first sight of her, when she listened with such humility to the boring old man in the third-class dining-room, when she stood at the rail with her head thrown back, her skirt blowing, her thin arms braced to hold her weight against the ship's roll. For some reason, he thought of his mother, in the black cave of their kitchen: 'Girls are different from boys, Gilbert, they must be protected'; and a skinny Arab girl, a year older than he, shinning with practised strength up an orchard wall, her bare dirty feet an inch from his nose. Lala Elkhoury. One by one they went to her, up behind the disused well, where a crooked fig tree grew. And then he thought, there is no point in inventing complications in one's life. And that water melons, when they split open upon the ground, are red and wet inside like a human being.

'You have no conception of it, you in Europe.' The spectres are there still, hidden behind the relics; photographs, gravestones, stories told to the young. That's Uncle John, he was killed at Dunkirk. And in Malaya, in Africa, in Italy, in Greece. There's the tin hat in the air-raid shelter at the bottom of the garden, there are the old books, the magazines, a recipe for a pie with no meat and no vegetables, a pattern for a dress cut out of curtains; there is the challenge of it, 'Of course, you young people, you don't remember the war, you have no conception, no conception at all.' In films, in the theatre, in songs and poems, the old fears parade still, driven underground at the very end by the pervading triumph of good; in the back of his mind, tucked far away, there is still the reminder of danger, of threat to life, thought, existence. 'What would you do if you were attacked? If you saw your mother, your sister, your lover attacked? If you saw your child? How would you be a pacifist then?' The old questions, raised to justify what was done, remain open-ended, unanswerable. I am accused, with a whole generation, of having no conception. For Gilbert it is easy, having been born to persecution, having fought, having survived; he knows who he is and what he can do. Beside him I am a wraith, blown on the wind from one kind state to another, never to be rid of my question, never to understand. There is a square, a long brick wall high enough to obscure the sky; I am standing against the wall; the light is dim, greyish, as if at dawn. A uniformed man is coming towards me across the square, a weapon outstretched. Sometimes it is a gun, sometimes a knife. Everywhere there is complete silence except for the steady crunch, crunch of his steps forward. I wait, to see what I will do next. And he comes on, and on, and on.

Last night three people were killed when a mortar bomb exploded at Tel Katsir. The Syrians shelled a kibbutz at Ein Gev and shot two fishermen and a tractor driver. The boats are not running across the Sea of Galilee today. And so I am sitting alone in a café in Tiberias, waiting for the bus, which will take me there, to Ein Gev, to the other side.

3

SHE is there with three others, crouched in darkness, the only light an old torch grabbed in passing from a kitchen drawer. Around them the unknown spaces stretch to be explored, the great empty rooms in which the door of an abandoned wardrobe will creak open, a rat run across the floor, a window rattle in the wind. Tom, his black head lifting at her elbow, whispering 'Why don't we go home now?' voices her fear. One of the others answers sharply, poking his face forward to peer into the gloom. 'Quiet. I heard something. He must be in here somewhere.' The man they followed down the narrow path along the dyke, between the waving bleached grasses to the empty house in the fen, the unknown suspected man who was looking for something, the wavering ring of light from his torch searching the banks; somewhere in the house, in the rooms close to them, he is at bay. It is hard to say now what the original intention was, whom they believed him to be; for everything has changed since they threw down their bicycles at the roadside, since Fergus cried, 'Come on, let's track him, he's up to no good', since the cold grey glow of a winter evening faded to foggy darkness and the known patterns of fen landscape, celery fields, mangold heaps, pollarded bare willows, vanished to merge with undiscovered space. She is shivering, with cold, with apprehension; Tom chews at the inside of his cheek, his lips screwed together. It is essential that Fergus and Andy must not see that they are afraid. She puts out a hand, picks at the peeling wallpaper, pulls away a long strip, damp and malleable; picks at it again, with concentration.

'One of us ought to go and see.' There is always a leader, expecting something. Fergus, the eldest, folds his gloved hands around his knees. 'The rest of us could stay here and somebody could go and report. They could take the torch, of course.'

Silence. The wallpaper comes away in smaller pieces, the plaster goes in under her nails. She hears her own voice, 'I'll go.'

Sighs, of relief, of acceptance. 'All right, Jo, you go. Just see what he's up to and then come back and report. Don't let him see you though.'

Carefully she stands up, stretches her arms, braces herself to contain the shaking, takes the torch, flicks it on and off plunging them into the darkness shocking them into light.

'Hold on, I've got some matches here somewhere.' Tom fumbles in his pocket and she knows, from the closeness, the hardly divisible air between them, that now she has said it he wants to be the one to go. He glances, his black eyes opaque. 'We can keep lighting them till you get back. Then you'll be able to find us easily.'

The yellow light of the torch moves up the door, showing cracked whitish paint; space is already behind her, between them and her unsteady movement as she steps between the big curled sheets of torn wallpaper, the bricks, the piles of rotting wood tunnelled by insects, that lie about on the floor. The door swings, creaks, stays open, the beam makes a fragile passage through the darkness, outside is a hall scattered with candle ends, with more wood, with the broken remains of a couple of chairs. A black shape hangs on the wall, a beast's head, horns arching to the ceiling. The yellow light shows mouldy hair, black rotting nostrils, the shine of a glass eye; upward, the sweep of antlers. A stag's head, to preside over decay, relic of a day's shooting fifty years ago. The eyes, the only imperishables, stare yellow and hard straight ahead, signalling nothing. She steps past, out into the main hall, past an open door showing caverns of black; stops, listens, hears nothing but the movements of an old house in the wind, a faint rustle, a faint stirring of walls, of foundations, a slight tremor in tune with the movements of the softer earth outside. The stairs ascending to the sky are wildly lit beyond the window at their top. A door opens to rooms, to further doors, to green baize tables lying shipwrecked, to curtains falling like old banners, to sculleries left with only a cracked plate, an old stained copper pot, a sink of spiders. She stands quite still, the choices appalling. How long before one can go back and say, he is not there, I did not find him? One could have stayed behind, waited just a second longer after Fergus spoke, till another voice said, 'I'll go.' One does not have to risk this far; only a buried compulsion surfaces, takes control, speaks with one's voice, breaks the silence and drives one out here into the dark. She pushes the door, hears it creak further ajar, shines the torch swiftly around the room. A book case, sunk to the floor, books tumbling out. A heap of cinders before the grate, cold ashes of former fires. Another door, shut, and therefore more intimidating. She draws back, deciding upon the stairs, for at least there is that window, that comforting square of sky, clouds, dim winter light. One step; another step; the wood springs, groans under her feet, the banisters slide past softly dusted under her hand, a smooth slope and then a knob, another smooth slope and then a knob. How far does it go, this climb, this placing of one foot before another, up and up, toward the terrifying rooms at the top? She pauses before the window, lets her eyes take in the line of the dyke, the branches of an ash tree that grows near; and sees a light move steadily, quickly back along the path. A man walking with a torch, purposefully, having found what he came to seek. Not a will-o'-the-wisp, not marsh fire, not a ghost blown on the wind. She stands, watches, sees the straight progress, the slight wobble of a torch held in the hand of a man walking fast, hears the utter silence around her, the absorbent complete silence, and knows that she has not cheated. Returning quickly, almost casually down the stairs, across the hall through the half-open door, over the sticks and papers and pieces of dirty old junk, she holds in her mind the image of that receding light. The house holds nothing now, it is a shell, discarded by men, a fragile enclosure of walls and roof, of rooms that will rot away and at last, in a year or two only, be extinct. It falls silent before the increasing confidence of her step, its breathing quietened under the sharp passing crackle of paper, crack of wood, its menace gone with the departure of the light down the dyke, with the malice of human intentions. She crosses the last patch of floor, moves through the last door, comes to where they sit hunched around a match light, their faces pale. 'He's gone. I saw him go back down the dyke with his torch. I went through a couple of rooms and up the stairs, and saw him go from the landing window. If we want to follow him back, we'd better go fast.' There is such superiority in this, such relief, as the tension falls away from their uplifted faces and she sees there mirrored her certainty, it does not matter now, this she knows; the thing has been done, one of them has done it, and now they can go home released from an adventure that has gone on too long. To follow him back along the dyke will be a pretext for departure, but none of them will bother to pretend too much. They follow her out, coming one behind the other in the wake of her careless step, and she enjoys this, to let them believe that it was easy, it was nothing. And the way is free now, the dyke nothing but a familiar pathway dimmed by darkness, the surrounding fen a world that may be easily known and conquered. Behind her, they even sing in loud experimental shouts, and slash at the grasses with sticks. The boots go noisily through puddles, kick against stones. And yet something persists; the house is empty, she has explored it, she has brought them all back to normality so that they can breathe easily, and sing, and stamp. But he will always be there, that man waiting in the heart of the house, crouching behind the billiard table, slipping in to hide behind a curtain as soon as a door is opened, moving unseen across an opening to stand flat against a wall. There will always be that progress through the house, not knowing. There is still the confrontation and the close accusing stare of his eyes.

The kibbutz is all asleep; Ein Gev, sleeping exhausted after its day and night bombardment. The children are in the shelters, the adults sleeping above ground, the guards dozing upright with their guns at their sides. Curfew at seven, after an early supper in a dining-room quiet with their fatigue, their tension. We borrow a mood, we slip it on like gowns. I walk straight-footed, careful, as if in church. I am one of a trio, suddenly, the others an Australian girl and a Dutch boy; we all have our reasons for coming here; the kibbutzniks welcome us with shocked, bleared eyes and have no energy to speak; we are shown an unused hut, whose door is hard to open, and three beds are dragged out, three worn blankets handed silently. We must sleep only inches apart. Others who would pass in a moment, their thoughts unknown, must all at once be admitted to be real.

'Well, I must say, they could have been a bit more friendly. I feel more like a bloody prisoner than a tourist.' The Australian throws down her haversack upon one of the beds, bounces beside it to test for springs. 'Christ, we might as well sleep on the bare ground as on these.'

'Better than nothing, surely. Why did you come?' It angers me, coming from Gan Hagar, that she cannot feel the weary tension of the kibbutzniks nor understand their curtness. 'Are you going to work here?'

'Christ, no, it's on my route, that's all. I stopped in Tiberias to do some water-skiing, then I'd planned to take a boat across the lake, have a look at this side, and go on up to Safad to see the artists' colony. I'd no idea all this was happening. I couldn't even get a boat across, they didn't seem to be running any today and that was a real drag as I shan't get another chance. Only that god-awful bus. I've got to be back in Haifa in a week, then I'm getting a boat to Europe. You're from England, aren't you? I thought you must be, you're so goddam polite to everybody. Eating that egg at supper that was like a bleeding bullet. I'm from Melbourne, Australia. Rowan Rattigan, pleased to meet you. Be a good name to go on stage with, wouldn't it? Who's this kid?'

'My name is Jan van Rysing. I am from Utrecht.' He blinks at us, a mere child, sixteen or seventeen; unfolds his sleeping-bag, rolls it out flat, gets into it fully dressed and turns his face to the wall. His voice sounds muffled, effortful. 'I think we must sleep, as they send us away tomorrow.'

'What d'you mean?' In chorus, we are viragoes beside his inert form.

'Six o' clock. We can't stay. A lorry comes for us. Good night.'

'Good night.'

'Good night.'

'Why did you come, then?' Rowan turns to me, her sharp whisper giving way to her ordinary voice. 'You don't seem too surprised by all this.'

'I suppose I just wanted to see what it would be like. Being somewhere dangerous.'

'Well, okay, here you are. It's dangerous, what's it

feel like? Then you can go home.'

'Nothing, nothing particular. I suppose we'll just spend the night here, and then they'll ship us off, and that will be that.'

'Talk about looking for trouble,' she says. 'Have a cigarette. D'you smoke? I've only got these rotten Israeli things that go out all the time, but I suppose they're better than nothing. Christ, it's hot in here, I must take my shirt off. D'you mind? God, I can't think how he can lie there in that sleeping-bag with all those clothes on, can you? I suppose he thinks he might be raped.' She pulls off her shirt, turns towards me a deep brown back with knobbly backbone and safety-pinned brastraps of worn elastic, rummages in her knapsack, discards socks, a tiny crumpled dress, a teddy-bear with no eyes. 'I always take my bear, I know it's childish. It's for good luck. Here, they're a bit crumpled, but I've got a full pack. I've got some Tarot cards here, too, I'll tell your fortune if you like. We might as well do something to pass the time.'

The walls are wood, pitted with the marks of drawing-pins where somebody once pinned family photographs, cuttings from papers, Israeli football teams. No one has slept here for months, years; in spite of the heat of the night there is a smell of mould, the single blanket on my bed smells of disuse. It is such a small hut, even for a ten-hour night until they fetch us at dawn. I sit beside Rowan and watch her lay the cards out on the bed, tipped by the rucked-up blanket this way and that, the kings and princes, the strange old symbols of man's fate.

'D'you believe in fate?' Her long nose casts a shadow on her cheek, her mouth purses as she lays the cards, her pointed chin very pronounced.

'I don't know, there doesn't seem to be any other explanation of what we do. I suppose one ought to believe in free will.'

'I knew for years that I'd come to Israel. We had this very strong Zionist group in Australia, went off and practised digging, learnt Israeli songs and all that. I suppose you must have guessed I'm Jewish. You're not are you? I thought you weren't. You look fantastically Anglo-Saxon. Though of course here that means something else. I've never been to England, never been to Europe. I can't wait to get to London, get myself some new clothes. Israel's pretty different to what I expected.' – 'It must be different if you're Jewish. What did you expect?'

'Oh, I don't know. I couldn't stick it when I got here. I left the group and took off on my own. I suppose it was cracked up to be something terrific back home, heaven maybe. And we landed up in a religious kibbutz and they shot us a load of crap. I'm not orthodox, you see. I don't believe in God, do you?'

'I don't know.' Here I am nothing, know nothing, but record messages. I see her fleet glance of suspicion as I let her go on.

'Hey, look, the hanged man. Well, you said you weren't superstitious. I suppose he's only a silly old geezer hanging upside down. I don't know why, but I believe these cards. I have to believe in something, being off on my own like this. I'm not going home for a year or two, you see, I'm going to travel, get about as much as I can. I thought I'd go to Spain, I know a guy who's got a house there. You ever been to Spain?'

'No.' The foot of the hanged man curls exquisitely, as if he enjoys his discomfort; I turn his head away. 'No, I don't fancy letting Franco have any of my money. And I'd hate it, knowing about all those people in jail.'

'Christ,' she says, 'you don't want to be squeamish. Everywhere's the same, you know that, don't you? There's men in jail everywhere. Ever heard about the way we treat the abos back home? It's as bad as a concentration camp. You'll end up going nowhere.'

'Maybe.'

Two of her cigarettes remain and we have eaten the last crumbs of chocolate from my pocket. The conversation goes on, her ebullience, my secrecy, and is repeated somewhere else. She gives out with both hands, carelessly, cigarettes, advice, anecdotes, confessions, she is spread right across the room and her particular smell fills the air; I am closed, quiet, in spite of some other will I hold myself apart. Gilbert is miles away. I am alone again. There is no approaching another, not through the mind, not through the body. Rowan says the English are aloof, the Israelis so hard. She is Australian, from another continent. I am a child on the green grass where the gargoyles spit breath into the empty air. My watch says one o'clock, our shutters are closed, the door is locked, the night outside, moon, trees, Syrians, all is invisible.

In the morning the voice wakes us, the door is thrown open; a shout, 'Autobus! Ha'yom ain avoda! No work today! Autobus, hurry please!' and half asleep, clutching together our random luggage, we stumble into blinding dawn light to where an army lorry stands and a man impatiently revs the engine, waiting to take us away. And down there beyond the trees, where the rough road curves round to the right, we see Kinneret lie, a lake of mercury, the shallow fishing-boats tied bobbing at its shore. A lake of peace, undisturbed in the pure early light; and we travel around its edge, beside the soft uncurling ripple of its water, back to where we began. In the evening another man is killed there as he draws in his fishing-nets and in the excitement of the catch, counting the flopping bloody-mouthed bodies in the bottom of his boat, his miraculous last haul, forgets perhaps where he is, floats too close to the muzzle of a hostile gun upon the shore, is picked off quickly like a poised bird, drops to lie face downward among the fish, who survive him by minutes. I hear it on the radio as I sit drinking my iced coffee in a bar in Tiberias, still wearing my ignorance like a charm.

'My name is Jo. Jo Catterall. Yes, I am English. No, I have not been here before.' An old man on a boat, sucking at his false teeth, sailing east for the first time too. Gilbert, at the boat rail, in a post office in Naples, standing at Gan Hagar with his back to me so that I still know how his face looks. Gilbert, Rowan, Zvi Mosseri; Naphtali, Gina, Larry, Lee; the names, the fleeting faces, indicating the existence of other worlds; Francis, Zvi, Rowan, Gilbert; I can only say that a situation recurs in which I am inextricably bound, which is, in spite of death, in spite of distance, never ended. My brother Tom, upon the sea-shore. A fat girl who smelt sweet. Gemma, a cousin who was in love. Their profiles remain turned, staring, they are the cards hidden in the pack to be laid upon the table, to make up the patterns of a life. They hold the past and the future. I am amazed that I put such trust in them, not knowing who they are. And each one signals, I exist, I am real, I am not your invention; but how may I be sure? The man in the empty house is real. The man I believed Gilbert to be is real. The girl on the train that chugs through the beech woods, she is real. The dead are real. It is I who have been invented

'How do you like Israel? How long will you stay? Are you Jewish? Why did you come here? When are you going home? Have you been to Tel Aviv, Haifa, Jerusalem, Eilat?' In this small country perched on the edge of sea and desert, we move in slowly inscribed circles. A tragedy, a joke; we share it within minutes, meet a stranger telling of it within hours. Another has always been this way before. The same story circulates, told in a dozen different ways. Have you heard? Is it true? Are you real?

And in Safad, as in Tel Aviv, Haifa, Jerusalem, Eilat, a small group has come together by chance, here I have joined it by chance, I am drawn by chance again into the moving caravan of another's world. A town lying coiled like a spring upon a hill, all its roads and streets join to make the spiral; some of its houses are blue as the early morning sky, painted against flies, against the evil eye. At the top – but I have never been to the top; the house is halfway up. Each night the sun sinks into the valley below our parapet, each night land becomes liquid, a lake of gold. There are other houses higher than ours, with yet more to see, poised in a more complete estrangement from the earth; and below there are the abandoned Arab houses set upon the slopes, that change from honey white and lose the light from their windows and turn blind black eyes down the valley, further still. Each night, hardened again into the outlines of rock and hill, the lake dries and becomes earth once more, stony, uncultivated. In our courtyard the mulberries drop from the tree and spurt juice from the stones, leaves part and another face appears. There is a man stretched in a wicker chair, a paperback book held over his head, a dog stretched beside him, patched fur mixing with the shadow of wicker and leaf. A woman perches upon the low wall, painting her long nails with dark maroon; her head held sideways to survey a hand catches at the sun glow, is lit like a cotton wick. There is a short man with a guitar, crouched on the doorstep, a tall blond man beside him, tapping out tunes on a tabletop roughened by weather, faded by sun. The tree covers them all with its mottled shade and they are edged with gold. This is how I see them as we enter first, Rowan and I, as we come in here having travelled from Tiberias. A self-absorbed world, a tiny society isolated in a city that only tolerates, that is how I see them as we go away.

'I'm sorry if you mind mess. We're both rather untidy

people.' We cross the paved yard, a huge tree's rafters spread to shut out the sky. Inside, the walls lean together, yellow and bumpy and bare. A guitar sticks out from under heaps of clothes on the bed, trousers, shirts, pyjamas spread like an organic growth across bed, chairs and floor. Plates lie across the table, margarine-smeared crusts, cigarette ends, cheese rind, spilt Nescafé and sour milk. Newspapers furl and flap and are in wet piles beneath the sink. A thin dog, its eyebrows raised, slides out from behind the door and licks the dust from my toes; my fingers move to and fro across its head, finding each bone, each hollow of the skull.

'Coffee? If I can find a mug.'

'Oh. Yes please.'

To come back here we stride across cobbles and up acres of white steps gleaming towards the sky; and he is a frail short figure ahead of me, in his black shirt and trousers hardly cut away from the shadowed sides of the houses that we pass. There is a little trail of strange tobacco, a sweetish smell lifting with the breeze. Half of the words of his last song are still playing in my head.

'Its ages since we had any girls in here. That's why it looks so foul.'

'Oh? I don't follow.'

'What are you doing here anyway?' He throws himself back on the springs of the only chair and lights a cigarette.

'Doing? Well, we haven't much money, and nowhere to sleep, and your friend said we could stay here. Are you surprised?'

'Well, frankly, yes.' He throws a cigarette. 'Girls don't just go home with perfectly strange men. I don't know you. I don't know what you want.'

Freedom ends where it meets suspicion. 'I told you all we needed was a bed for the night. You needn't have offered. Offered Rowan.'

'That kind of tough Australian,' he says. 'I've met

them like that before. They just travel around on their backs.'

'I think that's unfair. You don't know her.'

'I know a come-on look when I see one. And anyway, how do you think kids like that survive? She'll be on the move for three years, four years. She'll get the itch to travel and she won't go back home easily after that. Everybody she meets will take her for a whore and the only way she'll get along is by behaving like one. How d'you think she'll get across Europe from here otherwise, hitching rides with gentlemanly truck drivers who'll indulge her in conversations about Proust? I've seen the whole bit before. Nice Jewish kid, mother back home gets her all mixed up with the local Zionists, cheap trip to Israel, mother tells all the neighbours about how daughter's working her little heart out on a kibbutz, planting trees like mad, while daughter takes one look at it, does a bunk, leaves the rest of the party stranded, claps eyes on some beautiful Aryan bum like Lee and makes for the high life. If you can call Safad high life. But there are a hell of a lot of men like Lee around, and most of them not so pleasant.'

His face all shadow and teeth; ugly, pale, eyes that on stage seemed to hold tears. 'So everybody else is just one of a type? You've type cast Rowan and now Lee. What about me?'

'Christ. Trying desperately to kick over the traces. Good school, good family, am I right? Identifying like mad for some reason with Jewish Cause. Dying to be screwed by Jew, scoobi-doo. Playing at being bohemian, plenty of money to fall back on.'

'Not bad.' But the ache of tiredness comes back, the taste of ash. 'What about you?' He has made me want to inflict cruelty.

'Oh, me. Typical East End Jew out to make money. Chip on shoulder, hence longing for fame and wealth. Did you notice, they're coming all the way from Jerusalem to hear me? Larry Feinstein started in a small way and ended in a small way. Sorry it was a bad night.'

'I wondered why you sounded so angry. What the hell's the matter? You were fantastic. They loved it, specially that last one. So did I.'

'Did you really? Well, I suppose that's something. Coming from the cosmopolitan whirlpool of London. I've been here so long I was beginning to think I was quite a big fish; and what am I, a tadpole, a water beetle. This is rather a small puddle, as far as the music world's concerned. Still, I suppose we had a few cognoscenti tonight. That's what depressed me, I can do so much better than I did this evening. It suddenly seemed so hick, with those white shirts out front. And bloody Manny taking off his shirt halfway through as if he was still driving his tractor.'

'Who were they?'

'The Jerusalem crowd? A guy who does music criticism in the *Jerusalem Post*. I never dreamed he'd descend to pop, but then I suppose anyone's entitled to go slumming. I rather hope they might make us part of next year's tourist attractions. Real beatniks in Safad, you know. Then the woman with him, the one in red, works at the theatre, I think. So there's another possibility. The others were a mad professor you may have heard of, called Zvi Mosseri, and his wife, who I think is some kind of a doctor.'

'Zvi Mosseri? Yes, I have heard of him. Is he really a revolutionary?' The thin face, the stare of impersonal curiosity that contains no embarrassment; the sudden smile; and then he turns away, whispers to his wife, orders another drink. They wear full, light dresses, the women, and I catch 'Madame Rochas' upon the air. The men are both tall, dark, their shirts open at the neck but ironed and white. The Canadian, Lee, already has a hand upon Rowan's across the table, says, 'You could stay with us. We've got half a house.' The glances pass across me, mocking yet friendly. 'Yes, thanks very much.' The party from Jerusalem at the next table settles itself for the interval, Larry drinks water on stage, the bass player stretches his arms and yawns. 'What'll you have?' Lee handles our empty glasses like a waiter, 'Coke all round?' I turn, looking for Rowan. The man from Jerusalem leans his arms along the back of a chair, smiles, friendliness darting out and in again without warning, like a lizard. I turn my back, receiving the cold glass; and he turns simultaneously to the woman at his side and begins to talk rapidly to her in Hebrew until she laughs and shakes her head. 'Actually,' I tell Larry, 'he's a friend of a friend of mine.'

'I should think he's a friend of a friend of practically everybody. A friend of a friend, but not actually a friend. When the chips are down. No, I was joking, of course. He's just a bit of a thorn in the flesh of the government at the moment. Stirring things up at the University. A tiny pin prick in the tiger's paw. His students are supposed to adore him, of course. I believe he tells them they're going to be the inheritors of a united middle east, outnumbered a hundred to one by their Arab neighbours. It's not really bound to be a very popular doctrine, as you can imagine. Come on, have some coffee, it's getting cold.'

The long valley turning from gold to grey, nightly; the empty Arab houses like honeycombs, sucked of their honey, littered upon the hills. I ask him, 'Well, I suppose they did leave of their own accord? I mean, nobody forced them out. They could have stayed on.'

'Who? What the hell are you talking about?'

'The Arabs. The ones that used to live here.'

'Christ, it's a bit late at night to start talking about Arabs. Of course they could have. It was the landlords, the big guys in Damascus and Amman, who sold them out, sold the land to us. It was quite legal. But I do find the whole Exodus theme balls-achingly boring, especi-

ally at two in the morning. Let's get to bed, shall we?'
'Where?'
'Well, I didn't think you would particularly want to sleep with me, so I thought you could have Lee's bed and I'll curl up with the dog outside. Then if they come in, they can have mine. It's bigger.'
'Is that all right?'
'No it's a fucking nuisance, but there we are. I quite like sleeping under the stars, and the dog has to, because otherwise he pees in the room. Good night, then.'
'Good night.'

The song ends, the crowd wakes with the spread of applause, the clapping grows strong, certain, breaks into cheers and shouts for more. He creeps back on to the stage, sweating under the lights, his black clothes clinging to him, his hands bony and white, gesturing his acceptance. Lee at his side draws back, allowing him the centre. Tonight the club is full, every table used, the low stone ceiling of this ancient Arab house pressed with smoke. The hands rise to clap and wave, feet stamp under the tables, faces are flushed and damp with the heat and crush though the stone flags underfoot remain cold. Outside there is the cool breeze of the hilltop night, on the bald surrounding slopes there are jackals and wild dogs. The streets of the city rise towards the sky and stop before precipices, before stars. The Cabbalists turn and live in the shuttered houses, listening to God. In the ancient timbers, between the stones, rats run at night down to the wells. Outside the nightclub the cars are parked at the roadside, on rubble and grass. Around the tyres and the shining metal mudguards and the white rubber bumpers the weeds grow high, are tangling into the chrome as the night air, the passage of time, eats away at the metal. Everything is to be gnawed to the bone, left white as rocks in the moonlight. The town has been here, huddled upon its hill, and all has passed before it and gone away.

I come in again as the clapping falters and Larry takes a backward step, bowing. The air is damp and choking after the clarity of outside, my skin is wet at once and my throat filled again with smoke; but Rowan flings out her arms, clasps my hands in hers, cries, 'God, those two are really good, they're so *good!*' and her hair flies back from her bony face, and for a moment I see her carry her enthusiasm through Europe, a torch which all will try to extinguish because it makes them feel their lack, their darkness; I see her at last silenced by a coldness she cannot understand. But she is away, in a bound she is on the stage, hugging them, crying, bringing both men laughing, protesting, together, into the firm circle of her arms. And I stand, and want to move, and cannot. A voice behind me says, 'Who's the girl, then? Is she part of the act?' A deep woman's voice, touched with irony.

'Well, wouldn't you have liked to run out and hug them? I must say, they deserve it.' The man answers in a murmur; turning, I see the couple from Jerusalem, Zvi Mosseri and his beautiful pale wife in her summer evening dress, and with them another man whom I have not seen before; and then Zvi stands, leans propping himself on the table with one hand, calls out clearly above the last fragments of sound, 'Encore! Encore! Give us some more!' Faces half-turn to encourage, to support him; and Larry bows slightly again, smiles in our direction, including the Mosseris and myself in the same glance, catches Rowan and Lee each by the hand, waits for silence, breath held, and then calls back, 'Thank you, thank you. I would like to sing you a new song, one I wrote a couple of nights ago. This one is a lullaby. A song for a sleeping child in war time, who does not know what is going on.'

The audience waits, is silent. And he motions to Lee and Rowan to sit down, and they sit together, still holding hands, at the corner of the little stage. Three days ago we were in Ein Gev, a week ago I was with Gilbert. Time winds tighter and tighter, nothing takes long, Lee and Rowan are sitting holding hands like children, unselfconscious. There are no preliminaries, no rituals. Zvi Mosseri turns and smiles at me and I am sure that I have met him somewhere before. Yesterday is a year ago, tomorrow rushes in through the dawn. We stand at the edge of the precipice, at the end of the street where it falls into the sky. There is no time for sleep; the song lasts only for a few seconds, it is the dropping of a seed into the mind; and before I can turn the audience will be gone, broken up into separate people with separate places to go, Rowan will travel on towards Europe, Lee find another girl, Larry spring back into the shell of his irony, and all will be changed. It is as if scene-shifters rush about, bandaged with black and stockinged in the dark.

The last note sounds, the same as the first, so that in our minds the tune may go on, as if nothing has happened. I hear the woman behind me say, 'They really ought to come to Jerusalem. Wouldn't it be marvellous?' and a man's voice reply, 'I wonder if they would come. I wonder if we might be able to do something.' It is the visitor, the Mosseris' friend. And the woman, Ruth, says, 'Such a shame Hannah couldn't be here tonight, wouldn't she have loved it?'

'I'm sure they would come to Jerusalem if you asked them. If you could find them somewhere to play.' I hear myself, my interruption; and they are surprised too at my sudden turning and intrusion into their conversation, their faces are blank for a moment, I see them struggle like people who have been asleep, to reassume a conventional pose.

'Oh, do you think so? Oh, that would be good, wouldn't it. Are you a friend of theirs?'

'I'm staying with them. At the moment. I'm travelling

round Israel. But I'm a friend of Peter and Ella Lind, too. They told me to come and see you. You are Zvi Mosseri, aren't you?' It is a clumsy introduction; but he smiles, a sudden whole-hearted acceptance, the heavy lines of his face lifted, and she leans forward to hear more clearly, and all at once another door is opened, they want to know more, they are claiming me easily, suddenly, as a friend; I must tell them about myself, say exactly how the Linds are, I must come out for a drink, I must stay with them in Jerusalem. It is as if everybody is potentially a friend of everybody else, as if one only has to give the password to establish the right connection, turn the numbers to the correct sequence to be instantly admitted.

'Peter and Ella—' Now their faces are dim, I try to remember them, hear only his stridency of voice, her sudden laugh, see only wide trousers, flowing dresses, earrings, suede jackets, their trappings. 'Oh, you're going to Israel? I must give you some addresses. Great friends in Jerusalem. Love to see you. Simply must have their address.' A large house in Chiswick, a walk with perambulators in a little park. Aeroplanes overhead. Tea in a garden outside, children, cats, tortoises, wine in the early evening in long glasses, talk of a last trip abroad. Ella returning from the house with a notebook. Telephone numbers, assurances, and I depart like a messenger. Yet their faces evade me.

'Peter and Ella, goodness, how extraordinary—' And are the Linds' faces as remote to them as they are to me, or do they see, across all that space, a particular mannerism, hear a particular intonation, making the Linds dear to them, a smile, a way of saying hello, the curving line at the corner of a mouth; are these the things I bring back to them? Or are they a name, simply, written in an old address book – 'Oh, you're going to England, I simply must give you the address, great friends of ours, the Linds, in Chiswick, marvellous people' – are they

just the mechanism by which I am here?'
'I'd love to.'
'What'll you have? Ruth?'
'Oh, another vodka and lime please, darling.'
'I'd like the same, please.' They are the first people I have met here who drink alcohol; after weeks of drinking coffee and eating little, I feel the first mouthful touch my stomach like fire to kindling. I turn to Ruth Mosseri as her husband goes to buy more cigarettes, I am light with alcohol, I am stunned by her beauty. Hands like wax flowers, curved without a bone, a face so perfect in proportion, the short straight nose, long upper lip with its clearly marked cleft, the line of the mouth drawn with unusual distinctness, curving as she smiles at me into a deep declivity at its corner, as if long ago as a schoolgirl she studied habitually with a pencil point pressed there, at the corner of her mouth. Tonight she is wearing green, so that I see her eyes are also green; and her dress is cut away at the neck so that when she leans forward I notice the slight pale mounds of her breasts, securely pushed upward. For the first time I am aware, and afterwards I cannot be oblivious of the contrast; she, cool and curved as a swan, I holding tight my sunburned hands with their short cracked nails, tucking away my legs, hairy and brown, my dirty feet in their dust-stained sandals, here in my one dress, washed and hung out to dry a dozen times, bleached an uneven sky-blue by the sun, patched and marked with sweat and grease. I run a hand through my hair, trying to smooth it. 'Israel seems to suit you,' is what Ruth Mosseri says, her mouth drawn down its deep corners so that I cannot tell, cannot ever tell, whether she is serious.

And Zvi tells me, offering cigarettes, 'You look like a pioneer. Have you been slaving away on a kibbutz?'

'At Gan Hagar, in Gaza, and before that in the Emek. But I left Gaza – oh, it must be a week ago already.

I went straight to Ein Gev and then came up here. From Tiberias.'

'What the hell did you go to Ein Gev for? There's been bloody murder there these last few days.'

'That's why I went. But we were sent back.' His smile darts out and in, his eyes narrow in amusement or curiosity. I want to push Ein Gev under his nose, to force him to understand. But he says, 'That was why, was it? Oh dear, I see.'

'Well, I'd hardly have seen Israel if all I'd done was sit about in nightclubs drinking vodka, would I?'

His hands lift, Ruth looks down into her glass. People are leaving the bar and shout to each other and the glasses pile upon the bar top. On stage, Manny is dragging away wires. The floor is clammy, there is foam from spilt Coca Cola, trodden cigarette ends, bottle tops; I glimpse Rowan in the doorway, waving and then pushed on out of sight, and Lee's head white above the others under the light at the door. The stone walls drip with sweat, like a cave. Zvi says, 'You'd have seen it. You'd have seen what it ought to be like. Normal, you know, quiet. Somewhere where people can sit around and enjoy themselves in the evening without thinking about being blown up. Where one wouldn't have to talk politics all the time. Like England. I imagine England's still like that, isn't it? You haven't yet had your Algeria, have you. But I guess it'll be gentlemanly enough when it comes.'

'Algeria?'

'France was like that. I remember it. Wine, theatre, civilisation. Food and conversation. Everything battened down, hidden away behind the scenes. And now look at it. Torn in half, nearly wrecked by this Algerian war. And now everybody knows what the French are capable of. No illusions. I suppose the same could happen in England, but somehow one feels – no. Even the end of the Empire wasn't too nasty, was it, really?

Tea and cakes and Sunday afternoons, a great virtue.' And he smiles still, so that I am lost and smile back, in self defence.

'I thought you were meant to be some kind of revolutionary. You don't sound much like it.' And he puts up his chin and laughs, rubs his beard and then his eyes, glances across at Ruth, stares at me with that curiosity, daring me to go on. 'Well, that's what I heard, anyway.'

'Not from Peter and Ella, surely?'

'No. Not them.'

'Then who?'

'A man I met. A kibbutznik. And other people, too.'

'Ah.'

'Then you're not?'

'No, I'm just a historian,' he says at last. 'I lecture in modern history, political theory, that sort of thing. Not even very revolutionary lectures. Most of what I say has been said a dozen times before. Sorry to disappoint you. Were you expecting me to be waiting in the shadows with a bomb under my cloak? Or to be wearing battle dress or something?'

'No. No.' Ein Gev, embattled; stripes of moonlight distorting the ground; the enemy who will not come out, who will never disclose himself, the footsteps I am waiting to hear. In the end I only ask him, 'Why don't you come round and see Larry at the house? Then you could ask him about playing in Jerusalem. What about tomorrow?'

'Tomorrow, then.' And we say good night.

'Who was that you were talking to?' Rowan waits for me against a wall outside, smoking a cigarette, enticing a stray cat out with a whisk of a twig.

'Zvi Mosseri and his wife. I told you about him. The one everybody seems to disapprove of.' The cat leaps away stiff-backed and vanishes into shadow. 'Where's Lee?'

'He and Larry wanted to go over some song. They went on home.'

'It was nice of you to wait.'

'Oh, Christ,' she says, discounting it, 'That's okay. I wanted to say something to you. I think I might stay here, that's all.'

'For ever? With Lee?'

'For ever?' She is dazzled. 'Hell, I don't know what that means. For a while.' Our sandals go slapping over the cobbles, the way is familiar now, the town rises around us, silent in the small hours, even the sky no longer surprises, with its extraordinary brilliance of stars. We are easy-going, passing the dark alleyways that we have passed before. A deceptive familiarity, a surface ease. The cats scuttle in the dark and press up into doorways, somewhere in the heart of the town, unseen, somebody is still awake. We exaggerate, as if we have known each other for years, we drag our feet lazily and forget to speak.

'I don't think I will.'

'No, I didn't think you would. But it suits me fine. He said he'd teach me guitar. And I could get work here, perhaps.'

'What about Europe? Isn't your passage booked?'

'Oh, Europe.' And she turns on me her ironic smile. 'Europe can wait. What's the hurry?'

'You're staying for Lee, then? What'll you do, move in with him and Larry?'

'No. We thought we'd try and find a room. It's too crowded at the house. And you can hardly stay in bed all day if people are tramping through all the time.'

'But, Rowan,' I say, risking friendship, 'you've only known him about three days. Are you sure?'

'Listen, whose grandmother are you? Ever heard of love at first sight? Well, this is lust at first sight. So what, I've only known him a couple of days. All the more time to get to know each other, right?'

'Larry won't like it, if Lee moves out.'

Kicking a white pebble, deliberate yet careless, she replies with a laugh, 'Well, Larry isn't going to get it, is he?'

The gates are ajar, we pause in the yard where light pours over the cobbles from the open door, we come in noisy and refreshed from walking. Larry and Lee sit silently, raise their eyebrows at us. I look at Lee again, to understand; a large blond man, hair and brows bleached by the sun, skin deeply tanned, body hardly contained in faded denim and a tight black sweater; something slow and unruffled there, like a big slow-moving animal shouldering, chewing, through grass. His hands close over the guitar strings, over Rowan's hands, over fragile objects like wine glasses and cigarette lighters, with gradual care, as if he long ago grew used to the thought that he must approach everything in this way or break it at first touch. He waits, he accompanies Larry, he smiles at what Rowan says and often does not answer; he sits in a corner, squashed into a small space as if in apology, and answers questions in monosyllables and rolls carefully constructed cigarettes. Tonight he looks to Larry to speak first; and Larry screws up his mouth and points a thumb towards the wall, the thin partition wall between us and the next room, where Gina and Naphtali live and are shouting at each other in Hebrew. We crouch, guilty, disturbed, trying at once not to listen and to discover what is happening.

'I suppose we'll have to go. I can't stand this sort of thing.' Larry murmurs to Lee, ignoring us.

'What the hell's going on?' Rowan asks, unintimidated, her chin jutting with curiosity. 'What happened?'

'He's bawling her out for letting us stay here.'

'But you rented it, didn't you? God she sounds hysterical.'

'Well, yes, I rented it. Only I'm a bit behind with the rent and Lee's been living here for three months, and now you two are here, and he's suddenly got pissed off. So much for being a non-profiteering, non-capitalist landlord. But it's probably more to do with his work than anything.' Naphtali's latest sculpture, shrouded in sacking, a great rough column of stone, stands in the corner of the courtyard, hardly touched.

'Oh. Maybe we ought to go.' I glance at Rowan, she narrows her eyes and shakes her head. 'We're probably the last straw.' I sense once again the fragility of it, the little outpost built by a few people, the tiny frail society into which individuals group themselves; which at one gust, at one departure and another failure of nerve and another disagreement, will fly apart, disintegrate as if it has never been. I am here at the end of the act; my only reason to be here is to witness it, all Gina's hysterics, Naphtali's final decision, Rowan and Lee departing. And then I think that I know the Mosseris, that they have a solid world in which they have invited me to stay; that I shall leave and go to Jerusalem. And at once I am cheered, strengthened; there is an exterior reality, beyond tonight.

Rowan says, 'Shit, she'll get over it. It's probably her period or something.'

Next door crockery falls in a long gust of sharp sound, a voice begins to scream and sob. The dog, Naboth, gets up from his place on Larry's bed, nearest the wall, as if afraid that the house may fall upon him, and walks to a far corner.

'That's his dog. Only as soon as we moved in he came to live with us.' I remember how we sat in the courtyard on those evenings, how we arranged ourselves. Naphtali alone, the dog and Gina curled up against Larry; Gina's hand inside Larry's shirt, tickling him. Nothing shows, not until the surface is cracked. I think of Naphtali, his long slumped body, its apparent repose, his eyes half closed against what is going on. And around me, around us all, the heaps of dirty clothes, the remains of meals and empty bottles, the holes made in the walls by the repeated thumbing in of drawing-pins where pictures of Larry, torn out of newspapers, are pinned; the kicked, scuffed paintwork, the dog hairs matted everywhere. The cakes and bottles of wine that Gina has brought us, when he is out. The things we have taken.

Through the partition a door slams and something unbreakable thuds to the floor. And our door flies wide and Gina comes in, her face streaming, scored with tears, striped with rubbed mascara, her blond hair in tufts so that the dark roots show, her thin hands clasped, perhaps to prevent each other from flying out in further violence. 'I must come in, you don't mind, do you? God, that bourgeois pig, how I hate him.'

'Coffee.' Larry, gentle as never before, guides her like a lover to his chair.

'Oh, thanks. I'm sorry, everybody. Oh, that stupid pig, that stupid bugger.'

'We ought to go.' Larry takes her the cup, moves her hands to hold it.

'No, no. Hell, no, the whole point is, it's my house, I like having you here. I love it, the music, the people from the club, you all coming and going when you like, I love having you around. It's him. He can't really live a bohemian life, although he likes to pretend he can, with that beard and everything. He's just a bourgeois little shopkeeper at heart.'

And she takes a cigarette from Larry, lights it, puffs smoke through her nostrils; 'tragic finality', 'desperate calm', these are the phrases that come to mind; everything she says appears in inverted commas, as if she has rehearsed. I hear the echo, 'bohemian', 'bourgeois'; what I see is a painted landscape on which she plots her illusory search. Rejecting both European middle-class traditions, and the puritanism of the pioneers, she has decided to create a bohemian life for herself. She will pay us to stay here, to furnish her illusion; without us, without supporters, she is lost. And yet we are ordinary, Larry a young man with a minor talent, Lee a footloose Canadian on the make, Rowan and I ordinary girls, also looking for the extraordinary. What each of us has seen is not the other, not the limited human face and form but the shadow, glamorously large upon the wall. 'Don't go,' she pleads with us. 'Don't leave, please.' For we are a part of her life, chosen, deliberate, like the long blond hair, the Americanisms, the incessant smoking and drinking from bottles, the jerk of her thin body twisting to the music, late at night. Naphtali was deliberately picked too; she lives with an artist, she tells people, hinting that she might be his inspiration; and nurses up his contrary moods, encourages him to be wayward, unpredictable; until at last he begins to threaten the very structure she has created; and it is at this point that she has to make him stop. Why do I scorn her now, where before there was only envy? Because she pretends, to cover up a need; because a need exists where I did not perceive it. Because she is not strong, admirable, self-sufficient as I thought.

Larry says, 'Well, I must pay you the rent, anyway. And, if it'd make things easier, I expect Lee and the others could make some contribution, couldn't you?'

'Oh, it's not the money.' Her hand sweeps sideways in a cutting motion, refuses such considerations. 'For heaven's sake. I just think we're incompatible, after all. All he really cares about is security, work. A snug little nest with nobody wandering in to disturb him.' She gives the word 'security' a full weight of scorn. I think of Naphtali, his silence, the angry energy with which he sets at pieces of stone; I remember her spending a whole morning arranging dried flowers and grasses in a vase, constantly asking him how it looks, humming, flitting to and fro. I think of her sharp little sigh of annoyance as he stands over her, asking something, and she looks up from her game of patience, flicks a card down suddenly, indicates that it is all spoilt. How will they see us, if they think of us at all? The people whose arrival finally split them apart, faces unmemorable, names perhaps forgotten too. Birds of prey, poised above a death. We come and go, using the house, vaguely involved. It is they, the Israelis, who must stay. And when we are all gone, the house empty, the courtyard silent, the last western light dropping upon a cracked table scattered with leaves, broken chairs left empty through the winter months, gravel sprouting with weeds, the vine drooping from the wall, she, Gina, will be alone. Tonight I see her feel it with her nervous fingers, breathe it in on the warm air; while her mind ranges on, planning, ordering, and her swift talk never pauses, even now we are all poised to fly from her. At the time I feel little for her; people should not make incompatible marriages; it is better that they should part. Later only I hear her voice, saying that if this had not happened, if that ... if only ... if not ... and begin to estimate our carelessness, her loss.

'It's all rather different, now.' Before, as I woke in the afternoons from a long sleep, people would be singing. In the torpor of early evening, people gathered outside to eat sauerkraut, tinned beans, cake and cheese, to drink coffee and watch as Uri the bass player from the club stood braced against the cobbles, feet apart in dirty sneakers, aiming his knife at the trunk of the mulberry tree. As I came out, still clammy from the heat that filtered through broken shutters, still feeling the nausea of afternoon sleep, the sour after-taste, Gina would be crouched at the table, reading fortunes in outstretched palms, knitting long pallid costumes for herself to wear, telling a story at Naphtali's expense, or Larry's, or Lee's; as Rowan and Lee appeared, half naked still, half asleep, half entwined in their last embrace before sleep fell, Manny the drummer would make a space for them, they would curl quietly into the little group at Larry's side, or on a bench under the window, or propped against the curves of the long cane chair. And on some afternoons we would go out into the street, Larry and his guitar leading; and then shopkeepers, wakened, would come to their doors, and couples emerge from cafés where Turkish coffee was served in corners in the dark; and a chanting and leaping would follow us home, halfway up the spiral of the city, to where the iron gate stood open. It was this world that I wanted them to share. 'There were always people here,' I tell them. 'All singing, telling stories, you know.' A story I have invented, to tell to myself and strangers.

'Oh?' Ruth Mosseri's clear eyes question me, she looks around her involuntarily, at the courtyard deserted by all but the dog. Larry is asleep, Rowan and Lee have gone out; the others, as if warned by telepathy, have not appeared. From the house I hear the voice of Eartha Kitt on record, where Gina lies with pads of witch hazel on her eyes and her face rigid in a white face-pack so that she cannot move or speak but only lie like a mummy, suffering unseen. Naphtali is taking his things, fetching bags from the attic. The dog crosses the courtyard and lies down panting at the table leg, Ruth Mosseri moves her own smooth leg further away.

'You could ask him,' I say to Zvi, 'when he gets up. He'll probably be up soon.' The silence around us hums; mosquitoes are beginning to float beneath the branches. I am tense with my failure, and wish that they would go, or cease to exist. The assorted cracked cups hold the pale remains of our Nescafé, the ashtray holds the butts of our cigarettes, Ruth's marked with lipstick. Zvi seems to jerk himself awake, making an effort. 'Who? Larry Whatnot?'

'I expect he'll be up soon. He gets terribly tired.' Like a nurse, protecting. I am doing this for him. And yet it seems that the Mosseris have set their seal on it, the end of this little community; as if with their elegant clothes, their cosmopolitan Jerusalem air, they cannot allow the existence of anything so simple. Today I am ready to believe that it is all their fault, so uneasy am I in their company, as we wait for Larry, and he does not come. I think of Gilbert, working from five in the morning on the harsh land of the Gaza strip, of the meals eaten by the kibbutzniks, porridge, peppers, bread and yoghourt. 'You look like a pioneer. Have you been slaving away on a kibbutz or something?' As if it were a fault. And yet in the nightclub he stood and called for more in a different voice, made boyish in his enthusiasm. Now, trying to reconcile these conflicting thoughts, I am full of aggression towards the Mosseris, who took me so easily, so uncritically, for a friend. I am not like the Linds, I want to tell them, I do not live in a big house in Chiswick; they are not really friends of mine, therefore I cannot be a friend of yours. It is all a mistake. I am not who you thought. Let us go back to the beginning, before we ever began this charade. And then I remember that it was I who spoke first, Zvi who merely smiled, as one might at a stranger who is enjoying a performance too; it was I who imposed, being so sure of myself.

'What's the matter? You look furious.'

Unguarded, surprised at having been so quickly discovered, I answer without thinking, 'You think it's ridiculous, don't you? You're just having fun, doing a bit of slumming, seeing how the beatniks live. You don't really care about Larry, do you?'

Close to me, his face appears to set in concentration; light from between the leaves flecking his hair and beard throws shadows under his eyes; it is a curiously shuttered look, as if he is hiding; a look I have seen before, in the club when I asked him about his politics, and on the first night, as he listened to the music, before I knew who he was. It is as if he begins to think seriously, to judge the fairness of what is said, and becomes so engrossed with some other thought of his own that he cannot think what is going on around him; as if his reality is so remote that words, looks, allow no communication. 'No, I don't think it's ridiculous,' he says at last. 'The boy's got talent. I thought he was marvellous. I don't see why he shouldn't go down very well in Jerusalem, and I thought I might be able to provide a connection, that was all. Forgive me if I seemed patronising. But it occurred to me that all the rest of you are just camp followers really, aren't you? Clustering round, trying to identify with a particular way of life. I suppose it's always happened to artists. They tend to become the honey pot for a lot of envious flies. But I was just struck by, well, a certain rather alarming conformity, if you want to know. Forgive me for speaking frankly. Anyway, I suppose being a neo-beatnik in an artists' colony in Safad isn't a bad way of identifying. At least you don't try to achieve anything.' He says 'artists' colony' as if we are penguins, identical, lost on an ice floe, crouched upon our eggs. And I feel once again the sense of loss, experienced once already when he spoke of kibbutz life with that irony.

'I've only been here a few days. And I'm leaving, anyway.'

'Don't take any notice of him,' Ruth says quietly; and I see that her part must always be to soothe, to accommodate. 'He's just a cynic. And, after all, what are you, twenty?'

'Yes.' And what, I want to ask, is so real about your lives, what is there that is missing here, at Gan Hagar, at Ein Gev? What is your experience that it so invalidates mine? I am ready to forget last night, to say that it never happened; the dance will go on, the song ring out, in a minute all these people of whom I am so proud will come into the courtyard, begin their masque, in order to prove me right; they will take up their attitudes, and there will be no dissent, nothing to disturb. But I stare back at the Mosseris, and remain baffled.

And only Larry comes out, drying his hands upon his black jeans, his hair sleeked back into its quiff for appearance on stage, his black shirt unbuttoned, a large silver medallion swinging upon his pale chest. In the daylight he looks small, shabby, his black clothes funereal. As he comes closer I see that he has been squeezing a spot on his chin. In England he and I would never have met or, if we had, it would have been to assess, criticise, note only externals, reinforce prejudices, and move on.

'Hello,' he says now, putting out a hand, first to Ruth, then to Zvi, with a formal gesture that seems strange here. 'I'm glad you came round.'

The look on Zvi Mosseri's face could be relief, but he is still guarded with Larry as he never is with me, a child. They begin to exchange addresses and the names of people, to draw street maps of Jerusalem on the backs of envelopes, while Ruth and I, sitting well back in our chairs, exchange a smile every few minutes and find nothing to say. Down in the valley the empty windows of the abandoned houses are black, like holes; it is only the light of the sunset that makes them appear beautiful.

'Shalom,' it is more a warning, barked out suddenly, than a greeting. Naphtali comes out of the house, dragging a large cardboard suitcase and a leather bag full of tools. What he sees is a group of strangers sitting in his garden, watching him; we see him move across before us as if we are the audience, he is the actor, until he is at the gate; and somehow each of us is powerless to speak. The dog stands up, drags its hind legs out of the dust, rattles its claws against the rounded stones as it follows him to the gate. But there it loses its original intention, gives way to habit, to inertia; slinks back to the known table leg, cool in the evening shade. Once perhaps it knew some allegiance, but now it is a creature of the place, looking only for a comfortable spot in which to lie. Naphtali reaches the gate, his exit, refusing all the time to look in our direction. A few hairs show in his beard, on the backs of his hands; his shirt pulls out of his trousers as he heaves the gate, and we all see its ragged ends. The gates swing open, the iron bars patterning the ground, casting Naphtali into shade; and then it shuts behind him, clanging, and his wide shoulders and dark bent head are outside it and he is gone. Indoors loud sobbing sounds, the record stops suddenly with a scream as if something has been thrown at the gramophone and the needle dragged an inch across the grooves. A few mulberries, shaken from a branch, thump sodden with juice to spurt dark red upon the stones. I see the Mosseris silenced, their fingers moving about on the table their eyes questioning each other. For a moment is upon us, there is no stopping nor drawing breath nor reflecting on what has been; now they are saying to me, abandon this, take what we offer, see things our way, accept explanations. 'And so, you will come to Jerusalem?'

'Soon, yes.' Perhaps I have learned to establish a small gap for myself, just enough to breathe in. Ruth looks annoyed, for some reason, as if she has some plan that I have refused to fit. In Zvi's face, I can read only a new and rather surprised respect. Bolder, I tell them, 'Quite soon, I will come to Jerusalem.'

4

NOTHING has been kept, nothing thrown away. What is here was always here, a bald earth pitted like the surface of the moon. A man here would look strange as a martian, casting his brief shade. The mad prophet only, crouching under the long tent of his robes, watches for the V-shadow cast on the earth by a nearing raven, bringing food. Black birds rise upon a blue-black sky, signs from a fierce God showing favour. The idolaters are in their temples, incense burning before their columns of brass, their cow-gods cast in bright metal swallowing men. The train winds between pathless hills, among the scarred rocks and close-growing scrub, climbing to Jerusalem. And the first marks that man has made are blocks of concrete turning white sides to the sun, wrecked American taxis, runs and tangles of barbed wire, cans thrown in heaps. The first humans are children playing in the dust, in the full sun. Jerusalem, an immigrant housing estate thrown quickly together, a bleak suburb built of haste and need. But from the station the bus climbs again into the open and there are broad streets, trees, a clean wind from the hills; the skyline curls, hilltop to hilltop, the shapes carved by men to dominate their oldest holy place, the rocks that have always been, the steep slopes that are become graveyards, the mountains built of bones. Across the city, man-made too, the long cicatrice of no-man's-land, the torn open buildings, empty yards of stone and concrete, whorls of barbed wire tangling among weeds, ruins, corrugated iron sheets. An Arab soldier lies flat upon a sunbaked roof, behind sandbags; upon us, the long stare of his binoculars. Beyond him the old city is closed, invisible within walls, its domes alone moving in the sun like planets; and the villages of the other side of the valley are steeply shadowed, the houses honey-pale, silent and uninhabited in the glare of noon. Somebody is always telling me how bare the earth is there, how green and rich is Israel. The closed streets are another land, another world. The men there move like moles, underground. The horizon shudders, light fires a sudden gold on a far roof. It is hard to look across at the old city, to believe in its existence. There are the roads going to Jericho, to Bethlehem, to the Dead Sea, to Hebron; roads to places which only exist in dream, in the earliest moments of childhood, which are inaccessible. The maps stop, leaving a gap; the way is sketched only vaguely; at the back of the mind an image remains, from a story told long ago. Jericho, the walled cardboard city; Bethlehem, with thatched huts and cotton-wool snow. The childhood pictures remain, there being no alternative. The border draws the eye with a terrible persistence, the other side is always there, lying spread across the hills yet invisible, closed, only the slight movement of heat discernible. Half a city; half of the picture; the clap of a single hand.

'First time you've been here?' The taxi-driver turns downhill again, after showing me; in a street of trees and square houses like small fortresses I leave him the rest of my money and begin to walk past the numbers in search of the Mosseris' house, the number nine that has been in my address-book since I left London.

'Yes. Yes, this is the Mosseri house. I am sorry, they are not here. Can I help you, please?' The gate opens upon a paved garden, from under a trailing plant a woman looks up at me, a pale, worn face, sepia beneath the brown, veined eyes. The hand raised to shield her eyes from the sun as she peers at me is weighted with dull rings and stained with ink.

'I was invited. They asked me to come and stay when I was in Jerusalem.'

'Everybody who lives in Jerusalem always says that. It doesn't mean they're going to be home, though. But I suppose you'd better come in. What's your name? As a matter of fact, Zvi might be back tonight. I don't know. I am a cousin of his, by the way, my name is Lydia, Lydia Volkovsky. I am studying at the university. Are you interested in ancient history? Of course, they are barbarians here, the students, utter barbarians.' The deep breathy voice, its rapid English, faultless but heavily accented, the exhausted brown eyes hold me there in the courtyard, my suitcase in my hand, my mind blank. 'Do you know, they think nothing of marking the manuscripts, documents hundreds, thousands of years old, with a blue biro? As if they were marking off a shopping-list? There is no respect for our heritage. Not any more. I, I had no chance to be a student, you see. I had to wait until I am old. I know what it is to long for knowledge, to be locked away, despised, refused entry to places of learning. I say to them, these students. But nobody listens. Oh, well, come in, I am sure we shall have a lot to talk about. Tell me, how do you know Zvi? Do you know Ruth too? Ruth has gone to Paris. Zvi was to go for a few days, but his work keeps him here. Work, he says, I call it meddling. I don't mean his lecturing, you know, I mean his politics. Writing pamphlets, talking, what's the use? Napoleon never had any use for pamphlets. The great men of history, the great politicians, men of action they were, pamphlet-writers none of them. Ah well, my dear, sit down, and I will prepare some coffee.'

We drink Nescafé, the grains floating unassimilated on the surface of pale liquid thickened with condensed milk. I make room for myself on a chaise-longue littered with papers, pages and pages of tiny writing; a few sheets detach themselves and float evenly to the floor.

'You know, of course, that ancient Hebrew had no punctuation, no vowels even. The sounds were understood from the consonants themselves. But these students are not content with that; do you know, I even found that somebody has put in punctuation marks on a manuscript that dates from the time of Judas Maccabeus? Illiterates, that's what they are, vandals. Zvi, he doesn't mind this. He thinks nothing of sitting on a desk to lecture to them with his feet on a chair and his students sitting about on the floor. But then, that's modern history, that's different.'

'Did you say he'd be back this evening?' I imagine myself sitting here, days hence, tied fast in words like a fly in her web, the Nescafé cold before me.

'I should think he might. He only went to see somebody in Tel Aviv. Something to do with a newspaper, I don't know. He's a fine historian, though, so they say. If you ask me, nobody recognises the importance of historical evidence any more. The things people throw away. When we ought to keep every telephone directory, every laundry list. What will future historians know about us? Everything is thrown away, into the dustbin, into the fire. Do you keep letters? Do you keep diaries? I write down what I do every single day. Actions, thoughts, meals, everything. I know what you will think, you will say to me, Lydia, is your life so important? Will future generations be interested in what you do? And I say, study the ant and you will understand the anthill, that is a microcosm of the world.'

'But you must have led an unusual life, anyway?' Somewhere in a diary I have written the exact time and the exact place; but how much has escaped between the words?

'Things happened to me that have not happened to everyone, that is true. Do you know, I never sleep at night. Not a wink. I have not slept since 1935. That is when my husband died. I have to take pills, to calm me. I am neurotic, the doctors say, that is to say, my nerves are abnormally sensitised. I sit in a chair to rest, I cannot lie flat because my back is weak and would not allow me to get up if I were to lie down. I never take sugar, it poisons the blood. First thing in the morning, I drink an infusion, a tisane. Without this the kidneys will not function properly. And when I take a bath I always put salt in the water.'

'I'm sure future historians will be interested in all that,' I murmur to her, and hunt in pockets and bags for cigarettes.

'No, thank you, my dear, I have not smoked since 1948. When the state of Israel was founded, you know. Ah, is that a car at the door? It could be Zvi already. Would you go and see, my dear, I feel my back a little weakened.'

The scene is never that which I have prepared for myself. Zvi and Ruth together, a meal served, the talk easily flowing from our memories of Safad, from some common ability to survive the wreckage of others' homes, that is what I imagined. A repetition of what has already been. Lydia, unexpected and irrelevant, claims no sympathy now; it is only later that I remember her with curiosity.

'Ruth is in Paris?'

He is already across the courtyard before he sees me open the door. I am empty-handed, standing like a forgetful hostess, I have to say something.

'Ah, Jo! what a nice surprise. I hope Lydia has been looking after you? Lydia? Yes, Ruth is in Paris, she went to visit some friends. There's a Zadkine exhibition on, and a play she wanted to see.' He leads me into the dark interior. 'Ugh, whatever's that? You call that coffee, Lydia? Let's have a drink, there's some vermouth somewhere, I must say I could do with it. Well, and what do you think of Jerusalem? Have you been all round Israel yet? And why aren't you back doing your bit on your kibbutz?'

'Kibbutz, she doesn't want to go to a kibbutz, what are you telling her, Zvi?'

'Shut up, Lydia. Well, where have you been?' Surprised by his aggression into an obedient answer, I tell him, Caesarea, Acre, Tel Aviv, all out of order, the places of interest.

'So, you've been quite a good tourist? Why haven't you been to the Negev, you must see the Negev.'

'I want to go there last. I am saving it to the last.'

'You must go to Eilat, there's a good beach, marvellous water-skiing.' As if he is testing me, or only wishing to mock. I am beginning to wonder why I am here; suddenly there floods in the familiar sensation of complete loss of courage, breaking out like sweat all over; I am wrong, this is wrong, I want to retract. He is distraught, almost frantic with something, I have come at the wrong moment; or, I should not have come at all. 'Everybody who lives in Jerusalem always says that. It doesn't mean they're going to be home, though.' I am a trespasser, found out.

'I don't want to disturb you, Zvi, if you're busy,' I tell him carefully. 'I'll look round Jerusalem on my own. I could stay in the youth hostel easily. There must be one, isn't there?'

He looks across at me, vague, raising his glass of vermouth. Lydia says, 'Youth hostel, you don't want to go there.' My warm fingers take the chilled glass before me, a slice of lemon swims up against my lip, there is the chink of ice in big blocks from that refrigerator that purrs in the kitchen, filling the room.

'No, no, of course not. Stay here, why not? We've plenty of room. I have to go out this evening and I must work tomorrow, but you take a guided tour round Jerusalem, you will see more. I will treat you. Otherwise you will see nothing. And then in the evening we will talk.'

'A guided tour? But I don't need one, thanks. I always just walk round places on my own. I don't care about seeing the sights, I just like to get my own impression of places.' Now I know that anger has been growing in me for hours, fermenting while I waited for him and listened to Lydia and heard myself put off and put off. 'I'm perfectly capable of looking after myself, thank you.' But what is it that I expected, what right have I, walking into his house, to require anything different? Only a word reminds me, a thought, a smile, something small which seemed to indicate once a recognition, interest, a common pleasure in each other's company. Something so slight that the balance is only just weighted, this way or that, Jerusalem or the Negev, to stay or to leave; something too fragile surely to cause so profound a disappointment.

'Yes, I'm sure you are, Jo. But please do Jerusalem the honour of looking at it properly, not just wandering about the back streets dreaming up stories and confirming your own prejudices, will you. Don't look so angry, you look so childish when you do that I'll feel I ought to send a nanny out with you.' His hand covers mine suddenly, squeezes it upon the table, making me jump. 'Of course, you could always stay here with Lydia, and I'll go round the city with you in a day or two, if you like.'

'I could show you my work,' Lydia says, 'tell you about my manuscripts. If you are interested—'

'No it's all right, thank you. I'll take the guided tour. It'll be a new experience, I suppose.' Beside me I see Zvi laugh into his drink, blowing bubbles, beginning to relax.

Of which Jerusalem am I telling? Of the tour, in which we crawl over the surface of half the city, examining data, building up theories, learning the history of new monuments and recent battles? Of the other half, silent, submerged? Of dialogues woven through the night and into the small hours of the morning, in which ideas present themselves, collect to form attitudes, are questioned, dispersed; in which the argument goes on, to elicit what may appear to be the truth? Or is it of the silences, the pauses between words, between actions, the movements which never take place; of the gaps between buildings, where mortar bombs tore down masonry, of bullet holes, of the spaces between trees and walls, the invisible line between mirage and solidity when the sun is at its height; of the short hours between falling asleep and waking, in which dream creates the patterns of our lives and a whole city lies open to be explored? I have waited so long for Jerusalem; since, a pre-literate being, a savage upon the shore, I buried my hopes, knowing I would find them again, since I first heard the name, the word, given to what we search for, since my brain told me of the city built upon rock, the infallible pure form, the end of man's creativity. I have waited so long that I do not know what it is; I stumble out into the streets, blind as a wakened owl, waiting to be told.

Today, at the tourist agency, I find a young South African, two Brazilian ladies, a middle-aged English couple and myself. It is as if we have been sent, to act. Slowly we grope towards our parts, establish our idiosyncrasies, reveal our prejudices, become fluent with our lines. The guide, a student in dark glasses, grins with his mouth, veiling his dislike of us; he is the stage manager, rushing about arranging things, standing back with his smile of irony. It was from this encounter that I wanted to protect myself; but I am doing what Zvi suggests, I am being taken around the city, I am passive to receive. We set off after lunch in an old Buick, jammed together buttock to buttock on the sagging springs. The young guide drives with his arm laid along the edge of the open window, one hand upon the wheel; plastic dolls bob upon the windscreen, the radio shouts at us, a song sung in London a year ago, and where I sit I feel the force of the wind upon my face, drying skin, blowing hair, making all else hardly audible; I love it, this narcotic wind, blurring the edges, removing the proximity of that fat thigh against mine. And the indigestible past presents itself, in fragments, in layers, perversely jumbled. Excavations, roads, towers, hills, walls holed like Emmenthal cheese, wire, stones, the exhibits. 'History repeats itself,' our guide tells us smugly, making himself a charmed child of coincidence, safely at home with paradox. We stand in a row, at one edge of the city, where the stones at our feet are the floors of Rehoboam, recently dug and pored over, and the walls that stand are those of a former kibbutz. Beyond the excavations the buildings and white hills of Jerusalem stretch and flow to the horizon. I am looking at the mosques, the steep streets, the unfamiliar, the untouchable. Somebody says again, how bare it is, how dry, on the other side; it is the South African, his profile turned like a bird's to search only for worms in a whole world of other creatures, his eyes palest blue when he looks towards me, surprised perhaps by my stare.

'You need money to have piped water, here.' I have broken the silence, the truce.

'But they are lazy people,' he says. 'They will not work. That is what I have heard. Give them the machinery to cultivate their land, and they would only leave it to fall apart. Isn't that true?' His voice is slow, careful, he appeals to the guide as to a prosecuting counsel. The guide snorts through his nose and folds his arms and sighs, having heard it all before; a student, he is earning holiday money, paid to maintain the peace.

The South African persists, his pale eye of anger fixed on me, his hand laid out to touch the guide's forearm like an insult. 'Isn't that true? That's what I've heard.'

And, shrugging his shoulders under his light shirt, the guide says in a flat voice, 'How should I know? I have never been there. And prejudice, you know, exists everywhere.' He takes off his dark glasses and looks at me, frowning; and I am discovered, driven as I was by something simply in the blond young man's stance, in his accent, to attack. The student guide is like a school teacher, calming young children, not showing who is right; I look in vain for sympathy, a preference, and he puts on his dark glasses again so that his face is impassive. 'There you see again Mount Zion, there the Wailing Wall. The road to Jericho. The Mount of Olives. The Intercontinental Hotel.' He turns away from us, one arm gesturing. And the others, who all watched and listened as we stood on the edge of dissent, looking down, begin to pay more desultory attention, as if they can no longer concentrate. One of the Brazilian ladies begins to fan herself with a newspaper and the English housewife in her cotton print, sturdy against the sun, says to her husband, 'Isn't it lovely, George? One really can't imagine that anyone should want to fight over it.' And makes a little hat out of her handkerchief, to cover her head; not out of deference to the view, but because the sun after all is too strong. Cameras flash, recording, people pause, stiffen and exclaim, after the shutter's click. And I stand apart, I listen, I judge, I am looking for right and wrong, black and white, the absolutes which I must have come here to find.

And there is another day, another journey through Jerusalem; on foot, sandalled and alone, I shuffle down the hill into the valley of Hinnom, where the paths are sheep-sized, strewn with boulders, where dry bushes jut from the hillside and there are black-eyed children hopping away like birds. At the bottom of the valley, men are building a road. The yellow earth is cut and levelled, tarmac pours in a sticky stream. The men look up and I greet them and go on; they are construction workers, Arabs, young men and older men, eyes narrowed against the sun or against intrusion, I do not know. At the bottom of the valley the rocks are sharp, and as I begin to climb again earth falls away beneath my feet in a stream, pebbles and dust. The hills are all around me, the hills of Jerusalem green with flowers and young grass, the sky above is a washed, April blue; colour has returned, yellow daisies with wide open faces, mimosa, poppies, the tangle of scarlet and red in the deserted gardens, the live pine-cones set in a fur of green; clouds sail where there was no cloud, drawing their shadows smoothly across the hills. The city is made of pine trees, flowered lichen, the sound of bees in grass. I reach the base of Mount Zion and climb the Hativat Yerushalayim, almost empty of traffic in midafternoon, to reach the Jaffa Gate. To my left the walls still stand, there is still the wire, the rusted iron, the pocked, torn stonework of the place I knew as no-man's-land. A room has been torn away, on the remaining one wall there is a fireplace, a shelf. Grass grows here now, tall weeds climb, there is a gentleness in ruin. And along the grim grey walls that flank the Jaffa Road, where nobody walked and no hand ever drew, somebody has chalked a long mural, a smudged festival of red, blue, yellow and green. Children, perhaps. Students returning home after a party. An artist maddened by the last grey expanse. And in a moment I am through the ancient gate and into a little square, I am drawn on down, into narrow darkened places, into an intimacy, a warmth of smell, a cluster of people, a descending passageway, on and on past stalls of hanging leather, embroidery, fruit, calves' heads, their bloody closed eyes, bananas green upon branches, butts dark with olives; spit, urine, breath, heat. The Street of the Chain, a voice says; and I know that this is a lie, a dream, a return to the dark tunnel from which I was born, from which we are all born, and which nobody may remember, to which nobody may return. A dream of Jerusalem. That is all.

'I don't understand. Why d'you have to be so cynical?'

'I am not particularly cynical. I am simply much older than you.'

'But nobody of your generation seems to have any ideals. That is what I admire so much about the kibbutzniks. They seem so certain. I'd never met anybody who was, like that.' Gilbert at the boat rail, spread flat upon the grass at Gan Hagar; Zvi drinking his vodka late at night upon the balcony, in Jerusalem. The same flowery skies of stars, the strange light midnight. Only the winds grow a little cooler in September.

'It's romanticism,' Zvi says, 'the way you see it. Not bad, not good. I find that those are words I need to use less and less. What does it mean? The idea, this is good, this is bad; a mind divided against itself. In the kibbutz the majority decide what is good for the individual, and that is what I cannot accept. But, of course, when I was your age, I thought much as you do.'

'When I was your age. . . . But you are cynical. Patronising, too.'

'I'm sorry.' He leans his forearms on the balcony, the white sleeves of his shirt rolled up. I want to look to see the number printed there, but dare not. 'You believe, though, that the majority has the right to decide for the minority, for the individual?' He is enjoying this in a leisured way, drawing me on, a teacher to a student. And I plunge in always, unregarding.

'It still seems to me the best way of life I've seen. They do decide right, you see, don't they? They may decide for the individual, but what they do decide is good.'

'So you believe in good and evil, after all?'

'Well, I don't see how one can't. I mean, how could anything mean anything, otherwise?' I sit back in the wicker chair, my legs tired with standing, and see his face turned back to speak to me, in half-profile. The carob trees beyond the courtyard, the row of little cypresses, bend in the wind. There is a smell of warmed stones, cats.

'Do you believe in good men and bad men, then? The heroes and the villains of the piece?'

'No, obviously, they're mixed in all of us. But on the whole I think man has natural vices, selfishness, ambition, covetousness, things like that, which he has to control. They're glorified as positive virtues in the west, they're what one's taught to accept. And here, I suppose, in the cities. But in the kibbutz they're curbed, because everybody believes in something higher.'

'You good little socialist,' he laughs. 'But what if the set-up is exclusive? What if it only applies to a few hundred people? That's not very just, is it? And anyway, to go back to what you were just saying, why must you talk about vices and virtues? Why can't they just be attributes? Attitudes which people take up according to the circumstances they find themselves in? What a passion you have for self-castigation. Tell me, what do you think the state of nature is, then? Pure aggression? Pure selfishness and bloodthirstiness?'

'Yes. Yes, I suppose I do. A state of chaos. Well, that's how it seems, doesn't it? I'm sure people's vices outrun their natural virtues, or attributes, or whatever you want to call them. That's why the kibbutz works so well. I'm sure that if I lived in a kibbutz and found I didn't get on well there, I'd blame myself rather than the kibbutz. It wouldn't be the system's fault.'

'Just that you weren't sublimating hard enough? But in that case why aren't you there?'

'I'm going back. To Gan Hagar.'
'To live? You aren't serious.'
'I don't know. I might. I want to see.'

'Well, he says, his back to the balcony now, hands spread wide, his face dark and invisible against the black trees that line the street, 'Well, well. I wonder if you will. I wouldn't have thought you were a joiner, a bender to the common will. Rather more of an individualist, I would have thought.' Again I am in the Emek under Gilboa, cracking the hard earth with my hoe, sweat running into my eyes, the bodies of others around me; the silence, the effort of work; sun, burning up excess energy; something so demanding that there is nothing left over, no excuse, no criticism, no room, no time for thought. And in Gan Hagar, where there is rubble to be shovelled, concrete to be laid, wood to be fitted to wood. I am longing again for the freedom to work, to be totally absorbed. The night in Jerusalem is all at once too airy, upon the hills; and on the balcony, between us, there is restlessness, unease.

Zvi says, watching, 'Shall I tell you what I think? You can laugh if you like, you with your cynical view of man's potential. I believe people can create a perfect society, not beg to have it forced upon them, and that it needn't be rigid or exclusive as the kibbutzim tend to be – no, don't attack me yet, not all kibbutzim, but some, not yours I am sure – but as some of them tend to be. You make me feel I am walking on eggs, do you know that? I think the state of nature, on the whole, is a happy, profitable, mutual situation. I think that, once he's free from fear, man is no longer aggressive, selfish, all those things you so rightly condemned. But it's because he's accepted those things in his own nature, not outlawed them, not repressed them. Because he's forgotten the terminology of good and bad, acceptable and non-acceptable, the old Judao-Christian dualism that separates and categorises. When a man is afraid, the fear is something he invents. It is more than the simple reaction of alarm to a dangerous situation; what we live with, fear, anxiety, is really a fear of nothing, of what might be in the void. But look into the void, face the centre, and what do you find? Nothing. Fear is illusion. And once a man is disillusioned of his fear he is free. He no longer has to act aggressively, to gain power over others. You see? A revolution, but from within. It sounds easier than it is, perhaps.'

'But what if one tries to look into the centre and it evades one? If one tries to look at the fear, and it escapes to somewhere else?' At Ein Gev, the enemy who is not there, the Syrian lying like a lion along a branch.

'It's just what I said, Jo, it doesn't exist. There is no evil, outside ourselves. No spooks in the night. We invented the whole charade, evil, the devil, death, punishment, sin. We have made complex what is simple. Death is simply the decay, the non-functioning of the organism. It is endemic in life. We all begin to die, we just do it differently. We invent a hell for ourselves, in case we're enjoying life too much, in case we forget that all good things come to an end. Come on, you're shivering, let's go inside. I'll make some coffee and then perhaps we ought to go to bed.'

He thought, here I am, talking like a professor again, what bad habits teachers grow; and how can I ever get used to it, be hardened to it, that limpid vulnerability of the young; and that on faces, some faces, one watched the moving patterns of thought, one thought following on another and another, as the shadows of clouds moved, momentarily darkening a landscape. One said things and thought that one believed them, having said them before in other places and at other times; and not until they were visible on another's face, passing, clouding, did they seem suspect. He thought, sometimes I realise the onset of age, suspecting the facility of my own thought. But she did not appear to judge him but sat considering, taking him seriously. He sensed a restless hunger for information, certainty, fact. She looked dissatisfied still, having asked for absolutes and been offered his middle-aged ambiguities, the paradoxes which suited him, his convoluted ways of thought. The position was familiar; slightly bowed head, hands locked, mouth a little open as if to speak, as if the arguments to defeat him, to prove him utterly wrong, might only be a moment away from winging through the brain. But his students, he felt, were more robust; apt, with common sense to rebuff him; arguing from the irrefutable evidences of their own lives. Her life was shadowy, remote. He could not guess at what it was. A calm English country house, perhaps, a boarding school, holidays beside the sea; that mixture of gentility and physical toughness, that was what he remembered of England, something hidden beneath the surface of faces, of landscape; a shuttered ability for feeling; but it was only a foreigner's view, he thought.

'But what if one tries to look into the centre and it evades one? If one tries to look at the fear and it escapes to somewhere else?' She followed his line of thought closely, she knew what he was talking about. It was not, then, mere solipsism; it was comprehensible to her. But what had she meant, by this fear? He sensed, thinking about it, some definite anxiety, some channelling of generality into the particular. 'If one tries to look into the centre and it evades one.' There was some episode, some unresolved thing that she wanted to talk about; and he, insensitive, academically pompous, had not noticed until too late, until they were going indoors, leaving the conversation behind them; and where he should, as an older man, a confidant, have asked her gently what it was, that she wanted to talk about, what fear, what nightmare, he had simply followed his own train of thought into the familiar, blunted statements it had formulated. There is no evil. Death is endemic in life. How could one say this, to a pretty nineteen-year-old visitor, who asked for help? He thought, it is time I gave up teaching, before it is too late. And as he stood and watched the water for the coffee boil up and the dark froth spurt all over the stove he thought for the first time in years that in him was a fundamental falsity. There is no evil. And yet he knew evil, knew it intimately. It had stood opposite him, inches away. It stayed, watched him, made mockery of all the tenets of a liberal education. And the only way he had been able to accommodate it, all those years ago, had been to decide; it is in that man, therefore it is in me. That man is myself, in uniform. I cannot hate myself, and so I cannot hate him. Evil is accidental, like a buck tooth, like hairs on the back of the hand. It is a possibility for all of us, like birth, like death. Only the circumstances, only the roles change. He had been nineteen then, or twenty. When he came out, these thoughts had slipped to lie in the back of his mind. There had been so much else, his arrival in Israel, work, marriage, the war, freedom. The acquisition of the trappings of freedom, the proofs of individual existence. Even his name had changed.

'Would you like another drink?' What he wanted to say, as he laid a hand lightly on her shoulder in passing, was, 'I'm sorry I misunderstood you. I'm sorry I did not remember. What was it, please, that you wanted to say?' But one could not whistle up confidences nor hide to oneself the fact of insensitivity. He lit a last cigarette and heard the kitchen clock strike twelve, as they sat with their mugs of coffee balanced, awkwardness between them emphasising the lateness of the hour.

At last she said, leaning back, tipping a sandal from a bare and dirty foot, 'Do you ever wish you were somebody else?'

'No. Not any more. I used to, when I was young.'

'I do. I still do. I can't bear the fact of not knowing so much, of there being so much I don't understand.'

And when he said, 'But it doesn't change, I feel the same, there is so much that I do not understand either,' he knew that she did not believe him.

Knowledge waits, a limited quantity, waiting only to be explored; we will eat it up like food in a larder and know it all. The cleverest woman in the world, they say Miss Sparks is; she holds the keys, I believe it utterly. The forms that she imposes will be the true lineaments of life, linguistic and scientific. As small children we see her, high up, we crouch by the stairs to watch her ascend; straightbacked she drives in her baby Austin, aloof and powerful she comes through the front door, one at a time her feet lift, she walks up the stairs, we stare, and there they are, her spats. A proud head nodding from eight feet off the ground, hair scraped into a thin grey bun at the back, rimless glasses, a man's collar and, in winter, spats. A pink nose, large for her face, arthritic hands that one day in winter close completely like boxing-gloves, can no longer hold a pencil; a voice that shakes as she reads of how Horatius held the bridge; she is an ordinary woman of sixty, teaching in a small school in a house in East Anglia in the 1940s. I see that she has an outside lavatory and things on saucers in the larder waiting to be used up, but my eyes are blind to these things, for she transcends them. When she dies, it is a shock to know that this is possible. That little house, a starting-place for journeys; Miss Sparks ascends the stairs and until one is summoned one may only guess at what her room is like. It is used for painting, when she is not there, and needlework; but the essence of the room departs with her, the dust and chalk smell of serious study, the acridity, is lavender-coloured like our French teacher's blouse, is languid, conversational, feminine; it brings a perfumed unreality to life. We are to believe that the airy noise 'chou' might apply to a solid dirty garden cabbage, that one may count 'treize, quatorze, quinze'; that England is not the centre, nor English universally understood. It is easier to pretend that this is not true, to look out of the window at the English sky and laugh. And during French, painting, needlework, one may discover an indiarubber left behind by a girl who was this morning taught by Miss Sparks; one may pick it up and strain, through its warm tactility, to reach the knowledge of what it is like to be in Miss Sparks' room when it is truly hers, when she breathes the air. There may be incomprehensible words left upon the blackboard, Latin, Greek, and scraps of paper upon which the same incantations appear, diagrams roughly drawn on loose sheets, books left about, hieroglyphs, containers like the genii's lamp. One does not go in there alone. It is as if the spirit of pure number, the ghosts of a dead, powerful civilisation, lurk there still, somewhere in the cupboards behind the boxes and books, beneath the trivial paraphernalia of painting and sewing; as if the strong heady essence I seek to capture may suddenly surge out and capture me.

One begins as a small child, downstairs; knowing the back door, the cloakroom with low pegs at a five-year-old level, the downstairs room, the worn boards, the particles of coloured chalk dust rising as rabbits and pin men are drawn; the sun in one's eyes from the stained windows round black shapes of letters dancing out of place. Downstairs, it is possible to guess only vaguely at upstairs, at its different scales and perspectives; once upstairs, there is still the mystery of Miss Sparks' room, the green room reached like a burrow from behind the board, the teachers' bedrooms, their walls shrinking and stretching, containing whole worlds beyond. There is the slow exploration, the seven years' search; and beyond the knowable confines there is the outside world, the possibility of other schools, other environments, a world finitely extending, bounded only by the limits of experience, a universe one may possibly come to know. At five, the first room is large, wide, its walls untouchable from a seat one dares not leave; the blackboard, slanting, the aeroplane trail of chalk bumping the surface, the piano, a window showing kitchen gardens, trees swaying behind in a line; there are french windows, opening to a tiled place where deathbed scenes are played, wild horses corralled for the night, a green lawn too, and one silver birch tree worn smooth to four feet up by hands, jail for the captive, gateway to forbidden lands, and visible raspberry canes from which wild dogs leap on winter evenings. There are tables, each one a stage in a progression, to be reached as one ages; the movement is from right to left and then backwards, until the door is reached, the way left open to the stairs and the kingdom above. On the way up and out is a room in which two ageing bulldogs sit on armchairs, their eyes bigger than saucers, than plates, than millwheels, their claws long and yellow as human nails might be if never cut. Their pink tongues suck and drool, they cannot close their mouths nor point their noses; their faces remain squashed, indeterminate. Like Cerberus, they sit to guard the world beyond. And everybody passes them, stupid children, crippled children, for everybody there is a way out. The world is knowable, we hear. The world is ours.

And this afternoon I have been to the cemetery. 'It must have been enormously expensive,' I say to Zvi. 'All that money for a cemetery, when it could have been irrigating the Negev'; and I hear him laugh, kindly, teasing me with affection now that we begin to know one another, so that I need neither shrink back nor apologise.

'Don't you like cemeteries?'

'Père Lachaise and Highgate, yes, but this was so neat.' He smiles at me, says, 'In Israel we aren't very good at romantic wildernesses,' and I see him think, the English, the sentimental fools; or perhaps he is thinking not of the English but of me. I think of the graves on Mount Herzl, the tomb, the letters, photographs, plays and books in manuscript, the Balfour Declaration, all the relics; the green turf, the trees pointing dark fingers upward for silence, the gravel, the tiny pebbles; the sun sinking, turning stone to the colour of peach. Myself, restless, seeing that for the others it is not enough; that they would like to see Herzl's nightshirt, his toe clippings, something to tell them of his mortality. 'One ought to keep everything, throw nothing away,' says Lydia; in order to tame the mysterious and threatening past. They were not greater than us, they were human; see, the laundry lists, the unpaid bills. It is the little things that remain from the concentration camps that make people turn away in tears, the little personal things, for they are recognisable, they assure us that nobody is of heroic dimensions, that we have nothing to emulate; that our only duty is to gather up our own small bundles of possessions and escape from the descending hand of fate. I have seen, in a castle in France, two historians turn to each other, laughing and incoherent with relief, at the sight of Napoleon's bedroom slippers.

'What are you laughing at?'

'Nothing funny, except in a hysterical way.' But I tell him the story, because it seems to establish another tie. I would do anything to make him listen, now, to recapture that grave attentive stare; drag up a slight story from the past, falsify, embellish, plainly lie, in order to be remembered.

We return to the balcony, to a breakfast of orange juice,

coffee and cake, and the sun burns my forearms as I sit smoking. Our conversations are ever afterwards contained for me by these four walls, the shadowed stucco wall of the house, the trellises of wood where climbing plants grow out of boxes, the low wall of the view of the trees at the courtyard's edge and the street beyond.

'One is always being made to remember: this is how things were, this is how they are now. Don't you find this?'

'The past here is recent,' he says. 'Yesterday crowds up on today and before you know where you are, it's tomorrow. Yesterday is the past, tomorrow is the future. Today is terribly brief. Or that is how it seems to me.' His hair, wet from the shower, is drying fast in the sun, sticking up in tufts; I see that he has shaved around the edge of his beard so that the contrast is sharp, skin and hair; and that he is wearing another clean shirt that smells of rough linen, as if it has dried in the sun. 'There are reasons, you see, why nobody, anywhere, is allowed to forget. And that idealism you were talking about, that is part of the myth, too. People know that their predecessors were idealistic and so they believe that they are too; whereas in fact they're often simply materialistic, chauvinist and sentimental to boot.'

'You're very harsh about it.'

'Well, it may sound harsh. But you see, people have all these qualities in them. It is simply what comes to the surface that counts. I sometimes think that here one has more of a chance to be either a hero or a complete bastard than one does anywhere else. Or run the gamut, inside oneself, between the two. And I was brought up to believe in the moderate man, the golden mean, the balance. It's what I'm still trying to achieve. So, I think, are most thinking people. But it's hard for them. There are so many opportunities to allow the extremist in one to come out.'

I am chewing bread and honey, my own thoughts catching at me in the gaps between his words. 'So you think everybody is a potential extremist of some sort?'

'Of course. Otherwise, why would anybody succumb to it?'

'I don't know, upbringing perhaps, some trauma in the past. You can't think Hitler was everyman, can you?'

'Well, I don't believe he was supernatural, that's for sure.'

'And then, people think of you as an extremist. That was what I'd heard, a revolutionary of some sort.'

'That is because', he says firmly, 'what I am trying to do is misunderstood. I have to believe that.'

'What is it exactly?' The question, held beneath the surface for so long, comes up like fish for air.

'What is it, exactly. Well, I am a socialist. There is this state, founded on socialism, but first, to establish itself, it had to make homeless the people who were here before. They didn't have to go, they could return, there are endless arguments about this. But they felt they had to go; they are gone. And then, justifiably, comes the pride, the self-satisfaction, look, we have made this miracle, nobody else could have done it. Nobody else has suffered as we have, nobody else has our moral stature, nobody else can achieve such a just society. But what I find unjustifiable is the exclusiveness of our socialist society. So, I am not a socialist. Anarchist, nihilist is what you hear, what you may have seen in the papers. I spoke to some students and they got excited, in the Hebrew University that was, about a month ago. Zionism is suicidal, I said, it means moral and possible physical suicide. It was supposed to be a closed meeting for a university society, but somehow the press got in and somebody from the *Jerusalem Post* made mincemeat of it. Perhaps I shouldn't have done it, but on the other hand how can one be a teacher and not speak the truth when students ask what one believes?

Sorry, I am going on about it, are you interested?'

'I wouldn't have asked, otherwise.'

He smiles, suddenly selfconscious, and reaches for some more coffee. 'The famous Mosseri lecture kit. Well, you see, unless we stop the immigration policy, we'll be flooded. There'll be no room for taking refugees back, even if we decided to do so, even if the Arab states let them come. And then the Arab leaders, Nasser, Hussein, won't even talk of peace till the refugees are taken back. There are about nine hundred thousand of them sitting in camps being fed by the United Nations – down there, near Jericho, and on the Egyptian border. And then Ben Gurion says, no repatriation until Israel is allowed to dictate the peace settlement. And the Arab leaders find them useful, too, a sitting grievance, a proof, look what the Israelis have done. But meanwhile, what are they going to do? Can you imagine spending your life in a camp, with no rights, civil or personal, just a number among a thousand others? How long do you think it'll be before some of them just explode? Well, all I have been doing, and this is no secret really, has been to get in touch with men, Jordanians, Lebanese mostly, a few Syrians, who believe as I do. That the state and its leaders must not be all-powerful, that we must make a fait accompli of moderation. That any form of nationalism, Arab or Jewish, must end. That is all.'

'But what about the people being persecuted in the rest of the world? Like the people from Morocco, Algeria, Russia, South America? What happens if Israel suddenly starts saying, you can't come here?'

'Well,' and he peers into the coffee-pot, finds it empty, replaces the lid and leans back, dissatisfied. 'I don't know. I don't know the answers. I know it's a choice of evils, but the most important thing surely is peace. And it has to be a realistic peace, not an imposed one, with the United Nations guarding us like a nanny looking after a sick child. Otherwise it's only a matter of time before there's a major war and the Arabs either push us into the sea or we go on a little longer, shored up by American arms and money. It's unrealistic, to live with one's neighbours as we do. They are not savages or madmen, as some people make out. There are thousands of Arabs who want peace, I am sure.'

But, in spite of him, I pursue my question; thinking of Gilbert, of Larry, of Rowan, foreigners who discovered in themselves the buried need to come here; of myself. 'I think it's something deeper, even than the fact of persecution. I mean, why people want to live here. I've not really thought about this clearly. But it's a need to identify with something, to belong, to be accepted, to find some sort of reality one can connect with. In the West, whether you're Jewish or not, everything's so diffuse. So out of control. You can't have any effect. Nobody's doing anything direct. D'you see what I mean? It's ironic, in such a besieged situation, but here one feels one might have some control over one's fate. I think Israel is a dream for more than just persecuted minorities. Unless one person alone can be a persecuted minority.'

'In that case, it's a pity you missed the Second World War,' he says. 'You'd have enjoyed it.'

'Well, you can laugh, it's easy for you. I know it sounds absurd. But the whole point is, I did miss it. I just grew up hearing people endlessly talking about it. It was a reality for them, at least. For me, for people of my generation, it just served to point out how much more experienced our parents were. I just remember one siren going off and, when I was afraid, somebody told me it was a cow. I wasn't even allowed that experience straight. I knew it wasn't a cow. And then we were evacuated and lived with an aunt. And then it was over.'

'Well, you were lucky.'

'In a way, in a way not. We kept a sort of innocence,

I suppose. But at a price. I know all sorts of horrible things happened to you,' and he inclines his head, a polite bow. 'But here you are, you exist, you know about it.'

And again he leans toward me, takes my hand, holds it a minute, speaks to me as I imagine he might to a daughter. 'I know. But don't go getting involved in somebody else's battles because there doesn't seem to be one of your own. You think the situation here is reality. Well, so it is, but not for you. Your own is waiting somewhere. But if it's more complex and less final than direct physical action, then that's the way the world is going.'

'But surely,' and now I am more aware of the pressure of his hand than I am of my own thoughts, 'one can effect things. One must. I mean, look at you. Working on behalf of the Arabs. What are the Arabs in the camps to you? You're fighting somebody else's battle, aren't you? You aren't an Arab.'

'No, but it's different. First, I'm not working on behalf of them, but for a state of peace in which to live my own life. Second, perhaps because I spent some time in a place like that. I don't care if they're Arabs or Eskimoes, they are outcasts, and I live here, in a house, in a street, where they once lived. I came here for my own reasons, I'm not accepting the right to take another man's house and lock him in a camp. Why should my freedom curtail his? It makes me ill, knowing it. Maybe there are Jews in other countries suffering the same situation, they are not directly my responsibility, I can sympathise with them but I cannot essentially change things. But that was a thing I did, I chose; I came here, I accepted the state, I love this country in spite of what you may think, and now I am a citizen of Jerusalem. But I ousted that man, I sent him where he is. Do you see?'

'I think so.' Breakfast is finished. The dusty sediment

of the orange juice settles back at the bottom of the glasses. Crumbs of spiced apple cake scatter on the table top. Ash blows among them, the dead matches lie about. And I feel myself invaded by tiredness, eyes aching after that short night's sleep, stomach slightly nauseated, feet cold in their sandals; too confused, too tired to think any more, I am aware only of the sensation of a burned-out morning, when all the breakfast is eaten, the last cigarette smoked, conversation comes to an end; of hours unspoken for, a move to be made. 'I might go down and cash a traveller's cheque, see if there's any post for me.'

'Yes.' He accepts the end of discussion as at the end of an hour's teaching, when his students are evidently tired and can assimilate no more. 'I've got a few letters I must write. But we could meet for a drink? Have you been to the King David? You must, it's historic. I'll show you some more bullet holes. At twelve, then, in the entrance. Beseder?'

And when the breakfast things were cleared away, the stained cups and plates smeared with honey and ash stacked in a bowl in the kitchen, he sat down at his desk to work, arranged the letters in front of him that must be answered, poised his pen above paper and sat for minutes without moving at all. He was unsure whether or not she had left the house. There was never that finality of a closed door, of slapping feet downstairs and a fainter crunch on the gravel fading completely; there was not the relief of being left alone in the house. Ruth would go out noisily, singing, her high-heeled shoes tapping firmly down the road, audible almost to the corner; her movements were those of confidence, for she knew him, knew that he liked to hear her go; for she could return. Now there was perhaps the creak of a door; or it could have been the wind lifting a window-catch. Somebody crossed the floor in the next room and walked towards the stairs; or a paper blew to the floor and settled there, a book slid from a chair arm, a newspaper came through the slit in the door. There was no telling. He sat tense, ill at ease in his own house. She was gone, she was down the street, she waited for a bus or strode on foot down to the centre of town; but no, she was there, breathing faintly in the next room, spread on a chair, legs flung out and crossed, lost in thought. A tatty, crumpled dress, limbs somehow childish in their unselfconsciousness. Light eyes vague, with pupils drawn to fine points as she stared at the light, unseeing eyes turned upon uncertain realities. A small brown dry hand tapping its fingers upon the arm of the chair, of one of his chairs. He wanted to go and see, to be sure of her. To say, why are you here? How much do you understand? For children saw and comprehended and did not speak; they saw the shortcomings of their parents and could not name them; perhaps if one had children, teenaged children, this was how one felt about them, curious, protective, stricken with guilt. And at once one might long, as he found he longed now, to tell the truth, to be completely honest; and one might find that the ability had gone, since through habits of years one found only complexity, paradox, compromise, the half-truths of experience. He had tried to tell her and had heard it sound false, for this was not his language, this simplicity. And he saw her weariness, thought that his argument had worn her out even physically; and yet in his mind the words went on, he was telling her in spite of her tiredness, you must know more, you must listen to more, you must stay and hear all of what I am. There was the unacceptable, that he must tell her; that he was limited, inconsistent, as all men were. She stared back at him, from the other side of his desk, from the curtains, the opened windows, she was in the reflection of trees and sky that appeared within the big framed pictures on his wall, and her stare was completely open, frightening him with its total acceptance. Where there was such vulnerability, what could one do but wound? At last, as the rooms about him began to relax into silence, he put down his pen, rolled a clean piece of paper into his typewriter and typed his address at the top. Having said that he must write letters, he felt that letters must be written; there was this obligation to be truthful to her even in this; and what the hand would not do, machines must be made to do, in spite of all inclination. If in the smallest things honour might be kept, there was perhaps hope that it could survive the greatest. For habit, learning and experience were all still on its side.

The letter is a surprise to me; at first, seeing the uneven scrawl of the writing, its unfamiliarity, I think that it is a mistake, not for me at all. There is the crumpled brown envelope with its Israeli stamp, blue biro slanting all over it, the name written in childish roundhand 'Mlle Joe Catall', hardly decipherable, and the address in Hebrew. Inside, a scrap of lined paper torn from an exercise book, perforations ripped open down the side. It is written in French.

'Chère Joe, I hope you are well. I am well, also all the Chaverim. Esther has her baby, a girl, called Gabrielle. She was born in the new hospital in Beersheva. Tonight we have a party to celebrate. It is a pity you are not here. Perhaps we will dance outside the hadar ochel. The house you saw me painting is finished. Reuven and Yolande will have it when they are married. In the vineyards we are beginning to be very busy. Will you come back, I wonder. I think not, when you have seen the city life, which is more like Europe. I like to be with you, Joe. Shalom, Gilbert.'

There is half an hour left before I am to meet Zvi. I put the letter in my pocket and wander down the street, dazed by the light that strikes at me between the buildings, shivering still from the cool darkness of the post office; cold, then heat, flesh shrinking as in a fever. On the way, as I pause between shop windows and stare at objects and feel the new money in my bag, a jeweller meets me halfway, at his door. He is waiting for somnambulists, for the stricken wandering observers in the city, those with eyes drifting from object to object without understanding. I feel his presence but do not see him; in the window I see Arab gold, semi-precious stones from the Negev; in my mind's eye, my mother in Cambridge, faded English colours, the damp pavements after summer rain. There is a brooch shaped like the sun, a delicate model of that which burns me where I stand.

'Come in, come in. Yes, it is beautiful, isn't it? For you, two lirot less. You are English?'

'Yes, yes. I'm not sure. I must think about it. It's for my mother.'

'Perfect. You are beautiful, your mother must also be.'

'She is, in a way. I'm not like her, though, not at all.' The anonymity, the dark interior of the shop; heat, then cold, the welcome compresses. My fingers extended touch soft surfaces, leather, cotton wool, worn velvet; and then the cold hardness of the jewels themselves, the hard little separate points. The relief of retreat from the sun's glare; I am weak, wanting to sit down, ill perhaps; I bathe my eyes in the easy dark.

'Are you well?'

'Yes, I'm all right. Just a little tired. I hadn't realised how strong the sun was. One forgets.'

'Yes, it is strong. I never go out in the middle of the day. You see, I am from Russia, only five years. Come, I fetch you some coffee, some water?'

'Just water would be fine, thank you.'

'Sure? No coffee? Or some tea?'

'Sure. Just water. I don't think I could drink anything else.' In my pocket, crumpled under my hand, Gilbert's letter. There is no answer, not yet. I dare not read it again, as a child away from all that is familiar dares not reread the newest letter from home, for fear of nostalgia for all those certain things. The road to Beersheva, the known dust track; the pattern of the huts; the hadar ochel, the cowsheds, the trenches themselves; there is a small, a possible life, easily comprehended, easily lived.

The water is warm and tastes of rust, but I drink a couple of mouthfuls to be polite.

'You have a very interesting face,' the jeweller says, his hands resting upon his apron as he gazes intently, with an interest that seems professional.

'Really?'

'Would you like that I tell your fortune? I do it well, I have a gift, since I was a boy.'

'It's strange, how often people want to tell my fortune here. How do you do it?' It is tempting to succumb, to hold out my hand in the gloom and close my eyes as his voice tells me of journeys, of strangers, of luck and love and danger as his hands trace my lines, perhaps scrupulously, perhaps lecherously, and I sit there not caring.

'From hands, from faces. From handwriting too, it is possible.' There are too many ingredients already, all the things he could tell me of are already there. I no longer want to know who or what will arrange them, whether my own free will or a fate set out for me before ever I was born, whether decision or circumstance. 'No, no, thank you, really, I must go. I'm late for an appointment already. I'll just take that little brooch, though, if you'd like to wrap it up.' Already the quiet twilight of the room is oppressive, I am cold again in my thin clothes, his solicitude grows all at once suspect. Something changes, in a second all is not what it was; as if a magnet has moved and everything is drawn after it. My ease and relief are gone. All that is left is irritation.

'You go already?'

'Yes, I must. Which way is the King David Hotel from here?'

'The King David? You must take a bus. Wait, I show you. First I wrap the brooch. And I would like to give you a little present. To remember me. Here. And you don't mind if I kiss you? Like an uncle only.' His dry cheek brushes mine, I think of his lips, the mauve edges; an absurd, annoying person who only minutes ago was kind and sympathetic. In my hand something is loosely wrapped in tissue, besides the little jewel box with its tight rubber band. When I am in the street I thumb aside the tissue and glance down to see that I hold a tinny Star of David on a thin chain.

'Oh, thank you. Thank you very much.'

'Is nothing. Just to say, I enjoyed your visit. I shall not forget your face. You will wear it, yes?'

'Yes, of course. Thank you very much.' Now that I am in the heat again, the clarity of sunlight, I am reassured; and know with a moment's guilt that if there is a small rebuke in his voice it is because I have set this distance clearly between us, because I am thanking him as if he were a servant. It does not matter, though, in the next moment, what he is feeling; I have already turned a corner and am out of sight.

In the King David Hotel there is the silence of extreme comfort. I walk about cautiously in my scuffed kibbutz sandals and perch on the arms of chairs, looking for Zvi. There is headed writing-paper in a morocco leather case, a pen and inkwell, envelopes, a blotter, all laid out on a broad desk top for guests. I will not read Gilbert's letter again, not risk that pang, but will write back immediately, from here; not because I know what to say, but because of that paper. The crisp white folded square will emerge from its pure envelope in the middle of the kibbutz day; I see Gilbert's brown fingers, his broad dirty nails. 'King David Hotel, Jerusalem.' The heading will tell him. The letter will be to say that I shall not return. 'Cher Gilbert, je vous remercie de votre....'

'Excuse me, but you are sitting on my newspaper.' But I am translating my thoughts into French and the sentence springs at me straight out of a phrase book; hardly looking up, I reply, 'The postillion has been struck by lightning.'

'Excuse me? I'm afraid I don't understand.'

'I'm so sorry, yes of course I am, how silly of me.' I feel, pull out his *Jerusalem Post*, hand it to him straight-faced; and see above me a puzzled, handsome American face, a face from an old Hollywood film when heroes were heroes, the puckers between their eyes suggesting stupidity rather than moral doubt.

'Was that some kind of password?'

'Oh, did you think I was a spy? No, it was just a joke, not a very good one. I'm sorry. "You are sitting on my newspaper" just suddenly sounded like something out of a conversation phrasebook, that's all.'

'Hey, you wouldn't like to join me for a drink, would you?'

'I'm sorry, I'm waiting for someone.'

'You mean you were just pretending to write a letter?'

'No, I was really going to write a letter.' Now my watch-face says twelve-thirty, I am thirsty and tired. 'Yes, all right, I will have a drink, but I may have to abandon you rather suddenly.' I take four sheets of headed paper and two envelopes and put them in my bag while he watches.

'That's okay. I wouldn't expect a lady spy to behave any different. What'll you have? Scotch and soda?'

'Fine.' The deep leather armchairs are all at once accessible now that I am accompanied; I sprawl into one, take my drink, wonder idly what he will say.

'Of course, this was quite a place, during the war. The forty-eight war, I mean. It was blown up, did you know?'

'Yes. The Irgun Zva'i Leumi.'

'Of course, that seems another life now, doesn't it? Old history. I don't think I introduced myself. Howard Helpmann, from Philadelphia. Are you on holiday here? I'm on business, technically, but then I always believe in mixing business with pleasure. I'm a representative of a food firm in the States. Baby foods, dried foods, coffee, all that sort of thing. We've just put through a big deal with an Israeli firm, so I'm here to tidy up the ends.'

'Don't they have baby food here already? I thought babies needed orange juice. There's lots of that.'

'Well, yes, sure they do, we can give them greater variety, greater convenience, better equipment to produce the stuff on the spot. Israel needs our capital, you know, it isn't just the end product.'

'I'm sorry, I wouldn't know, I'm not a capitalist.'

'Excuse me?'

'I'm not a capitalist. I don't believe in it. Capital means exploitation, haven't you read Karl Marx?'

'Well as a matter of fact, no, I haven't, I'm sorry, I didn't know you were a Communist, I'd never have....'

'Spoken to me? Oh, it's all right. One gets used to capitalists speaking to one. Buying one drinks. Although technically one shouldn't accept drinks from exploiters of human labour.'

'Look, I only said we make baby food. Now couldn't we talk about something else?'

'I'm sorry, I did say I'd have to go.' Zvi is at the bar, turning slightly this way and that to look for me; I see him stand, his back towards me, the shirt drawn tight across it as he leans his elbows on the counter; he looks thin, relaxed, self-contained, he pulls out a packet of cigarettes and places one between his lips and raises his head to move it into place in a gesture that is already so familiar that I nearly cry out to tell him, warn him that he is watched; and the American sees him too, and glances at me and says in a sour voice, 'Oh, that's how it is, is it? Well, another time I shouldn't be too keen to drink another man's whisky, if I were you.' Like the old jeweller, he is left behind, forgotten. I have mumbled something in apology, suddenly ashamed of my behaviour, and am at Zvi's side, greeting him so that he turns in surprise. His smile is the sudden social movement of somebody who has been jerked out of thought; yet it becomes pleased, relieved.

'I've been horrible to people all morning. I was kissed by a revolting old man in the Jaffa Road, and I've just been very rude to an American who bought me a drink.'

'It sounds as if you've had a busy morning.' But something has soured, I want to tell him, some confusion and lassitude have driven me into a viciousness I do not recognise, that it is not I who am like this, that I am, like him, full of integrity.

'Pointless, really. I just felt bloody, I suppose.'

'I'm sorry,' he says, as if this bores him. 'Would you like some lunch? Let's have lunch here, shall we?'

'Not here. Outside, I'm cold in here. Let's just get some falafel and eat it in the street. God, I need the sun, I feel as if I want it to burn me up.'

'Are you ill, Jo?'

To burn, to purge, to eradicate; today it is one hundred and twenty degrees fahrenheit; this summer is the hottest that Israel has had for twenty years. After minutes in the street, the trickle of sweat pours down my spine, my upper lip is wet, my hair damp at the roots. My arms and legs protrude like brown sticks, coated with dust, hairy, unrecognisable. Down by the Red Sea, the sun has twisted up the rocks themselves as if they were putty. I have heard too that people go mad in the sun, they froth like dogs and die. I am fragile, in the sun's passage, under the bland eye of the moon. We are all fragile, walking at midday with our short shadows, striding as if we, the insects, the burned leaves at the furnace mouth, can change the world by one degree.

'I have two tickets for a concert,' Zvi is saying, as we turn down towards the German colony, on our way home. 'Ruth thought she'd be here. It's a student thing, but the music faculty's quite good here. Would you like to go?'

The sun makes red patterns in my eyes, showing chains and hammers above the roofs, where there are none. 'Yes,' I tell him carelessly, 'Yes, I would.' If at this point I had said, no, so much might have been different. But I habitually say, yes.

5

ONE of these nights, when we sit out on the balcony, when Zvi pours iced coffee and tiny glasses of vodka, there is silence. This is in the gap between words, the current underlying conversation, when the traffic is quietened, the hour uncertain, the moon vast and high, holding us motionless. Between the buildings nobody moves; there are the great weals of highways, the toothgaps left between walls, the territories where no footprints show; I have looked at Jerusalem and seen the marks made by generations, the mounds of endeavour, we have talked until our mouths are dry, until all words mean the same, fact and fantasy blurred into one image, the inescapable pattern of life. Now there is the silence, the immobility of the present moment, in which anything can happen. The next move and the next, the words we will say, the actions of our bodies, all are wound up in this chrysalis of silence, in which the bones of the city also wait. The initial movement from the balcony to the room inside, exchanging this stillness for a frenzy of action, is there; the possibilities are infinite. A word, a small gesture, a glance recognised the world over, these are all that is needed to force that step over the edge into the mutual agreement of need. I am rawskinned as I wait, hearing only my own breath. Indoors there is a mat of grass, there is an oasis. Our hands are the fineboned bodies of small fish, fluttering along a river bed; our skins, shifting desert sand, the separate created cells, the infinitesimal grains. Blood beats in a pulse, the time marked; the moon's eye at the window, a supervisor, drags back the dark seas the world over, controls our movements and the suck and settle of the wave. Skin cannot remain dry, the rivers overflow, the sweat of the night, the sources of the body like milk; the soaked sheet is wound up at last, the night air cool upon exposed flesh as the streams dry. One hand is in another's hair, one arm along a stretch of taut sheet welcome as the arctic, a leg flung across another, a shoulder like a hillock rumpled with snow; and the slow fan turns, the light ticks, the summoned noise of the insects is audible again now that the silence is broken. The clock moves on, one hand passing another in disregard of its separate progress. The clock is broken. The night is endless. The moon never moves from the window but comes closer, peering, a bawd with her silver teeth. Outside the shooting stars thud to earth, burned out like old fireworks. There is suddenly an 'I' again, identity. I know it, being suddenly alone, eyes upon me. And there are the eyes rolled upward in a moment, hands pegged out across the sheets; something has been done; there is no other being any more, but an envelope. A voice says behind me, 'This is what you wanted'; and I am stopped, wondering between one heart-beat and the next, is this what it is like, the shell of a man? In place of explanation I am out in the street, where the boys shuffle towards the synagogue. A stone lands at my feet. In terror I tug at my brief clothes, to make them cover me. I hear a shout, Zvi's voice, 'Look out!' and now I am awake. We return to the balcony, to a breakfast of orange juice, coffee and cake, and the sun burns my forearms afterwards as I sit smoking. 'The past here is very recent,' he says. His hair, wet from the shower, is drying fast in the sun.

And Mahler's fourth symphony comes to its end and I have a pain in the base of my throat like a fishbone stuck there that will not be removed. Now we are at the Binyanei Ha'ooma, tucked comfortably away within the railway-station exterior, behind the raw concrete with its reinforcements poking through. I will remember the outside particularly; before, it seems unlikely that we will go in to listen to music, rather that we will hear a train announced, be hustled on to a platform, depart in some direction without a backward look; afterwards, I look up at that dumb lit façade and see how easy it was, how a man coming out of that building could be seen clear across the street, his shadow cast huge against the walls. But inside there is comfort, air-conditioning. The student orchestra moves restlessly, getting ready. A girl in black resins her bow, a young man wipes the mouthpiece of his clarinet, blows down it on one hoarse breath. The double bass stands big-bellied, dwarfing the boy at its side. There is the scraping and rustling of tuning up, there are the few pure accidental notes, the coughs from the audience. The theatre is sparsely filled, here and there rows are empty. Latecomers stroll, still talking to each other, their voices quieter as they come down the aisles, their mime growing more emphatic as those who are already settled glance over their shoulders, purse their mouths, stare intently at the stage.

'It's rather a strange place for a concert. Isn't it really a theatre?'

'They do a lot of opera here. And the university can't house a full orchestra easily. Sssh, they're beginning.'

He leaned back beside her and closed his eyes, trying to let the gentle notes of the beginning wash his mind clear, unknot the tension there. Several small things nagged at him; the thought of Ruth, of a letter he had not posted; and a man down in the front row who had turned and waved and raised his eyebrows as they settled into their seats, at the sight of Jo with him; and the fact that Jo had not changed her dress or put on stockings but was crumpled, bare-legged like a ragamuffin; and the thought of letters to the press that might appear in answer to his own of last week, of his own name appearing and reappearing, of becoming predictable, vilified, inevitably misunderstood. Jo would not wear stockings. Mahler was dead, but the music lived. Problems, themes, outlived people. Ruth preferred to be in Paris. The mind was a ragbag of impressions, hardly sorted, out of control. He sighed and saw her glance at him, her eyes with their startled, inquiring look. The music, spreading, made his flesh creep with its undertones of disaster; the surface, sunlit, beautiful, was yet transparent to the depths. He was always like this, hearing Mahler; he shivered to hear, beneath the gaiety and lightness of some of those tunes, the steady step of something inevitable coming nearer. Mahler's own death, perhaps. The artist's complete knowledge of the moment, of all that it contained. For a historian the moment hardly mattered, it fluttered and was gone. The march of time was what counted, minute building upon minute, the unerring process, cause and effect. Analyse. Account for. An examination paper set for students: give reasons for the rise of the Prussian state, assess the role of Henry IV of France. A conversation with a student: explaining the meaning of the word 'tautology', the historicist view. And across the border, in their mud huts, they lived, the inheritors. There was no way to justify it, no way at all. A conversation with Jo, imagined: justify your existence, prove yourself to be in the right. And he turned his head restlessly, to ease his neck muscles, and saw her glance at him again, just out of the corner of her eye. She sat very upright, her throat long and straight, and her hair seemed to him the colour of corn after a late summer storm. She was a child, young enough, as they said, to be his daughter. And Ruth returning, bringing him presents from Paris and greetings from her friends, laughed with him in the recesses of their home, that was grown comfortable again with her presence; Ruth, who was calm and beautiful and his equal in experience, who did not leave coffee cups all over the floor and handfuls of dead flowers in the washbasin, who did not demand, but existed, a grown woman, understanding him. And his mind turned, twisted, unable to be contained by the music. He should give up, that was it, give up teaching history, since evidently he no longer believed in history. Suddenly it was clear that he had not believed in it for years, but had shored up his old convictions, making them do. History consisted of facts, to be proven, and theories to be extracted from them; and suddenly all that he knew was as those dead flowers were, those grasses she brought home, shells whose inner life was irreplaceable; and all he wanted was to know one thing, one simple thing, to understand a moment from all sides, as Mahler had done. As he realised this, his whole body began to relax and he sat, drinking in the rest of the symphony, his hands lax on his knees, unaware of anything else.

There is a telephone call for Zvi, in the interval, between the symphony and the songs. A boy comes to tell him, from the box office. 'Friend of mine wants to meet me outside afterwards,' is all Zvi says as he returns, settles beside me again, turns up the programme to see what is coming next. From his voice, I guess that it is somebody whom he cannot easily meet by day, somebody who has perhaps risked coming through the Mandelbaum Gate, crossed no-man's-land, an outlaw of this society. There is a frown between his eyebrows as he waits for the first notes, but in a moment or two it clears, he sighs as he has often sighed, and leans back again, apparently satisfied. And for me, once again, the music fills all corners, washes away the surface, discovers a layer of acceptance where anxiety cannot penetrate. My unfinished letter to Gilbert is in my pocket still, with his to me; in the other I have a shabby

Star of David, half-wrapped in tissue paper; in my bag are sheets of blank paper from the King David Hotel and a pack of American cigarettes that Howard Helpmann, in his discomfiture, left on the table. Somewhere I also carry with me the image of a figure pegged out across a bed like the skin of a hunted animal; the moon's dial, the clockface; the sound of a voice crying out a warning; air cold upon drying skin. But the music reaches deeper, finding a seashore burial, a boy with ruffled blackbird hair whacking at the hill of sand. Afterwards I come out as if I have been asleep, full of energy.

'Wait; we'll let the rest go out, I don't want to get all caught up in the crowd. Jo, do you mind if I have a word with this person alone? Could you wait for me somewhere? It'll only be a moment, I just want to be sure of something.'

'Of course, that's fine. I'll just lurk about in the foyer, shall I? I might be able to get a coffee or something.'

'Thank you. I told him I was alone, you see. I hope you don't mind?'

'No, as I said, of course not.' I like it, that he should have a secret meeting; it is as if I were involved. I depart to join the queue in the ladies' cloakroom, to pretend to examine my unmade-up face, as if I cared about improving it, as if my mind could be on such things. And when at last the room is empty and a woman comes to polish the lavatory seats and lock the doors, I leave and go up into the foyer. There is nobody here, apart from a young man with a protuberant adam's apple, in the box office, who is locking away bundles of paper in a drawer. He smiles at me, comes out, goes in the direction of the men's lavatory, money jingling in his pocket as he walks. Standing here alone, after the crowds have gone, I feel the space stretch and grow around me, and watch each slight separate movement intently. They take no notice of me, the occasional people locking things away, it is as if I am invisible. I stand at the big glass doors, in the shadow, to look out. A figure stands by the roadside, poised on the kerb, looking this way and that; it is Zvi, with his white rolled sleeves, his tall thinness, the point of his beard. He is alone, waiting for his friend. It must be twenty minutes, half an hour, since the concert ended. I try to see my watch, hair hanging over my eyes, but find that it has stopped, that what it says makes no sense. I am about to call out, to go to him, to say, don't stand there, don't wait any longer, you are vulnerable, or, he is not coming. But 'Look out!' I scream, the heavy door swinging open with my weight; as a car rushes down the street, its headlights dipped to search the road, as there is a bump, a cry, and the lights show me a bundle rolling in the gutter, and then the car is gone, accelerating away with a hiccup of exhaust, turning the corner, a long American car, turning, flashing red rear lights, gone. The bundle in the gutter rolls and curls like a hedgehog in the dark. I hear the animal grunts, I am down the steps, tripping, falling, in the dark I find the darker stain, the soaked trouser leg, the sharpness of bone, I find hands gripping mine like claws, a touch of flesh, a grip of muscle, a grating of teeth, a long fainting sigh like orgasm, and then silence. I sit on the kerb, sick, unable to move, and see him limp in the gutter. What can I do? There is nothing to do. And then somebody else is running down the steps, there are people from the theatre who heard the brakes, the cry; there is a screaming telephone inside, a solid note of hysteria like all telephones here, there are hands lifting me, lifting him; I am shouting to somebody, terribly loud, 'I saw it, I saw it!' and there are more brakes, an old army ambulance, blankets, hands, the fast harsh chatter of Hebrew which I hardly understand. An accident. A car cornering too fast. A man alone. A girl who found him. An empty street. Steps, a kerb. The accident, the unforeseen.

'He'll be all right.' The doctor at the Hadasseh hospital speaks English, 'He was in considerable pain, but we've sedated him. It's just his leg that's smashed, and general bruising. I'll have to have another look at the leg in the morning, but I think it can be saved.'

Nobody has asked me. The journey is miles through the night, an invisible distance, the windows blacked. The ambulance climbing, a steep road. Zvi only moving his head from side to side, not hearing when I speak. The ambulance attendant looking at us, smiling, tired. And the hospital stands against the sky like a fortress, the earth around it falling away. There is a stretcher, there are men who appear, quiet and busy. Doors swing open, heavy glass again. Linoleum is soft to the feet. An old man sits at the door, his eyes heavy-lidded, watching. I sit on a bench, and shiver, and am wrapped in an army blanket, thick and heavy. There is a notice before me on the wall, listing the hospital departments. 'Psychosomatic gynaecology' I read, and look for psychosomatic accidents. Outside the blinds, the windows, animals howl on the far-down hills. And in here there is so much white, such brightness. I forget why I am here. And then I say again, out of habit, 'I saw it.'

'The accident?' He sits down facing me, his hands locked between his knees, a middle-aged man with deep creases down the sides of his face, stubble showing slightly.

'It wasn't one. I don't think so. He was run down. It was a big American car. An old one, perhaps. But he was on the kerb, the car must have gone up on to the kerb. And he didn't stop.' I think of the chicken-bone fragility, the splintering like matchwood, of dead animals spread upon the country roads in England. 'It wasn't an accident.'

'It's a difficult corner. Anybody could have gone up on to the pavement, cutting that corner too fast. He must have been drunk, the driver.'

'I've never seen anybody drunk in Israel.'

'It's true, there is little drunkenness.' The pride in the voice so easily summoned; this is the good land and we have built it; even as a man lies half-murdered. The doctor wears half-glasses, eyes fringed with the luxuriant lashes one sees so often here, so that the glance is veiled. His coat is whiter than I have ever seen. The linoleum between us and the door is spotted still with a few dark circles of blood. A man in overalls comes with a mop. There are benches, chrome chairs lined up to wait, at one end there is a rubber tree in a pot. The fans whirr.

I ask him, 'Do you believe there's an enemy?'

'An enemy? Do you mean the Arabs?'

'Anybody who wants to kill you. Do you believe there is an enemy?'

He frowns at me, puzzled, unsure if he has understood. 'Of course, who wants to kill you is an enemy. The man who hates you.' I see him think of sedation, injections, of remedies for shock; he glances sideways briefly to see if there are any nurses near.

'So the enemy isn't just inside one's head. There is a real one, outside. There is somebody one has to fight.'

'Well, of course. Why should we have such a big army, why do we survive at all? But Israel is strong now, we keep the enemy out. Now, I will give you some pills to take home with you, to help you to sleep. You are staying in Jerusalem? I will call you a taxi. No, there is no need to worry about money. You can come back in the morning to see him, there is a bus. Are you a friend, a relative, what?'

'Just a friend.'

The enemy is within the city, walks unnoticed in the streets. He moves quietly within the darkened rooms.

And yet there is nobody whom I can tell; not Lydia, who appears in the morning, not the police, not Zvi himself. 'I felt a little faint suddenly, I must have stepped off the pavement by mistake, and then I saw this car coming round the corner at a terrific rate, heard it skid, and then it hit me. It wasn't really his fault. I think he should have stopped, though.' This is what he says, to Lydia, to the police, even to me. The bed is scattered with books, the little tables thick with flowers sent by all his friends in Jerusalem. There is a telegram from Paris, to say that Ruth is coming home. His flayed leg hangs in a cradle from the ceiling, hidden from the painful touch of air; the doctors say that after all it will not have to be amputated. I sit and see his hands spread upon the smooth sheet, his wrists thin under his pyjama cuffs. In the next bed a dark man groans and opens his eyes to see us, and turns his face to the wall.

'I saw it, Zvi.' Nobody has asked me. I have brought him dusty bunches of blue grapes, a little melon, packets cigarettes, a bottle of vodka rolled up in a newspaper.

'I know you did. I saw you through the door, just before I fell. But you don't exactly know what you saw, Jo. You mustn't keep on saying that it wasn't an accident, you know. I'd never mentioned it to you, why should I, but I do sometimes have dizzy spells. It's a very mild form of epilepsy which I've had since I was a child, and since I don't like living off pills I take a risk occasionally. Now do you believe me?'

'But I saw it. Of course I believe you, if you say you have dizzy spells. But you didn't fall before he came. I saw him drive up on to the kerb and hit you. I saw it, Zvi. How can one doubt what one's seen with one's own eyes? Somebody tried to kill you, and you know it as well as I do, and I'm sure you know why.'

'Don't bully me.' His smile is a faint copy of what I remember. 'And don't be angry if I tell you what one sees, the message transmitted to the brain from the eye, is preconditioned by what one already believes. It comes from one's initial approach to the world, from one's upbringing, from what one expects, yes, from what one wants to see. Don't interrupt for a minute, I'm going to have my say. You're the one person in here who can't shut me up by sticking a thermometer in my mouth. Seeing is not always believing – or should not be. Think of a baby looking at, say, a spoon. What an extraordinary, new object. Yet when you look at a spoon you have definite ideas about it carried over from your previous experience of spoons.'

'Zvi—'

'And when you see a road accident in Israel, you have definite ideas about violence, about the victim, and so you think you see something which is not the truth. I don't know who that man was, but presumably he was too frightened by having knocked me over to stop the car. And who can blame him?'

'You may have convinced yourself that's what happened,' I tell him angrily, 'but you won't convince me.' Up and down the ward, with a slight glance of curiosity for us, the nurse goes with her tray; thermometer, list, rubber tubes for taking blood pressures; to make sure that all is normal. My voice drops, forced to a whisper. The man in the next bed turns his bandaged head again and sighs. 'I can use exactly the same argument on you. I know I'm not supposed to be tiring you, but it's too bad. You just can't accept that there's malice in anybody. You think everybody's kind and good and peace-loving like you, and that they only have to be treated in the right way. But they aren't. You have to see the whole thing as an accident, because you can't bear to think that anybody might want to murder you. Because you're so good, so unselfish, because you insist on seeing Arabs as poor dispossessed people wishing nobody any harm, and the government as just a little misguided, and the papers as just sadly misinformed. You can't accept what really happened, that one of your precious friends from the other side tried to bump you off, so you try to force me to accept an illusion too. Well I won't, and

I won't forget.' Tears pour down my face and drip on to the sheet. His clean hand with its cut nails grips mine and I look down at them both as if they are disembodied, for I cannot look at his face. There is silence, interrupted only by the squeak of trolley wheels, the breathing of others.

At last he says, 'Go on using the house for as long as you want to stay in Jerusalem, Jo. Ruth's coming back tomorrow, and she'll be pleased to see you. It looks as if I shall be here for a week or two, while they mend this leg. And come and see me again, won't you?'

Outside the hospital, where the red earth drops away into valleys, bald hills, an empty landscape, there is a launching-pad for helicopters, so that wounded men may be brought in quickly to the hospital from wherever they have fallen. I stand on its worn circle and look up into the dense blue of the sky at midday and wish to fly, to be transported suddenly and swiftly and painlessly, right away into another life. But the bus arrives and wheezes, waiting, while the passengers climb on; and instead of flight there is the slow bumping journey back to Jerusalem, instead of one clear decision there is the slow accumulation of many.

Somewhere there is a man hiding, nursing his secret, waiting for the money. Perhaps because Zvi is alive, he will not get as much as he hoped. It is easy to hire a car, to drive like a drunkard down a narrow street, to catch with the corner of the mudguard a man who topples towards the street, from the kerb, to see the flash of his face as he is hit, feel the thud against the tyre, to drive on without faltering, because this is expected, to leave that curled animal to howl in the gutter; to drive on, accelerating, disappearing round a corner again, to lose oneself in back streets, abandon the car, be once again a man among men sipping fizzy lemonade in a café, lighting up a cigarette after a job well done. It is easy, then, to be dehumanised; the driver may have been anybody at all.

The truth, the hanged man, staring at me always upside-down.

There is a bus, going south to Beersheva across the miles of grey land with no horizon, desert land or newly ploughed, ribbed by the winds or by a shallow furrow; it has come away from the hills of Jerusalem, from the plantations of young trees, the rocky outcrops, the shaded roads fringed by eucalyptus; sometimes it passes a deep hole in the ground or a twisted little hill that shows we are coming closer to the contorted landscapes of further south. And when it stops in the bus station at Beersheva and I walk out, past the girl selling sickly fruit drinks, past the staring man at the ticket office, I find myself in a windy dusty cowboy town, the flimsy houses set wide apart, the street for a wagon train galloping through. In a moment a man will stroll out from the deep shadow under that roof, behind that shutter, pistols at his hips, his hand flexing for a quick draw. But nobody moves; it is three o'clock, the town is in a deep afternoon sleep. Behind the bus station there is a camel on its knees, its eyelashes drooping, its jaw moving as it chews and chews. In the gutters, there are stumps of banana branches, yellow and dry. On one corner, under a flapping striped shade, a boy stands selling falafel; I wait and watch the flat envelope of bread filled for me, stained red, yellow, brown with the juices, and go to sit upon a post a few yards off, to chew like the camel and feel the heat rise in its layers from concrete and tarmac and dust. There is another, older bus to take me back along the road to Gan Hagar, and I mount it to find a seat among old men, their sunken hawk faces moving under the awnings of their headgear as they bite into the dried pips they chew, extract the sweet kernel, spit the husk with brown saliva to the floor. A young boy at the door, a kibbutznik perhaps, offers me a packet; and I take it and spit and chew with the rest. The old Arabs stare, their eyes dark as wells, ringed with brown, lined with dust, and speak to each other without moving their heads. Their hands clasp on their knees or lie palm upwards, open yet invulnerable in dignity. A woman mounts the bus, lifting her black skirts, holding a bunch of live chickens by the feet, and sits across the aisle from me. I see the helpless movements of the long scabby yellow toes, the flash of eyes from far down among people's feet. And the bus starts, a heave, a smell of petrol, a rattle along the road until behind us the rising cloud of dust obscures the desert town completely, and only the smells, tin and dung and bitter smoke, linger in my nose far out into the country. The music begins, a sustained wall of song; the windows are open and the hot air rushes in; the driver leans back, hands gripping the giant controls; behind me somebody pulls down the blind on his window and breathes hard, settling into sleep. The robed men sway as if carried still on camels, gently rolling against each other as the bus swerves. From a seat in front of me, a small girl dressed in pink leans out and is neatly sick on to the floor, and her father, muttering with rage, spreads paper handkerchiefs over the spot. Thirst is in my throat and the smells, the smells of humanity.

'Here. You want Gan Hagar, yes? Here, please.' The bus driver hands me down from behind his brass railing, a long arm reaching out to pass me my battered case, I am squeezed to the front and out through the door that wheezes and threatens to close too soon, down the steep steps, on to a stretch of sharp grass growing through dust, at a point on the straight burning road fifty yards from the nearest tree. The road is empty in both directions. The dented blue back of the bus retreats. I grow smaller, am lost to sight. And still Zvi waits upon the steps, his shadow big against the rough shuttered concrete of the wall, his white shirt clearly visible against the dark of his face, his beard. I see him from where I am, but only in outline, only in darkness. There are yards of darkness between us, there are steps descending, I cannot see whether he is on the kerb or standing in the street. The lights come again, dazzling, disturbing vision. The man who rounds the corner, driving his fast car home from a party, drunk probably, taking a chance, cannot see him until it is too late; he catches him with the long forefin of his car, sees him fall; is frightened, does not think clearly, follows his instinct to hurry on. He drives his car on around the next corner, believes that it was a dog he hit, remembers the bump against the wheel yet retains no visual impression, and disappears for ever. Zvi, subject to fainting fits since childhood, rolls in the gutter, his leg broken, the victim of an accident. There are traffic accidents, men are hit by speeding cars in cities the world over. I should be in Jerusalem, to visit him in hospital, to take him fruit and newspapers, to see Ruth when she comes back. There is no point in standing where I am, in the burning heat at the end of the long track that leads down to Gan Hagar, expecting something from a friendship that has ended. I wave after the bus, signalling for it to stop, for me to be carried on with it, to Tel Aviv, wherever it will go, but it goes further, becomes a small blue square travelling towards the horizon. And I have shrunk out of sight, I have completely disappeared. I have to stop waving and pick up my suitcase again, and walk on.

The huts of the kibbutz are white and grey against red earth, set in lines, their roofs indistinct against the low white of the sky; above me the fierce meridian heat is violet. The land around me moves like water. Again, it is like walking towards a mirage, the shapes I see receding and receding. Behind me, the fractured line of eucalyptus trees, the occasional rising cloud of white that tells of a car upon the road. The silence is yet loud with heat, that buzzing that one can never identify, that seems to come from within, from the blood. I put up my hand helplessly to shield my head, shade my eyes, to see more clearly; and the first solid object is a tractor parked beside the track, its great wheels white with dust, its seat dust-covered, for several hours unused. Then the first hut is past. I enter the kibbutz, expecting voices, movement; but there is nothing. A door swings on its hinge, creaks open and shut again, showing an empty room. Another hut, and only the peeling painted door, the cracks that the sun has made; a lizard running diagonally; nothing. There must be a group chatting on the steps of the dining-room, there must be swimmers in the pool, couples strolling back to their quarters, a man on a tractor returning from work in the far fields. A lizard; a cracked rock; ants in a travelling convoy; the battered door swings, fear mounts as I see that the place is deserted; my mind runs on to raids, to total devastation. But nothing is wrecked, all is order and silence. It is only uninhabited, a ghost village with the wind rushing through. I put down my case and sit upon it for a moment. The slight hills rise in layers. The blue flag is a sign, a summons. Soldiers wait there still, the blond men of the peace-keeping force, smoking their cool cigarettes. Disaster has not yet happened. There is control, vigilance, an awareness of the times. And then a voice calls me, 'Shalom!'

I turn, hunt the waste land. He comes from behind the huts to meet me, a heavy man, his body half-naked, his sandals scuffing the dust, his hat tipped forward to shade his eyes. 'Shalom. C'est Jo, n'est-ce pas?' The parched ground between the slight bow of his legs, the receding huts, the sky that threatens to fall between us; as he comes close I am nearly overwhelmed.

'Shalom. How are you? Gilbert is not here, I'm afraid.'

'Where have they all gone? What happened?'

'Oh, they've all gone to Beersheva, to the cinema. *Exodus* is on, it's the last week. They all went on the tractors, except that one, which isn't working, for some reason. You look exhausted, Jo, are you all right? Come on, I'll get you a coffee. They shouldn't be long, the others.'

'Exodus?' Gaston, his name is, Gaston, Gilbert's friend.

'The film, you know. I saw it in Tel Aviv when I was on holiday. I stayed here to look after the children. Come and see them, I was just getting them a drink and myself a coffee.'

In the newly finished children's house he moves about with slow care, giving out milk in plastic beakers with straws, his big farmer's hands adjusting bibs, briefly caressing heads. The four children sit and stare at me, their mouths pursed about their straws, their eyes dreamy as they suck; a boy of about five begins to blow bubbles, squints to watch the milk burst over the rim, sucks in again noisily, and as his grin breaks can no longer keep his mouth pursed but takes out the straw, sits back, dares me to comment. His round black shaved head tempts my hand; but he wriggles with aggression.

'This is Shaoul, these two are twins, Hannah and Ruthi.' The two little girls giggle and show their teeth and bend their shiny polls again to the milk. 'And this is David.' His hands touch the child's shoulders, a thin three-year-old with a fine pointed face and black North African eyes, the fringed oblique look already there, protecting him. 'And here is our newest child, she is not yet two weeks old. You remember, Esther was pregnant when you were here?'

'Yes. Gilbert wrote and told me she was born.'

'Ah, Gilbert.'

In a corner, in a narrow basket laid upon a table, something is moving. There is a red, domed head, sparsely furred with black, a mouth opening soundlessly in a yawn; small bright fists clench and open, a cat's paws kneading. The child is laid on her stomach, her head turned neatly to one side, the tip of her flat ear just visible above the tucked sheet. Gaston turns to watch a bottle of milk that is warming in a saucepan on the electric stove. 'She is nice, isn't she?' The pleasure in his voice is a father's, unselfconscious; his hands are used to this; he picks the bottle from the water, tips it to squirt a little milk against the inside of his wrist, wraps it in a small towel.

'Gaston, I want some more milk.'

One of the twins holds out her mug, is immediately copied by her sister. Shaoul sits drumming his feet, twisting his head from side to side, challenging and bored.

'Come, Shaoul, you can help me. Will you feed the dogs? You know where the new boxes of food are, don't you? And don't let the Wolf get at it before the others have had a go.' Shaoul goes, pulling on his hat, leaving the door ajar; I see him out in the brilliant square between the houses, walking like an adult, slowly swinging his arms.

Gaston says, 'She's called the Wolf because she's so greedy. But she's the best watch dog we have.' He sits, aproned in white, his stout brown legs coming out from the clean cotton, sandalled feet set apart. The new baby lies like a bound frog in the crook of his arm, arms thrashing to escape from the folds of cloth, aimless and imperative. Her features draw to a point before her mouth opens in a scream, and then she is all red, square hole, quivering epiglottis. The teat goes in, blocking the scream to a gurgle; her arms flail and drop, she is all sucking motion, tuned to concentration. When Gaston sits her up on his knees afterwards, his supporting hand cups her like an armchair and her head against the breadth of his chest is a frail egg, thin-shelled. Wind escapes from her in an adult belch, and when she sucks again I see Gaston's face make the same movements as hers, in his anxiety that she should finish, his cheeks suck in, his mouth move and tremble like a baby's. I find that I am looking away.

'We haven't got the children's house very organised yet,' he tells me when the baby has finished and lies back in a swoon of satisfaction. 'They used to live in one of the ordinary huts. You see, we have so few children here, compared with the bigger kibbutzim. When we arrived here, we were mostly not married. Some people have got married since. But there has been so much to do. But now I expect there will be more babies. If we have peace for a while.'

'You like children.'

'Yes, I do. Don't you?'

'I've never really known any. Since I was a child.'

'Oh.' He takes a cigarette from the crumpled pack in his shorts pocket, throws the rest down for me to help myself. 'Well, will you marry Gilbert, do you think? Marry Gilbert and have children for us?'

'Marry Gilbert?'

'We thought he wrote to ask you. And also I thought that is perhaps why you came back.'

A wounded animal, screaming in the gutter; sudden light, darkness filling the street; in my pocket a letter. The clean hands resting upon hospital linen. 'No,' I say, 'No.'

'Don't be angry. I didn't mean to annoy you. Ruthi, Hannah, do you want to go and see how Shaoul is getting on? One of the dogs has puppies, they like to see that. Go on, you can tell me if the puppies are fatter than yesterday. Take David, go on.'

The children go, the small boy dangling between the hands of the sisters. Their bottoms twitch in their brief shorts, their feet slap against heelless sandals. I tell him, 'I didn't mean to sound angry.'

And he accepts this, is unperturbed, laying the baby back in her basket, unpinning the nappy to expose a pointed behind, a mess of ammonia-smelling shit. As he takes the nappy I see the strangely developed female genitals unsheltered by any hair; Gaston comes back, wipes between the skinny little legs with a swab of cotton wool where the baby looks raw and swollen.

'I just thought that kibbutzim were founded and set up so that everybody could be equal.'

'So they were.' And he pats powder into the folds of skin.

'Yet you still assume that all women want to do is get married.'

'No, no. The girls here work as much as the men. Nobody has to marry, no.'

'Why should I want to marry Gilbert, then? Why can't I just be here in my own right?'

'Oh, that,' he says, 'there is no reason. I think he loves you a bit, that is all.'

'Oh, how do you know?' Dear Joe, I like to be with you. Outside the hospital, a launching-pad for helicopters; and the letter in my pocket all the time.

'He told me. Not so much, but I guessed the rest. Come on, little girl, lie down again, that's right, go back to sleep.' The pink translucent thumb wanders near the mouth, seeking, but the child has not yet discovered that it is hers. She falls asleep still feeling with her mouth, lies with it open upon the sheet, a small damp patch of dribble spreading. The hump of her body is so small under the cotton blanket that it is hard to believe in legs and feet; and yet she is self-contained. I think of her growing up on this strip of dry land, watching the trees grow, until she knows each stick and stone and may defend it with her life.

The beauty of a single person standing waist high among ferns. Gemma is a distant cousin, older by years, set apart, in love. The path goes on, deeper into silence; yards away from where Gemma stands and stares out towards the sea, they turn their backs and walk away from her. She is in love; and there is a particular man who is her fate but he is become faceless, nameless, whereas she is never forgotten. The sway of her body as she leans into the wind makes her into a figurehead, a ship's prow facing away; that perfect profile will not turn and bend, or if it does there will only be the vague kind stare at a child's interruption. 'What's the matter, Jo?' And there will be nothing to say, the question being wordless. Is it true, the question runs, that you are drawn helplessly after somebody, a man, a lover, that all you were, your childhood self, your habits and private thoughts and will are suddenly obliterated into this other; that you have become blank, waiting to be filled? But she moves away languidly through rooms, her hands trailing, fiddling, she runs down early every morning to find the post, stands by the open door with the pile of letters in her hand, and does not notice a child passing. There is the beauty of the green churchyard and there are the bones beneath; there are the living talking bodies, the people loved simply for being there, who may be snuffed out easily, one by one. There is Matt Ferguson, the smell of his tweed jacket, his red lips curved like a woman's; and there is his absence. And there is Gemma, at the crossroads, at the point at which happiness touches pain; at the centre, it seems, in touch. There are times when the child runs along the beach consumed in ecstasy, knowing this, racing the tide; as if nothing is ever present without its opposite. Later, she picks a photograph from a box, of the bent yellow Kodak packet that contains that year in Suffolk, to find a girl absurdly dressed for the seaside in a pale flowing frock, her hair hung in smooth loops shining in a patch of sun; the girl, twenty-one, holds a kitten and poses at the back door, a beach-bag at her feet. Gemma smiles in answer to a question, just a little, as if she might laugh, and turns away in a moment to finger a hollyhock. It is just after the war. Barbed wire has been removed from the beaches. There is concrete, in lumps. The man Gemma loves has been a soldier. Families come from Cambridge, wrapped in khaki knitted clothes, the babies' faces red like sluiced apples. It is all there, such a time ago, everything in bud, in embryo; in the ways that people pause between sentences; in the glances that are exchanged; in the way that the sun makes patterns of the days, casting shadow clear and light pure upon the ground, mottling undergrowth and forest paths, throwing the reflection of bulrushes like pokers into the water, where the estuary flattens out; in the way that familiarities are created, and expectations; in the intimations that pattern differently each human mind, making a future where there was none before.

'Jo, I want to ask you something.'
'What?'
'Perhaps I will ask you tomorrow.'
In the swimming-pool late in the evening, the water is oily black, appears to slide back over the head and shoulders of the swimmer. I no longer see Gilbert at the far end, only his white eyes as he turns, the flick of a long spray of water from his hair. I am at the shallow end waiting for him, the top of my body in the night air colder than the part which is submerged. He comes back to me, under water, invisible until he is a yard away and rising blunt-headed. We play clumsily, flapping as seals on land, our bodies nearly naked and close under the water, physical intimacy accepted with no overt glance or gesture; as if we are not alone or, if alone, not adult. Tired with racing and splashing we lie stretched along the white edge to the pool, limbs dark against pale concrete, water streaming. I raise

myself slightly on my elbows and look down at him, the long back, the runnel of the spine banked with muscle, the bunched shoulders and black round drooping head, Shaoul's head I remember, and the hair cropped like soaked fur. His wet swimming-trunks bag with water and are drawn down half an inch over his buttocks so that there is a paler margin, a slight curve of flesh upward, a faint division; behind me his legs are stretched straight, the black hair drawn like weed. I know his feet, they are straight-toed, they move like hands; they are there, frank and everyday, in his sandals as he walks about. I know so much of him, of them all. There are never any jackets, shirts, trousers, socks and shoes to remove; the comparative mystery in which Western men move is an archaism; here each person presents himself, herself, without artifice, there is flesh everywhere, brown, sunwarmed, well-shaped, unselfconcious. I have stopped looking in the mirror, and plod in my working boots to dig in the sun. And after a day, less than a day, his naked chest before me at meals is as ordinary, as expected, as the plate and knife and fork. We see, we are perhaps aware, but we do not touch. We wear our few clothes, lie out under sun and moon, but are never naked with the vulnerability of deliberate nakedness, which makes an appeal. Only now, under cover of water, our limbs accidentally touch, inhumanly wet and slippery, to dart away again like fish. And on the concrete, drying quickly in the night wind, shivering with the coolness of mid-September, we place our hands only inches apart but we never move them nearer. I remember a time on the grass when some buried convention in him vibrated with alarm; and I keep away. Upon freedom, it seems, a ritual must be imposed, upon nakedness the restraints of taboo. Naked and together, we must obey a code of behaviour almost Victorian in its demands. And I am sighing and walking up and down while he like a child performs somersaults on the rough surrounding grass; I am sighing and looking towards Gaza where one light shows the border with Egypt and a flag droops and flutters under the moon.

'The Chaverim say I mustn't work tomorrow. They say I'm a guest. But I'd rather work.'

'You are a guest. You needn't work.'

'But I'd like to.' I imagine the kibbutz, day-long, empty, with no purpose to the passing hours; heat and inactivity. 'What are you doing?'

'I've got some carpentry I must do. Then I was going to finish painting these new huts. You could help me if you like.'

'Yes. Yes, I will.'

We return by way of the cowshed, our damp towels hanging upon our shoulders; and dip the tin cup into the milk buckets, drawing it up with cream on its lip to drink half a pint each without stopping to breathe. Gilbert straightens, his mouth moustached with white. The cows rustle in straw, breathe out their rich grassy smell, slobber their tongues in the dark. There is a bale of straw to sit on, sharp to the backs of the knees. My wet bathing-suit streams rivers on to the sloping floor, lying at my feet in a dark blot. Gilbert gives me the tin again and this time I only sip, aware of the animal taste and give it back quickly to him, wanting a cigarette. We smoke nearly all the time we are together, the ritual of lighting and puffing providing an allowed intimacy; the little kibbutz-made cigarettes, thin as roll-ups, loosely packed with wisps of tobacco, are always going out, my lips are always sore with drawing them alight.

'Jo, I want to ask you something.'

'What?' I think of what Gaston has said and am confused as a child at school.

'Perhaps I will ask you tomorrow. Perhaps we should say good night now. Tomorrow I will ask you, if you come to the menuiserie.'

'All right. But why not now?'

'Not now. But you don't mind if I kiss you now?'

'No, of course not.' The hesitant first touch, skin barely meeting skin; the taste, apprehension rather than knowledge; the brush of lips, a first kiss at a dance, curtained in dark before the lights go up, long ago; dry, shy, frightened, I remember; but now I am greedier and cannot let him go, I follow the bolder movements of his tongue, drink up the salt sweat, milk, chlorine, tobacco, and at last the rainwater taste of the insides of mouths, of people. At last he draws away, he protests, his voice falters on a broken note, he laughs but does not mean it. He is standing up, drawing me from the straw bale, leading me out again towards the kibbutz whose lights show like those of a kitchen where a parent is waiting up; and I am following, tired, irritable, full of physical discomfort, finding nothing to say.

'She is back,' he heard, and followed the crowd, aware that the smiles and the satisfaction were for him. A fleet look from a friend, Gaston's eyebrow raised as he told him yet again. 'I know,' he said, 'I heard it on the way back. The place is like a telephone exchange.' She waited for him outside the children's house and the door was open and a smell of boiled milk came out. The children ran about, dogs at their heels, and shouted at him. She said, 'Thank you for your letter,' and smiled; defensively, a lift of her chin and an irony in her look, baffling him. 'So you decided to come back and visit us.' He would give nothing away, he would decide to behave like a sabra, he thought, and let her run on.

'Yes, yes, I did. And here I am.' She would not say, this happened or that, or this is what I feel; not commit herself to a certain length of time. He walked away beside her with respect, and their silence was only broken by laughter, hers. She showed him his squashed letter from her pocket, the brown paper envelope where he had laboriously written her name. 'I've been carrying it round with me,' she said.

'Have you come from Jerusalem?'

'I have.'

'And how was Jerusalem?'

'Beautiful. C'est magnifique, mais ce n'est pas la guerre.' He did not know what she meant. He sat opposite her at meals and did not stretch to help himself as he would have, but passed her things, politely. When she spoke, when she smiled, her upper lip lifted more clearly than other people's, to show her neat front teeth. She shook back her hair with a gesture, held it with one hand at the nape of her neck so that her jaw was suddenly bare. Water turned about them on the grass, the circling sprays wet their stretched feet where they lay. At the swimming-pool her shoulder blades met like wings at the centre of her back as she straightened to dive. The water carried them both, separated them. There was a buzzing in his ears as if he were going deaf. He was all at once languid, with no energy left; he could hardly walk upright as they moved towards the cow-shed to take milk from the deep buckets, as he often did at night. It was absurd, and they had all warned him, with their curiosity and their transparent tact and their envy and their turning away. 'She will not stay,' Gaston had said; and she said, 'Here I am.' She would leave again, making a fool of him. To live here, in the kibbutz, with her, would somehow be impossible; he hardly formulated the thought, could not have explained it, but in the back of his mind he knew its truth. He would have to leave here and be homeless again, adrift again, uncertain of her, he guessed, always. The cows stirred, their breath foetid in the darkness. She raised her face decorated with a crest of milk. He heard himself; 'Jo, I want to ask you something.' And felt all at once, seeing her sink back beside him on the harsh straw, that he could force what he wanted to happen, make her fit in with him, with the kibbutz, with life as he had known it, draw her down beside him in a day-to-day closeness clean of dreams and aspirations, those unsettling visions that threatened to cross boundaries and make nonsense of the established borderlines of life. 'Perhaps I will ask you tomorrow.' All would be ordered, reasonable, and they would be married as people were, without fuss. And she had accepted it, perhaps, she had seen what he was really like and wanted that; there was the hope of this, and she appeared docile beside him, watching, even agreeing. He sighed and leaned back, letting some of the tension out of his back muscles. It would be reasonable to kiss her now, to seal that decision. The cows moved and munched and the darkness was very warm, like a womb, like a bed. After the first touch he drew breath, set his mind against his body as it leapt; he fought with her, with himself, and with the child Lala who rushed at him out of the darkness, who lay like a forked twig under the dead fig tree and seemed to split; with the sound of the cry that echoed from then on through his life; and with the sight of the watermelon, avatiyah, that cracks open and spills its red flesh out upon the ground when everything is done.

'Shalom.' This morning I want only to speak Hebrew, to throw off European habits and begin to belong; I want to be terse as he is, and preoccupied and hard at work. In the menuiserie he moves about in the half-dark between the gleam of light from the little window and the shaft from the open door. I stand for a moment watching him before he knows that I am there; he takes a plane and starts to work carefully, slowly, on a long piece of wood. The curls of white flake to the floor, longer strips hang like pasta. His back is towards me and in the twilit place, in the dark and sweat, I see the muscles move, the beads grow at the base of his spine, I think how men have bent like that, concentrated and sweated and worked, for centuries. It is incredible that he does not know or care that he is watched; that what matters most is the piece of wood, the straight line. When he finishes and the last thin curl falls to the floor to lie soft among the hundred others, he looks up, smiles, replies, 'Shalom.' White eyes, white teeth, the white nakedness of wood; and the smell of the place again affects me powerfully, the wood smell, the newness, the fine dust and fresh sweat; and it is cool as water after the heat of the outside morning that boils up fast towards midday. It is right, right; I have invented it, invented him, but it is right. A carpenter's workship in a small settlement in a desert in the Middle East, to which I have come by chance; and yet this morning, familiar, inevitable; the parts carved and fitted as a jigsaw. The just society waits, needing only to be discovered. This morning it is possible to change utterly. We stand side by side in our shorts and sandals, looking down at the planed surface.

'Gilbert?'

'What?'

'I don't want,' I begin in Hebrew. 'Oh, it's no good, I'll have to speak French. I only wanted to say, don't ask me what you were going to. What you said you wanted to ask me, last night when we were swimming.' Is that relief that shows in his startled eye, or an embarrassment quickly covered? 'I'd rather you didn't. I just want to stay here for a while and work with you all and get used to it. I don't want to be here for special reasons, because I'm connected with you.'

'You want to work here?'

'Yes, I do.'

'Why? What is the point for you?' Not relief, not embarrassment after all, but the defensive gruffness after hurt. I answer him gently, 'It isn't that I don't like being with you. I just want to be here as an equal, a working member, not as a sort of accessory of yours.

It's a good way of life, that's why I want to stay.'

'Good, yes; it is good.' He is still rough, abstracted; his anger shows in the stiff line of his neck. 'But why for you? Your life is so different.'

'Because of that. Because I've chosen it, rather than having it forced upon me. If they'll have me, that is.'

'I don't see why not. They like you. They said so.' He turns away and begins to count the smooth planks, under his breath, in Hebrew. When he speaks to me in French I am aware of somebody with a limited vocabulary and a strong provincial accent; in Hebrew he is himself, unlimited by culture or class. It is a language for an invented life, for cutting away the chains.

'But would you mind? Talk Hebrew to me, I want to learn it fast.'

'Why should I mind?' He kicks the door ajar and takes the armful of wood to dump it outside. Light patches the gloom, the cobwebs and corners are all shown. 'Excuse me.' I stand at the doorway, in his way wherever I stand, yet certain of myself, knowing that his mood will pass quickly as a child's anger and that in the end he will accept. For he will always shrink from me as he shrank in the cowshed, whatever our situation; this I know this morning, wakeful in the midday light as I was in the early hours. I think of the baby Gabrielle, the spread tiny legs and the red cleft; I think of Zvi again, and the flayed leg hanging from its cradle, and his calm voice refusing to admit to me the truth. It is not Gilbert, not Zvi. It is a hidden thing that draws me to each of them, to hunt it out. There is just time to admit it, this frail thought, before I see it merged again with a hundred others, become indistinguishable.

Before she came in, his lips had practised what they would say as his hands moved up and down the wood feeling for splinters. It would be calm but it would be decisive. 'I think we would get on well together,' he would say, 'I think we would be happy.' There seemed to be a contradiction even as he tried it; there was something he knew but had forgotten, some knowledge gained in Europe – a glance across a street, some exterior thing which gave him knowledge of himself – that would make nonsense of what he had decided. The kibbutz, he said, that is what it is; I cannot explain the kibbutz to her, or her to the kibbutz. There are two sides to my life now, where formerly there was one. The knowledge tried him, made his hands twitch unreliably. There was a paradox – and he saw it lie on the workbench before him, to be carpentered, to be cut down to size, grasped; and it was that he both wanted to share her with the others, with whom he had shared for so long, and longed to keep her jealously, secretly, for himself, as young Arab women were kept in Algeria, so that nobody else might know. The paradox was himself, his upbringing and the life he had chosen; it was himself that lay on the workbench, feebly struggling. The old life, that he had believed so firmly cut away, was there inside him and could not be forgotten. He stood back, wiped sweat from his forehead, looked helplessly at his work as if he hated it for the first time. He felt himself stretched over it, a big man, muscled, capable; and he knew at the same time, yet more intimately, the weak boy who waited on the steps of a café where men sat drinking coffee, talking in low voices, and who brought out the brushes and shoeshine pots to polish the dust from their shoes. The men's voices sounded in French, a small pile of coins collected in his box; there were the wheels of cars, trams, very close; there were scarred trees, there were orange peel and old cigarette cartons in the near gutter, there was the smell of petrol and a rankness of bodies. Upon the rooftops children screamed and were silenced. Women passing were veiled to the eyes and walked like ghosts. Only men inhabited this world, only aliens. And he was a lone child, indeterminate.

'Gilbert?' His mother's voice called him on an up-down note of anxiety, she screamed her tension at him from the dark interior of the house. And before the revolution, before those posters appeared on all walls, heads of wanted men turned face on and sideways, and feet began to run in the street, and the butts of rifles banged upon wooden doors, she was dead.

'Gilbert?' The English girl, Jo, spoke from directly behind him and startled him with her presence. He pretended that he had not seen her, that he was engrossed in his work. He saw her, from the corner of his eye, bend to finger the white curls that fell from the planed wood. He had forgotten what it was he wanted to say.

'And so, you will stay, Jo?'
'Yes, I think so.'
And the matter is settled.

At supper, Esther, Gaston, Gilbert and I sit together on the wooden benches, crumbling up the last of our bread. The question is asked and answered. I will like Esther, I think as she looks up, narrow face between falling locks of black hair, hands beautiful as she touches the salt and pepper pot, moving them about on the table; we will be friends. It is possible to love people simply because they are there, to discover them uncritically, because I am accepted. And I think that she looks tired, with the circles faintly drawn beneath her eyes and the little line between her eyebrows, since she went to have her baby. The baby is across the kibbutz in another hut, she is asleep, alone, neatly turned downwards beneath the white blankets. She will take what she is given and grow like a plant, needing only to be watered; somebody else will teach her as she grows. Esther, beside me, is a stranger who has had a child, hardly older than I and yet firmly cut off from me in her experience; there would be blood, pain, a rending of tissues, I guess at it dimly, having heard.

'Didn't you have anything particular to go back for?'

'Not really. I was going to do a course to be a teacher. But it doesn't matter.' The unreality is where I am not; London, England, the dim grey light.

Gaston says, 'You could be a teacher here. We need somebody to teach the children English.'

Nobody says, 'You must go home, you do not belong.' For each of them knows what it is like to leave, never to return, to be uprooted, to come here expecting something; and yet for them there was no return, it was impossible. A packet of cigarettes lies upon the table and we all help ourselves and begin to smoke. I am tired, I have found a resting-place. My head sinks upon my hands in silence.

'I can't imagine, now, having nobody to go home to.' She gives me her smile of open sympathy; what could have been self-satisfaction appears to me now as an enviable security.

Gaston says, 'We have our family here, now. Not the one we were born with, but the one we chose.' He too is gentle with me this evening, gentle and careful and welcoming. The figure on the boat could have been any of them, he or Esther or Reuven or even any of the others whom I do not know so well; Gilbert, his profile turned as he stares at the sea, going home. There is no place for an exclusive, a personal love. Zvi upon the balcony talks to me of abstractions. I love his voice, the angle of his head, the separate intricacy of each spread finger. His back is turned. Love is impossible, an archaism. And they wait, the kibbutzniks, to hear what I will say, and remain unsurprised by anything. There is a longing that goes beyond sex and beyond identity; and I tell them overcome with relief and emotion, 'It's marvellous of you to ask me to stay, I can't think of anywhere I'd rather be, it's so good that you want me to be one of you.' They only smile, a little embarrassed, and Esther raises her eyebrows at me and says kindly, 'No speeches, or they'll feel they have to make one in return, and that would break their teeth for them.' Marriage must be like this, the invitation, tension, commitment, exhaustion of relief when all is decided, only then the binding is to one person alone and not to a whole community; and I find that I am laughing as I see now that the whole thing, love, marriage, the secession of the personality, will no longer be necessary. 'I had a cousin once. A distant cousin, who spent the summer with us. The extraordinary thing about her was that she was in love....'

Sleeping, I dream of England, the swollen winter streams, sticks carried from the bank, the lushness of fields in late summer, the dark August chestnut trees ringed with gnats. Church bells, the springy lawns, all that one would have expected. The scoured slabs of earth, black birds descending from a rainy sky. It is as if one half of the mind cannot exist without the other, its disturbing antithesis; a temporary, welcome stability must be dislodged by other longings and unwelcome memories; the floodgates are broken each time they are erected, for the whole confused inconsequential river of one's being to come crashing through. On a wedding night the dream of adultery darkens and confuses one's waking. Loving one man, it is easy to call out another's name. Loving a face, a sound, a landscape, it is easy to carry it everywhere unbidden, making no choices free. I am divided and subdivided; chained to the few bars of music, the changing look of the sky, to a clink of cup on saucer, to the noise of London traffic on a wet street; hooked up to a face here, a word there, driven like a dog after this smell and that; inconstant, unsatisfied, ferreting down the alleyways of experience after something unnamed; needing whole cities, whole countries and their inhabitants, the patterns of geography, the configurations of the stars, to provide their assistance to my own small pattern; watching in tea-leaves, coincidence, the stray assurances of the palmist, marking the unheeding word of a stranger passing, looking for the tails of comets, the signs out of the heavens; I am free and have made myself unfree, to be tugged round like a leaf on the first whirl of current.

The first sign that anything had happened was the cluster of people in the middle of an empty space. Gilbert came towards it from the shower room and felt the night air faintly chill and yet welcome upon his warmed flesh. The damp ends of his hair touched his neck; since he had been in Europe he had worn it slightly longer than before and had avoided the travelling barber. Tonight he was alone, he had wanted to be alone; and to stand in the hot stream of water, see it sluice and sting his flesh, was what he had wanted too. He stepped outside, clean, confident, looking forward to a cigarette in his own hut and a book to read. The sky received him, familiar white light from the great stars, the high bowl under which he lived. The earth was still warmed after the day's sun. His arms ached. There was contentment still in ordinary things, within himself. And yet the little group drew him, he could only walk towards them.

'What's happened?' He saw in a moment that Jo was not there, and wondered where she was. And then she was coming from the opposite direction, with Esther from the children's house; and she carried a book under her arm too, showing her intention, and her mouth was open, dropped in an O of surprise as his perhaps had been, and she held back her hair with her free hand, as if to hear more clearly.

'What's happened?' There was Gaston and Reuven and the boy Pesach whose turn it was to be on guard tonight, and Ari and Menachem and Ari's wife Yardenna. The boy was at the centre, carrying the gun from a shoulder strap, trying to explain something against constant interruptions. Gilbert looked at Jo with sudden fear; but her face was simply open with curiosity.

'How did you bring him in? Where is he?'

'I got him covered with the Uzi, and shouted, and luckily Dov and Bernard were around, and they came over and we got him down, and we locked him in the empty hut, the one where the children used to be, you know. He wasn't armed, or if he was he'd thrown it away by the time I got him. He's still in there.'

It was as if he only knew what he thought, what he felt, from watching Jo's face; as if he had no real reactions of his own, or none that he could trust. She stared at him and he saw that she had not understood what had happened; that in a moment understanding would break. He could not think why it should matter; and yet knew that it all centred upon himself, upon the development and sudden birth of a new sensibility, one which he did not welcome; and he watched her, to see how he would develop. The voices ringed them round; he thought with revulsion that it was a man's life that was at question and that all that suddenly mattered to him was the appropriateness of his own feeling.

'What's happening? Did you ring the police?'

Plans, facts, the next action. 'Yes. They're coming over from Beersheva.'

'When?'

'Tomorrow, first thing. There's some special check. I don't know.'

Check, security; the euphemisms they used. But the houses, the rooms in which they lived, could be blown flat, like cards. He saw Jo look at him as if she were waking up, as if she had not noticed him before. His mouth opened slightly, but no sound came.

'What is he, a spy? Are you sure he had no grenades,

nothing like that?'

'Not when we searched him. I suppose he could have dumped them on the border, or come on reconnaissance. Dov and I held him, and Bernard searched. There wasn't anything.'

Jo said suddenly, turning her head like a bird, 'What's happened?' Nobody answered her for a moment, and then Esther, hardly sparing the time to turn to speak, muttered, 'An Arab,' her mouth pursed up with excitement. 'Pesach was on guard and he caught him creeping in. He was in the field beyond the water tower, wasn't he, Pesach?'

Somebody said, 'Could have been planning to blow up the water tower.'

Gaston said, 'Or simply rustling a few sheep or goats. They aren't all desperadoes.'

And Gilbert tried to hold Gaston's eyes, to beg him that this might be true; he was on the edge now, excluded from the feelings of the others, guessing at them, even condemning them in his heart; he had been to Europe on a ship, and come back, and it was not the same.

'But one can't take a chance on it.'

'You never know. Of course, they'd send one who looked harmless, wouldn't they?'

'I mean, he'd hardly come across with plans for an air-raid on Tel Aviv in his pocket.'

Several voices spoke at once, competing for attention. And then they died away, the words stopped; they were all turning slowly in his direction, waiting for him to speak, waiting to hear what he might say. He looked around him and at Jo, confused, and then looked down at the ground.

'Gilbert!' And there was no reason why he should know anything, or say anything. The man was nothing to do with him and did not appear as real in his thoughts. And yet they waited.

He said, 'I should think he's probably harmless enough.' And they waited, and he said, finally panic-stricken, 'But then, the police will find out. You have to tell them, after all.'

Jo stared at him and he could see in her look nothing to guide him. He was angry with them all, that they should make him speak. What he thought should not matter, since he was one of them; nor what Jo thought, since she was a foreigner, after all.

'Where did you say he was?'

The voices, ignoring him, seemed now to have a dead quality, a predictability. They were no longer the voices of the people he knew well. And yet this, this incident, this passing thought; it must not be allowed to matter at all.

'In the empty hut.'

'Let's have a look.'

'Come on, then.'

'Can't he get out through the window?'

'No, we nailed some wood.'

'Aren't you coming? He can't hurt you.'

'No, I'm going to bed early. No, thanks.'

'Gilbert?' Approval was what they wanted; because he had been away. He hesitated.

'Are you going?' She passed him, inches away, she looked up at him in disdain.

'Why not?' Why not. 'Leila tov, Jo. Sleep well.'

'Good night.' And she walked away, and never looked back.

He is the last to go, lagging a little behind the others at first, then striding to catch up, laying an arm along Gaston's shoulder in careless affection or perhaps out of simple habit, standing on tiptoe to see over the heads of the others, into the little lighted room. I see his head turn as he says something to Gaston, the line of his neck, the jerk upwards as he laughs. Their heads are round upon their strong necks. They clap each other upon the back easily, they cuff at each other in passing. They move through doors carelessly and never look where they tread. There are lines of white around their eyes from their constant easy laughter. And I see his wide back in its blue shirt, the lift of his shoulders, the characteristic tilt of the head backwards, as if he is longsighted or everything has come too close, I see him walk away and stand in clear outline against the light and then move to where the others are and merge with them until only his head appears. So many people, peering in at one man; and the Arab without moving, I imagine, his stare repelling their curiosity. Behind bars, looking out to see the nakedness of those faces looking in, the fear, the relief, the curiosity of one species for another. There are monkeys that grin and catch chocolate bars and one day are burned by cigarette ends; but their grin cannot change, for it is one of terror.

I go back alone, and am alone in the hut I share with Yael now, for she is out with her friend Jacky and has probably joined the crowd outside the prison window, the watchers. I am alone, among friends, among enemies. The two narrow beds, the cupboard, the bare table await me. To think as others think, to act as others act: it is still the most desirable, most difficult thing. I sit and condemn the decision that brought me back here alone, I sit rumpling the blanket, watching the mosquitoes gather upon the window, smoking a cigarette. There is no sound for minutes at a time, and then I hear a jackal bark far off; there are howls from the desert as something is killed and eaten; there is at last a pad of footsteps, a dim chatter, as people return to bed. Yael comes in, throws herself down upon the bed, exclaims with exhaustion and begins to undress, throwing her few clothes to the floor. She has a fat brown back, small breasts that look irrelevant. She pulls a nightdress over her head. There is a mole on the back of her neck. 'Did you see the Arab, Jo?' I am lonelier than I have been.

'No.' I'm sure that if I lived in a kibbutz and didn't get on well there, I'd blame myself rather than the kibbutz. It wouldn't be the system's fault. Just that you weren't sublimating hard enough?

'Didn't you?' I wouldn't have thought you were a joiner, a bender to the common will. 'I did, we met Pesach and he told us all about it. Did you know the police had telephoned from Tel Aviv? They said we must hold on to him till the morning and then they'll come and take him away.'

He is still here, still locked away behind me. 'What will they do?'

'I don't know. Interrogate him, I suppose, find out if he's a spy or not, and put him in prison.'

I ousted that man. I put him where he is. Do you see? I say, 'I'm terribly tired, Yael, I must go to sleep now.'

'All right. I'm quite tired too.' She is disappointed in her audience, I know. 'Good night, then.'

'Good night.' The irritation burns, unexpressed. We turn out the light and lie down to sleep, our faces turned away from each other by common consent; and still there is a buried need for privacy, that I dare not identify. She will always be there, somebody will always be there; that is what I have chosen. To wish for anything else is a failing, a betrayal. I suppress it and lie awake, thinking of Gilbert, his strange sharp recent look. There is the luminous movement of my watch and the moonlight that moves across the floor and up the wall, there is Yael's breathing, her smell. The taftaffit is turned on and its steady drip marks the seconds. The night is full of insects, I hear them blunder against the windows and feel their way up the perforated zinc that covers the space yet lets the air in; the great wings of moths, the long legs of mosquitoes; the feathery shrouds hang out there, trembling; there are bats in the night, carrying disease, rubbery, noiseless, and giant grasshoppers, little snakes, black lizards running up vertical surfaces. The night is alive and is poking its fingers through the perforations, prising open the cracks, leaning upon the flimsy walls of our cabins, rushing through the empty spaces; it is a power, it is waiting out there, full of animals and insects and its own creatures. My watch hands seem to have moved, they stand now at a quarter to two. Yael turns and breathes, her plump arms outside the covers. My feet are two bare bones, white upon the floor, my ankles weak as sticks. My hand wobbles towards the door, turns the handle. The crack wakes the sleepers, has made the creatures flee; but I push again and nobody moves. Outside the door there are squares of moonlight touching the grass like frost. The grass is hard, sparse, scarcely grows. In between the blades is sand, and the wind blows it over the grass; the lawns grow bald in September. And in the hut that was empty the light burns constantly, so that he cannot sleep, or so that he may be watched. It is not far away; I pass the showers and lavatories, the children's house, the huts where the Chaverim sleep soundly; the night air touches the mosquito-bites on my legs and I pause and spit on my hand and wet the places and feel the air dry them; the hem of my thin cotton nightdress floats against the backs of my knees, the stuff comes and goes against my body, touching it in patches. My feet are hard, walk without flinching from grass to gravel, the pads worn solid from walking in sandals, no feeling in them any more. Sweat dries under my arms with a particular coldness. There is nobody; a spiky palm in outline, a tangle of undergrowth, ferns and long-leaved burned-out bushes. The last hut.

At first the room is empty, it is all light and cracked paintwork and a bare bulb hangs; and then in a corner is a bed, covered with a khaki blanket, and a man sitting upon it. He is quite small in the brilliance, the tidiness, and he is loosely tied together like a bundle, he is all rags and loose joints and thin protuberance, wrapped up. I see the bare brown feet in thonged sandals set upon the floor, the legs stringy with veins, covered with dust, the unravelling hem on the striped robe he wears, caught up like a petticoat unevenly. His elbows are on his knees and his head upon his hands, so that only the soiled white of his headdress shows. He is motionless, a felled bird, feathers awry. In the room there is something ticking, an expectation. I lean, and a twig snaps at my feet, and I put out my hands to the window-sill to balance, there being a narrow ditch dug around the base of the wall, and his head comes up and he sees me. It is an old man's face, dry, brown, the dust marked as if by tears; the eyes are stained with brown veins, circled and circled again with wrinkles, deep set like stones at the bottom of a stream. Two deep declivities run from his nose to the sides of his mouth as if his face has been folded. His lips are pursed, purplish. And his eyes keep a fixed and steady look, as if they see nothing. I suppose that they see me, a round-faced girl with a fringe of light hair, curious eyes, a face whose features are all foreign; but apparently he sees nothing. I am transparent to his gaze as air. I look and look and my curiosity is as keen as any of the kibbutzniks'; I see the falling away of skin from the jaw, the lips part to show stumps of teeth set in very pink gums, the grey stubble, the hand raised, slowly, to shield the face, its black nails turned towards me; the sleeve fall away from the arm; I see the recoiling, the rejecting of experience. The fear. I see an old man drawing away from me in fear, from my light skin and the questioning of my eyes. I see the enemy as I look from the dark into the light, the enemy that is everywhere, that threatens us all. And in my dream I do not move again.

In the morning the police are there, they question him I am told and take him away. After a while, nobody speaks of him again. He has become an incident, like a birth, a harvest, a movement of weather. There are still the hundreds of yards of ploughed earth between where I stand and the Egyptian border, there are still the huts and the United Nations men playing cards, and the guns laid in readiness against the wooden walls, and the flags marking the boundary line, and the trenches dug in red earth where men may crouch to pick a mark or other visitors stretch themselves to lie in the sun. It is all still there, until the next time. The sky cups the earth firmly from horizon to horizon and men move beneath it. The earth remains the same; only the lines that are drawn upon it change.

6

'It's raining.'
'I know. I heard it. I dreamed I was in Israel.'
'I didn't know it rained in Israel.'
'Sometimes.' The sound of water falling upon a slate roof in England in a rainy dawn, the noise of home, damp days, inertia. The slow erosion of solids by water, old stones worn smooth. But the water is dripping through the rush matting they hang above the windows here to cool the rooms, taftaffit in onomatopoeic Hebrew. Between sleep and waking there riot impressions, water drip, mosquito whine, the moon's eye, the jackal's bark. I wake to think myself in England on a rainy spring morning and go outside to find the aridity, the black stillness, the different moonlight, to touch still hot earth after the day's heat; and in England, waking to rain, I hear the precious water drip and turn to sleep again, to dream my way back into the same Israeli night. In my dream, I open the door of my hut, walk carefully, leaving a girl sleeping rolled in a sheet. I go down a step from the wooden floor to the hard earth, and my bare feet make no noise. I cross the square of worn grass outside and move with strange ease—
'I didn't know it rained in Israel.'
'Sometimes.' Impossible to try to explain the tenuous connections of one's own mind to another whose mind is elsewhere. Midnight, one o'clock, two o'clock; the night is dense, wet, empty of traffic and the swish of wheels, it is the hour at which one still wakes painfully and yet finds it hard to sleep again. And he always sleeps fitfully at my side, waking me with his restlessness,

turning on the side light to read a few more pages of a book, beginning suddenly to talk, asking me staccato questions so that I will have to respond. To be woken regularly in the night, every few hours; an efficient form of torture, known to break down resistance in even the most stubborn victim; it is said that the only prisoners whose minds escape it are those who are already insane.

'Why do you have to wake me up to say it's raining?'
'You were awake, weren't you?'
'No, I wasn't. I told you, I was dreaming.'
'You were awake. You started talking about Israel out of the blue.'
'I was dreaming. You woke me up in the middle of my dream. I was about to find something out, something I had to know, and you woke me up.'
'It's bound to come back, in some form or other. It'll get through, some other way. If the unconscious mind wants the conscious mind to know something, it will manage to let it know somehow. Shall we have some tea?' But he is tender, attentive towards the lost dream where he cannot be to my lost sleep. 'Do you want to tell me the dream, or what you can remember?'

'No, not really.' Ordinarily, I never refuse. He is in analysis and finds other people's dreams comforting, he says. He lies back beside me and frowns with concentration, listening, and when I have finished smiles like a conjurer who has brought the string of silk handkerchiefs out of his sleeve, says, 'That's very good, oh, very good.' And I remain flattered and irritated at once; to have dreamed a worthy dream, to have been so easily understood.

'Are you going to make tea?'
'Oh, all right.' Full of the pain of being wrenched from sleep I lean and fiddle with the electric kettle that waits at our bedside for these nocturnal times, my hand carelessly shakes tea into the pot, I hide beneath the

clothes against the cruel sudden light, waiting for the room to fill with steam. 'Are you seeing Vidler tomorrow? Today, I mean.'

'Four o'clock this afternoon. For what it's worth.'

Trying to draw him towards me I find his tenseness, his wakefulness. He sits upright in bed, pink and white and bright-eyed as a schoolboy in his striped pyjamas. My eyes open again carefully, I stare up at the blank face of the ceiling, so high up there, since we are sleeping on a mattress on the floor. The Victorian room holds us at the bottom of a tall, closed box.

'Doesn't it help?'

'Oh, I don't know. He's all right, but he's out of date. All this stuff about one's childhood, when what one's supposed to do nowadays is to face the existential reality of the present moment.'

'Perhaps one's understanding of the past helps one's understanding of the present. The existential present. Existential reality. What was it you said?'

'Absolute rubbish,' he says. 'The present makes the past irrelevant. For purposes of therapy, anyway. Don't you see that using the past as the only explanation of the present denies any play of free will? That's the flaw in Freud. Existentialism showed it up. So Vidler's old-fashioned.'

'Francis, I must go to sleep, I'm exhausted. Oh, blast.' The forgotten kettle rocks its lid and the sheets are wet with steam. But the sound of water pouring into the pot, filling it up, is soothing now that the rain has stopped. The tea stands in mugs, brown grains floating to the surface, poured out too soon; the tray is slopped, I burn my mouth on the first metallic sip.

He says, 'You're exhausted. Feeling tired is an escape from reality. You can't face something in your waking life so you try to get back to sleep in order to find a comforting illusion.'

'Well, Christ, everyone has to sleep. Except you,

apparently. And you go back to sleep when I'm at work, don't you? And who doesn't need a few fucking illusions?' I turn away and pull the blankets up around my shoulders, but the light is still there, pulling at my eyelids. Tonight is different. Tonight I am more tired than ever, and he has woken me from my dream at the point where free will might have begun to operate, where there might have been some choice. Usually I am so careful, so gentle, I tread like a cat entering a larder, not to disturb him. The moments of our waking life are carefully constructed, not to jar. There are many questions not asked, many criticisms not made; it is simply that I am afraid to ask, to criticise, and that he notices nothing.

I live now in his rooms, surrounded by his books, in which he searches for a reason for existence; they are thick, they come from libraries all over London; people think he must be writing a thesis. Once, long ago, he told me he was writing a thesis. It was when we first met. I have forgotten what the title was. And one day I challenge him, saying, 'You only pick out the ones that tell you how hopeless and pointless life is and that there's no reason for living, just to back up what you already think. You're cheating.'

'But how could you think that anyone with any intelligence could find a reason for living? Why shouldn't life be hopeless and pointless? One is hopeless and pointless oneself. That's the beauty of it.' A reason for living; a reason for death; I think but do not say that I require both. And he reads aloud a passage from Heidegger. 'Listen to this,' he says, and in a monotone reads a long passage while I forget to listen, for he reads so often from old newspapers. Kant, Kierkegaard, Jaspers, Heidegger, Sartre, they live with us, like the old newspapers, they interrupt our meal times and when we are making love; after them we creep in the narrow way of sanity. We are alone, he says, because the rest of the world is mad. Sometimes in a moment of vertigo I see the doctrine turned inside out, see us in our insane asylum and the world move on uncaring. Sometimes this is exhilarating, like swinging upside down in a soaring car at a fair; sometimes it makes me sick with fear. There is no telling which way up the truth looks at us, not any more.

'When I was a child there was a beach where I buried a tin box with all my money in it. I lost it and then I found it again.'

'Did you? We hardly ever went to the beach. My father never took a day off as far as I remember, and my mother would have dropped down dead if you'd taken her away from the kitchen sink.'

'That's where you get your Puritan conscience.'

'Don't start pretending to be me. Listen to this. "The self-reflection of the human being of integrity which had culminated in Kierkegaard and Nietzsche has here degenerated into the uncovering of sexual desires and typical childhood experiences; it is the covering up of genuine, dangerous self-reflection by a mere rediscovery of already known types".'

'Who's that?'

'Sartre on Freud. And it's genuine, dangerous self-reflection I'm after. I ought to read that to old Vidler.'

'I didn't think he was a Freudian.'

'Nor does he. But he's all tied up in it. He's intellectually hog-tied.'

'Why don't you try somebody else, then?'

'But it makes him so stimulating to talk to.' The smooth mouse-brown head bows again, golden hairs lit up by pale sunlight; he is excited in spite of himself by his search, and again I know the strong but passing certainty that after all, at bottom, we mean the same things, we believe the same things; that we understand each other. We are allied against Vidler in our contention of Francis's sanity, allied and alone.

'You see,' he says after a few minutes, 'he really believes I ought to sublimate my despair. Instead of feeling it.'

On some days life is narrowed to a tunnel, all will tied to the hopeless suppression of meaning. But there is something else, always; the angle of his head as he sits reading, the mouth puckered with occasional disagreement, the long fine bones of his wrists and fingers; there are sudden sparks of gaiety, jokes and experiments, as if a current has been switched on. I remember that once he conspired with me to make every event of each day particular. And we have left behind cause and effect, we have abandoned the conventional pauses between actions, connections between thoughts. Living with Francis, coming to his room and finding no real home of my own, I immerse myself with him in the surreal. And it is willing, it is conscious, it is out of some kind of hope. At some point in my life I found that I wanted to rid myself of the split vision, the good on one side, the bad on the other; ever since childhood I have searched for a way out of causality. But now my dream of the border kibbutz is the first thing of my own for so long, and I am loath to share it, to see it broken up into his order of things. Five years after the reality of my being there, I am greedy to retain the certainty of that hot night, that strongly lit, marked place; to feel again as I did then, to step out not knowing but looking.

At breakfast at this time the papers lie about telling us of growing aggression in the Middle East, of Egypt arming itself, of shots fired from the Golan heights and across the Suez Canal; of raids and retribution, to and fro across the borders of Israel. Francis leaves his coffee till it is cold and drinks it skin and all, unnoticing, it is I who shudder as the skin swims upon his lip. The marmalade and butter left on his plate are flecked with little black specks of ash and the burned crumbs of toast. He picks up the paper and his eyes move quickly but without interest. 'There'll be another war, I suppose.'

I tell him, 'I somehow can't bear the thought.' Feeling that there was something, long ago, I should have done.

'Got to happen, I suppose. Still, war's as good a way as any.'

'For what? What on earth do you mean?'

'To die.'

'To die! How do you know, how do you know? You don't know what you're talking about!'

'We shut our eyes to it,' he says. 'It's everywhere. Death is the only sure thing. What does it matter what we do before we die?'

'You're wrong, Francis. It does matter.' There is a hard lump that has waited in the base of my throat for weeks, that will not be dislodged.

'Anyway,' he says, 'why get so worked up about it? It's none of our business. Newspapers simply manufacture hysteria. One can't possibly feel a real concern, from so far away. Cheer up, you're only suffering from what everybody feels when they open their newspaper. They'll always give you something to feel guilty about. Have you read about the man in the gorilla's cage? Listen to this, it's extraordinary.'

The chill settles upon me, the cold breath of a late May morning with no sun beyond the panes of glass. From our kitchen window we can see one tree in the small back garden of a house below our flat, one lilac tree with its white trumpet blooms dingy and its leaves matt with dust; and the smell of lilac still rises to our window when we open it on fine nights, when we lean out and see the glow over the river, the sun setting on the pink chimneys of the power station, the clouds trawling a windy sky. In spite of the cold, this early summer smells of lilac. All around the tree are the broken fences and washing-lines and ramshackle dustbins of the back-to-backs, and on long light evenings the children rush up and down between the brick walls and throw tin cans and play hopscotch and skipping games and fight. Now there is a woman hanging out her own pink underwear and the boiled vests of her husband and sons, in spite of the cold, the damp, the dirt in the air. And on the window-sill is a geranium in a pot, dying. It is Saturday and the children are in the street shouting and sucking sweets, rushing splay-legged with white and bony knees, roller-skating down the alleys. It is a Saturday and I am not at work, as there is no school on Saturday, and there is nothing to do. Morning becomes afternoon so soon, without effort. At lunch we eat rolls and bacon and read our books. I turn on the fire. I tell myself that it is cosy, that it is home, that I am happy, that I love him, that this is what life really is. At some point in life, one has to believe these things; for an hour, for an afternoon, just for a little time at least. When he comes to touch me in the evening I shrink from his cold fingers until my own mental effort has turned them warm; I shrink from them as from those of a corpse.

'Whatever's the matter?' he said, seeing her. It was as if a cat hissed from behind a sofa, backing away.

The light was on, he felt her weight shifting beneath him; he had just switched the light on, to catch her.

'Nothing. I'm sorry. I'm just tired, I suppose.' He moved his hands and brought her small nipples up into points, but her face never changed from its weary acceptance. 'It's the war,' she said. 'There's going to be a war.' It seemed to him hardly worth saying any more, this was so absurd; he rolled away, and took his hands away and felt himself lie back on a damp patch on the sheet. He found it boring, anyway, to make love to her once he himself had finished, and his fingers grew stiff. And so he slept, curled away from her, a tall thin man, his knees brought up to his chest even on this summer evening, for warmth.

*

There is a time I remember when every night there is a party somewhere; all night in the top-floor flats of big old London houses, red wine dripping from kitchen draining-boards, Merrydown cider, air yellow with smoke, floors between sagging sofas and hard modern chairs covered with bodies. The bodies clasp each other, kiss, fumble, sleep fully dressed; sometimes one has to step over them. It is a time when people return from other places, America, Turkey, Greece. The boundaries of Europe are splitting, opening at this time, to let out the yearly migrations of students and others, nobody speaks of France or Italy now but of a chance encounter in Yugoslavia, a little café in Crete. Afghanistan, India, the wildernesses of central Asia and further east, these are still untapped. There are plans, yes. Nobody will stay in England. A strange man comes in wrapped in goatskin, brown faced, talking of Samarkand. Another, in another top-floor flat, takes out a little pipe made in Morocco and hands it round, and people taste and cough. Men are seen with soft leather knee-boots and heavy belts laden with metal, but they are the initiators, scornfully temporary in London. The vast pilgrimages have hardly started, but already people know what is lacking in their lives; already there is a hint, a suggestion of where it may be found. Smells are the strongest reminder of this time, the sour wine smell, a particular man's jersey, the smell of sick upon the stairs. It is a time when there is always somebody crying in the hall, among the coats. And the words of songs expressing loneliness, a longing for communion, say without effort what everybody wants to say. There is a peculiar tenderness between strangers, a common hunt for an understanding love, and always the hope of a face in the crowd, able to tell one of a discovery, a step forward. As the year goes on, the ritual dance becomes ragged at the edges as the couples move away, names are loosely held, claimed by the strings of gossip and then at last they are lost.

He walks across the room, quite deliberately. 'Well, how do you fit in with all this?'

'I don't know. I just know people here. Everybody seems to know everybody a bit.'

'I don't. I just walked in. Extraordinary set-up, isn't it?' And makes himself a traveller from further than I can imagine. A tall thin man with a lock of light brown hair falling forwards, pale eyes in a pink and suntanned face, a look of innocence, surprise, thin wrists sticking out from the sleeves of a neat jersey. Clear eyes like a baby's, unblinking, the pupils ringed with white; a look of health, unusual here.

'Extraordinary? Is it?'

'All these people dancing and so forth. What are they up to?'

'What do you mean? It's just a party, isn't it?' The first of so many times, blankness in the face of his assessments.

'Well, what do you think of it?'

'I don't know, I'm enjoying it. Don't you go to parties?' He stands cool and apart, an anthropologist. I never know what I think when he asks, it is as if a slate is wiped clean, all the old marks gone. I suppose that what holds me there is the lure of a new way of seeing things, a sudden understanding; it is the lure of travel.

'No, not much. I'm not crazy about the human race en masse. I suppose I dissect too many not to feel that it's all a bit pathetic. Come on, don't look too horrified, drink up and we'll leap about a bit.'

Something is familiar, reminding me; the unrecognising stare of another man's eyes in a crowded smoky room long ago, last year or the year before that, that closed look of preoccupation; and, before it, the sudden falling away of the mind's habits, as if nothing were ever experienced, nothing known before. I turn and see the party change before my eyes, the people shrink to the stature of dolls, their actions, words, smiles become absurd.

'Are you a doctor, then?'

'Medical student. Bart's. I finish this year. You?'

'Teacher.'

'Oh, so you're supposed to like them too.' He gestures to the dancing couples. The music suddenly shouts; somebody has turned up the volume; men's eyes close and their hips sway and they pout in unconscious imitation of Mick Jagger. The girls leap, their arms above their heads, booted feet stamping.

'I teach children. I'm an infant teacher. They're fantastic, I love it, they're so excited by everything.' But perhaps I am saying it for the last time, for my mind clouds as I think of them growing up, of their world.

'Jo, are you drinking? Here, have some of this before it's all guzzled. It's not quite as bad as the red plonk.' A friend passes with a bottle, a former friend of mine suddenly grown surprising as he makes the ordinary movement of filling my glass with white wine from a slim yellow-labelled bottle. 'I'm sorry, I don't know your name? I'm Ben Bryant, I'm sort of the host.'

'Oh, well, in that case I'd better give myself up. I'm a gate crasher, I just heard the music and came up. Francis Allard. How d'you do.' I see Ben, surprised and insulted by the formal handshake, lose his composure.

'Oh, hello. No, of course, do stay. Have some wine. This stuff isn't quite as bad as the red plonk. D'you know people? D'you know Jo? Well, you two are all right there, are you?' He goes, the bottle empty yet still clutched. We are in a cupboard-like space which turns out to be the kitchen, with heaps of dirty paper plates smeared with pâté, some floating to the floor, glasses and coffee mugs stacked on the small sloping drainingboard, the sink full of grey water, on one wall a poster of John Lennon, drooping at one corner. There is a tiny gas stove encrusted with something brown, a smell of burned aubergines. Across the passage from here is a room, somebody's bedroom, the door open so that we see heaps of clothes, some of them inhabited. On the bed there are two or three people and before a tipped mirror a girl sits with her back to us, so that in the reflection we see her face pink-stained, and the cigarette in her mouth with its rising coil of smoke. She is a girl I know, who lives here, but I can no longer remember her name. I am wondering what Francis sees, and why it is extraordinary.

'Want to dance?'

'Not particularly. Do you?'

'Why don't we go for a walk?' he says. 'There's not much happening here, is there?'

'No, I suppose not. Okay, let's.'

Outside there is a cold wind, a few stars, paper blowing down the street. It is hard walking at first, as I am wearing a pair of cracked black patent shoes with three-inch heels like little weapons, but after a few minutes I kick them off and carry them and walk on, smaller at his side, in black stockings with my toes coming out of holes, my shoes tucked under my arm, as girls do carry their impossible shoes all over London, easily bohemian. I remember a tight skirt with a long black jersey pulled down over it smelling of cigarettes, and my ability to take only small steps, the skirt tugging my knees, my heels and toes still out of touch with each other; he striding, I trotting, my toes stubbing often against things, painful and cold; trees thrashing their branches in the park, benches empty, leaves pressed down in their wire baskets, bulging out, flying away. There is a bench ahead of us, under a tree, and we walk to it and sit on it as if by spoken agreement. We sit for only a few minutes, the huge tree overhead like a ship with tangled shrouds.

'Well, better go back, hadn't we? Not much point sitting here.' He leans back, long legs spread before him, head tipped to stare up into the darkness at the centre of the tree, one hand carelessly over mine, cold as a fish. But his breath against my ear is warm, and my cold hand turns to hold his better. When he kisses me later, there is a feeling of cool freshness, as when one breathes in after eating peppermint.

I can never remember the conversations, only their endings; the abrupt way he suddenly wants to move. There are no long ordinary periods of calm such as life usually furnishes, only interruptions, movement, the cutting motions of his hands. Nothing is ever finished.

'Are we going back to the party? My feet will look filthy in the light.'

'Might as well, don't you think? See if there's something left to drink.'

'I suppose so, yes.' On the way back he walks more slowly, an arm around me, yet this is not anything to do with me but is absent-minded, like his shaking Ben's hand, somehow insulting. In the common hunt for love, one takes what comes, unprotesting and grateful. By this time I have decided that I must accept, and go where I am led.

'Where's the drink, come on, let's find the drink.' Back in the cold bare flat, where couples are already beginning to leave, he hunts singlemindedly for an unopened bottle, finds one in a drawer, uncorks it and begins to offer it to others who pass. 'I don't think they really want any, do you? They're only pretending to want it, to be polite. Come on, you don't really want any more, do you? Awfully bad for you, you know.' And he withdraws the bottle, ignoring the protest of the girl who has passed her glass. 'Much better without it.' And he pours two mugs full, passes one to me; we go back into the kitchen again to drink it. Later, when we have finished the bottle, he says to me, 'Disgusting stuff, isn't it? I hate drinking, hate alcohol really.'

'Do you?'

'What we need's some food. I haven't eaten all day,

you haven't, have you? For God's sake let's go and find a restaurant somewhere. I'm starving.'

'I'll come and watch you. Actually, no, I could eat something.' The effect is always that of being pricked, goaded into activity. But at this point I can still say, after glancing at my watch, 'I don't think anything'll be open at this time of night.' Later, I will be saying, 'Yes, let's,' only to join in a late-night fruitless search around local restaurants, to know his brief flare of anger when they are shut, the knocking on doors and shouting up at closed windows, and then his almost immediate announcement that it does not matter, anyway. I will be sitting beside him in cinemas, anxiously aware throughout my own enjoyment of the film of his increasing restlessness, the recrossing of legs and sighing and irritated comments, knowing that in a minute he will say, 'Oh, let's go, shall we, this isn't any good,' and that I will rise to follow him out through the darkness while people mutter and angrily tip their seats to let us pass and coats and bags slip to the floor and the usherette swings up her torch to find us out. Now, I say, 'You could come back to my flat if you like, I've got some tins of ravioli and things like that.'

'Have you got any tinned snails and those bags of shells they sell with them? We could put them all back in their shells and then get them out again.'

'No, no snails.'

'Oh, well. I'll come anyway.'

And when we have eaten and mopped up the last of the ravioli with the stale remains of bread, and drunk mugfuls of Nescafé and smoked several cigarettes, we lie back propping our backs against the sides of chairs and look shyly at each other; and I see for the first time that smile of his, that crumpling of tension into relaxation, that completely open, delighted smile that I must always struggle to conjure back again.

This year, in Jerusalem, an elderly man is preparing to stand trial, charged with crimes against humanity. He is not the man to terrify one upon a dark night upon a street corner, behind trees on a deserted stretch of dyke. Rather, one would notice his small stature, his shaking hands as he tries to light a cigarette, and would move on, hardly remembering his features. For how could one stop, confront him, find anything to say? There is only the hope that he might drop into non-existence, that where he is there might be a gap. Between the man and the gap that would fit him, there is an action. Nobody wants to act, nobody wants to do it. Passion discolours after the years. And yet he has taken up so much room that the gap will be large; for a few minutes, for a few days. The last of the flesh-eaters, people say, the last one of that race which has polluted ours, the last to walk the earth unchecked. For now there will be created a system of checks and balances; now all will be different. Never again, never again, never again, never again. People say loudly that they do not want to do it, now.

'It's the only logical answer.' He lies stretched out on the sofa, the square of window behind him a bright sunless grey.

'You can't mean it, or you couldn't say it.'

'Of course I mean it.' His cheeks flushed, his eyes bright, mischievous.

'You don't regret having been born?'

'No, not entirely. I suppose it was interesting enough. But I know when I've had enough. And what is the point in living, really?'

'Just to live.'

'Just to exist?'

Silence. There is nothing if it is not perceived. I say to him stubbornly, 'I can see a point in living.'

'Well, what? Convince me.'

'Just the process of it, just life. What things feel like.

The fact of a new day every morning. Surfaces. Surprises. Tasting food, that sort of thing.' There are times when it is a struggle to feel anything. He sits, cheerful enough, enjoying the conversation, while I grow pale and terrified, feeling each thing, each talisman grow less real, each sensation less identifiable.

'And here we all are, turning rotten inside, breathing filthy air, making the world so disgusting that soon it won't be able to hold us any more. L'homme moyen sensuel had his day ages ago. He's the one who's fouled everything up, just living to stuff his mouth with food and cramming in sensations, as you want to do. What's the good of living another twenty-four hours just to put things off and have another pathetic little sensation? It's like being an animal in a sty, just waiting for some more swill. You can't really think that.'

He always looks so well; now his cheeks glow as he speaks, his lips are that fine red that one sees in young children, his eyes are clear and lively, his hair shining and brushed. His long clean fingers close upon the book that lies on his knees, stroking the cover, and I see that he has cut his nails carefully and pushed back the cuticles. From the table top stares the skull that he brought home to study and that we now use as an ash tray; the empty eye sockets no longer appal me.

'Maybe not. Maybe I'm just comforting myself with lies.' For now when we make love we clash together and fall apart, he to sleep at once, I to lie hearing the birds upon the gutters; I only remember, or tell myself, that there was something else.

'Do put the Bruckner on, would you?' I put out a hand to find the record, knowing that once I have put it on the turntable and surreptitiously turned down the volume there will only be minutes before he asks me to turn it up again, and we will sit drowned in noise, the room shaking, the woman downstairs helplessly banging on her ceiling. Once, years ago, he said to me in this room, 'I can see you again, can't I? I must see you again,' making it into a plea, and I lightly said, being in control, 'Of course.'

'I knew a man once, in Jerusalem, who believed it.'

'What? Jo, do turn it up a bit, it sounds so feeble.'

'That life was worth living just for its own sake. He'd been in a concentration-camp when he was young, and all his relations were dead except one batty cousin. And his wife was brought up in the Warsaw ghetto and only just escaped.'

'Well, good for him. We can't all have been in concentration-camps. Though I'm sure that it marvellously concentrates the mind. What did he do to justify his existence?'

'He had dozens of clean shirts hanging in his wardrobe. Drip dry. He had a clean shirt every day. He used to wash them himself and hang them over the bath.'

'Oh.' Humming the Bruckner bass, he strums with his fingers on the book cover.

I struggle to continue, determined now to introduce these two conflicting influences upon my life and let them fight. 'People thought he was a revolutionary, some people did, but it seemed to me that that was the really revolutionary thing about him.'

'Having dozens of shirts? Or washing them? What do women do out there?'

'Just doing everything as if it was incredibly worth doing, almost as if he was doing it for the first time. Or the last. No, he just really knew there was a point in living. He was a survivor. He said so.'

Francis tells me, 'The survivors are the people who have sold the rest up the river. Who got corrupted at the last minute. The people who are afraid to die.'

I shout at him, 'That's rubbish, you don't know what the hell you're talking about, you just talk a load of balls.' I never do this, I never contradict; but now that I have let loose at him I feel a constricted flow run again, an energy of anger rush through me, and he looks up in mild surprise. This morning, in the early hours, I dreamed of that night on the Egyptian border; now, for the first time in months I think of Zvi and Zvi's life, on this one cold day in early summer I feel suddenly the existence of the unresolved past, of something in me that has been buried. My arm flies out and an unsteady vase of tulips, their tight greenish muzzles still folded, crashes to the floor. Downstairs Mrs Collins bangs on the ceiling with her kitchen mop. The Bruckner symphony runs on like spilt water.

Francis says calmly, as I ram the flowers back and throw a sponge into the mess of wet, 'To go back to what you were saying. It's no good just liking food and sunsets and clean shirts. It's too late for all that.' I stare at him, beginning to giggle with hysteria, my trousers soaked and clinging to my calves, but he goes on, 'Millions of people are dead already, living dead, can't you see that? What's the good of sitting in the promised land wearing a clean shirt? It just means a few days more, a little more consumption of food – oh, for God's sake leave it, it'll dry off – a little more pollution of the atmosphere. No, the only logical thing is to kill oneself. To seek death. What we call life – Jo, leave those bloody flowers – what we call life is just scraping along, inch by inch, slower and slower, not feeling and not functioning, not knowing why the hell we do anything. Only death allows one to know. Darling, what is the matter?'

'I can't put them back, they won't stand up, they're all broken.' Tears flood me, the first time, he has never seen me cry. The new flowers stick out of the jug like fractured limbs, their heads turned up absurdly to the ceiling. 'Oh, God, I don't know what to do, I can't throw them away.'

'Sit down, don't worry. Damn that bag downstairs, what's the matter with her? And how on earth did you manage to knock them over in the first place?'

'What do you mean?'

'What, about death being knowledge? Death is a state of knowing, absolutely.'

'How do you know?'

Did Matt Ferguson just die, or did he do it on purpose? 'It depends what you mean by kill.' A year ago, when they sat down nineteen at table and opened bottles as they were opened today, there was one here who plummeted white one night into the dark binding weeds of the river Cam, never to be released. It was a first knowledge of death, this knowledge of a gap. Sir Edmund, Sir Gervase, Sir Ralph, Sir Edmund, Sir Gervase, Sir Ralph; now the dead knights rise up from their grassy tombs to walk through her dreams, smiling their stony smiles towards something that remains forever out of sight.

'I suppose that is a risk that one would have to take.'

Skin still feels the touch of skin, in the moment before the mind intervenes; meals eaten quickly, hardly tasted, drinks swallowed in a mouthful still pass through the digestive system and are assimilated. There is still sun on the water where we go, even though he sits in a closed car, reading a newspaper whose message he has already forgotten, while I stand among the tussocks of grass to watch the far-down wrinkle of the waves. The books lie heaped about, are restlessly fingered, left lying opened, their spines cracked flat. I see the emptiness between those printed words where no mark is made, where he searches. I am inside the cave now, watching the play of shadows on the wall, telling myself that they are made by the light of the sun that burns outside, that there has to be a light to make a shadow; and yet I cannot turn my head, nor see beyond the shadow play.

'Listen to this,' he says, throwing down the book upon his knees, jutting his head towards the page; and the language I do not understand flows over me again, meaning nothing, a repetition. There is no way out, not in time, not in distance. The images we have seen remain in our heads. Coincidence still exists to make the connections we could not, dared not make. That is why I am here in the cave, why at the moment there is no point beyond it. This is the present, for it will not pass away, however much one longs for its passing. It is the present towards which I have been moving. But I am lying, of course. There is always a next day, another time. It is just that I have not yet felt the rebound of energy, the turn of the tide. I am alone, facing these hard clear images of the present time, which have nothing to do with me, yet which are all I know.

Sun spreads in patterns on the floor again, longer, deeper towards sunset. The columns of the power station turn to rose, are bound in drifting smoke; the sash window is pushed up, the air that floats into our kitchen is stale, tastes of dust, yet is peculiarly golden, a heavy concentrate of light held between the warmed walls of buildings. Newspapers are spread across the floor, printed pictures, smiling troops, tanks, blazing towns, refugees, faces. The stories wind across each other, hysterically told. I have read all the editorials, all the accounts, have searched for the sight of names, faces, places, marks; all that I can recognise is the sickening upbeat of the heart, that is my feeling. Life changes, utterly. Preconceptions, ideas; they are nothing when the touched heart moves at a name. Francis lies slumped in a chair, reading, his alert head moving as he pecks up words. His bare feet coil around each other, separate from him. He lights cigarettes and forgets to smoke them, moving only when the long worm of ash falls down across the page. It is hot in here, between our walls after the day, it is hard to breathe. When the telephone rings it is like a cry of terror, to be answered by a panic run; I am there, breathing hard, still shocked by the sudden intrusion of noise.

'Can I speak to Jo Catterall please?'

'Speaking. Who is it?'

'Jo? Do you remember me?' A harsh sound, distorted vowels, a laugh hidden in the last words: 'Rowan Rattigan, remember? That time in Israel?' Isreeal, she says.

'Rowan! How extraordinary! Where are you? Of course I remember you, you fool. What are you doing? How did you get my number? Are you in London? Christ, this is peculiar.'

'Why peculiar? I went to see your parents in Cambridge.'

'Oh, it's just that I was thinking about that time. Why did you go and see my parents?'

'Well, that was the address I had, from Israel. They were great, they gave me an enormous meal and told me you were in London. They're dead worried about you, did you know?'

'Yes, I suppose so. I haven't seen them for a bit. But where are you, Rowan, we simply must meet, can I see you this evening?'

'Are you all right? You sound a bit weird to me?'

'Yes, I'm okay.' I am in the little hall, stretched on the floor, one foot pushing the door shut so that Francis may not hear, the telephone sweaty in my hand.

'Are you alone?'

'Yes, I'm alone. I've been thinking about the war.'

'War? Oh, you mean in Israel. Yes, isn't it fantastic they're doing so well. They're going to win, aren't they.'

'Yes. Yes, it's a relief.' On the front pages, soldiers cheering, young men grimed from fighting; an occupying force, riding their tanks down between the frail houses, an army come to camp on foreign ground and drive stakes into the earth and begin to make things permanent; Europe, riding into Asia.

'I'm in Chelsea, is that far from you?'

'No. Not far.'

'I'm living with a fellow and we're opening a boutique.

I've done stacks of modelling for him, selling stuff. We've got some really wild clothes, you must come and see. I could probably get you some stuff at a discount, he usually lets me. He's a beaut man, he's called David Dawson, have you heard of him? And he's so rich you wouldn't believe it.'

'This is Fulham, you must be just up the road.' My voice, beside hers, sounds flat and dead. I wonder how we have changed during these years; then think, perhaps it was Israel, that level ground, where we could meet and see each other without misgiving. The possibility of meeting, now that we have talked, grows fainter. But I decide to make the effort, force the connection. 'Shall we meet for a drink? The pubs are open, aren't they? It'd be great to see you.'

'Okay. Dave's out chatting up some man who's going to do some pictures for us. We might be getting something on the cover of *Vogue*. Shall I come round to your place?'

'I'd rather come to a pub.' Light, noise, the clatter of glasses, Rowan talking, waving her hands, laughing as I remember; I must take this evening and use it for an antidote.

'I don't know many pubs. We generally drink at home, but most of the time we just smoke.'

'Smoke?'

'Shit. Hash. You know.'

'Oh, yes. Well, get on a bus, can you, and come right down the King's Road to Walham Green, and there's a pub there called the Falcon. It's a bit less trendy and ghastly than the ones further up. Half an hour?'

'I'll come in Dave's car. You'll recognise me, won't you? I'll be wearing ostrich feathers and driving an M.G.B. See you, then.'

'Sure. It's only five years.'

'Five years, Christ. Let's get pissed out of our heads. Good-bye.'

'Who was that?' Francis asks me, his mild voice rising from the book.

'Friend of mine from Israel. An Australian girl. I'm going out for a bit, just to have a chat, you know. I haven't seen her since we were in Israel. Won't be late.'

'Okay. See you.'

'See you.'

Going out, I do not look at him, but carry with me an impression of a darkening room, a lit sky beyond, birds against the window-panes, the long curved slump of his body, a small light upon the page. As the door opens again, the papers shift and rustle and resettle in their confusion, their corners lifted, ash blurs across a chair arm, the thick air is just slightly disturbed by my going. Slapping in sandals down the uncarpeted stair, I pause for a moment, struck by the fact that somebody has pulled a long strip of wallpaper away from the wall, leaving yellow distemper bare. In the dark pattern of roses and stripes, stained by the constant friction of passing bodies in greasy overcoats, the pushing shoulders of tenants, there is a scar of pale yellow. The paper hangs down, torn skin, never to look the same. I pick up the trailing piece, try to fit it back, try feebly for a moment to see it as it was; but one would need time, glue, patience; and there would always be that mark, that torn edge, it would not be worth it. And the paper itself is so ugly, so dull – the olive stripe, the seedy purple rose. I am surprised that I have not noticed before how ugly it is, that I have lived with it all this time. And the dirty carpet, the dull green linoleum that we never clean, the curtains, beige, drooping, that came with the flat. Tomorrow, I say as I rush on down the stairs, flip-flap, slip-slap towards the air, summer London, tomorrow I will get some new curtain material and some white paint and make it all look different.

When I got back, he was gone.

'You look a bit washed up,' Rowan says, her wide eyes painted with black, her face so smooth, her long brown wrists coming cleanly out of her shirt.

'He keeps talking about death.'

'Christ. I'm not sure I wouldn't rather it was other chicks.'

'At least one would know, I suppose. Is that what you have?'

'All the time. At least, I think so. He's beaut, really, but he's a randy bugger. But I guess I don't mind all that, so long as he doesn't ask too many questions about me.'

'You seem to go for them, don't you?'

'Hmm. D'you remember Lee?'

'Of course. And Larry. And Gina and Naphtali and Uri and Manny. It was an odd interlude, wasn't it?' Viewed now from another standpoint, an interlude, safely tucked in between two other spans of time. At the time we never said, what is it, what is it like?

'And those people from Jerusalem. He was in the paper.'

'No, who, Zvi?'

'I recognised the name.'

'Zvi Mosseri. What was it about? The war?'

'You quite fancied him, didn't you? Did you see him again? No, go on, have one of mine.'

'In Jerusalem I did. What was it about the war?'

'The bloody war, is that all you can talk about? You sound as if we were in it.'

'I feel as if it were in us.' To commit some violence, see some absolute thing, to find a relief; young men, Jews and sympathisers are sitting at airports now, waiting for the word that will summon them to action, embryo heroes, their heads drooping with fatigue. One could go; simply buy a ticket, contact an organisation, be involved. Here, our dirty beige curtains flutter against the windows, the light June breeze touches us and retreats, the creak of his chair sounds loud as he reaches for another cigarette, another book, as I simply sit and wait. In the pub, young men in pale butterfly-coloured shirts flit and posture over a bar billiards table; before me a blond head gleams under the light, a watch glass flashes as a wrist turns, eyes follow the aim of the cue across the soft baize of the table, there is a pause, a clicked shot, and the white ball rolls gently into the hole that awaited it.

'He's quite good, isn't he. We ought to have a game. Come on, Jo, you can't get worked up about something that's so far away, for God's sake.'

I no longer know what is far, what is near. Seeing her makes it so long ago, yet makes it real again. 'About Zvi. You were saying something about Zvi.'

'Oh, some organisation with some Arabs. I don't know exactly. Drink up, and we'll have the same again.'

Rowan is twenty-six now, my age. I see her sit, sipping her glass of Scotch, her long thin fingers with their polished nails lifting a cigarette to her lips; lips drawn firm in a decided line, beneath a thin high nose with wide nostrils that flare with smoke. Her eyes, very bright brown, glitter to and fro, as she watches the bar billiards players, the tension of their backs and buttocks as they plan a shot, and flash across to the clock to see the time, and rest for a moment upon me, ironic and questioning yet not wanting to be told too much. She sits upright, her back straight, her throat with its lines of tension softened by the collar of her blouse. Against the dark sweep of her hair, the ostrich feathers she promised me curl in a straggly turquoise tangle. I see rings, earrings, a chain disappearing in a thin gold line between her breasts, where beneath the transparent material she wears I see them sit cupped in a half-bra, in small, rather pathetic points, as if they have shrunk. Now that I see her there, I can no longer remember the girl who sprawled on the bed in that hut at Ein Gev, telling the Tarot pack while the night crawled past, and the heat stifled us, and there were men with guns a mile away; the girl who ran with arms stretched wide open across the stage in that night club, when Lee and Larry sang, and cried with easy emotion, and was setting off, her pointed chin held high, to conquer the West. Her wide, loud Australian voice seems to have been clipped; there is a little line between her eyes; now, she does not easily enthuse. I wonder what happened before the rich boutique owner and the covers for *Vogue*, how much struggle there was in between. A phrase comes back to me, something about lorry drivers never quoting Proust. She sighs and moves restlessly and smiles at me with a small guilty smile, apologising, and sips the rest of her drink and sits with her hands folded waiting for my suggestion.

'We must do this again.'

'You must meet Dave, he's beaut.'

'You must come round to my place.'

There is a mirror tipped behind us, in it her neat white back and crest of black hair, and the fake ostrich boa, and then my face, pale and unmade-up, my light hair cut in a straight fringe and falling, as it has ever since my childhood, a black jersey of Francis', too hot for the room. Outwardly, at a first glance, we do not change that much. But seeing Rowan makes me know something I had not suspected, that there is something that passes, that makes certain events irrevocably past; a change occurs that alters the balance, swings the needle up and down, creates irrelevancies, makes new things important. We are different people, and in five years, when she writes to me from New York, or visits me from Mexico, or sends a card written in Tangier, I will have moved again, and all this will have somehow been assimilated; all we will recognise in each other will be a movement, nearer or further, on or back. In neither of us is there any permanence; and now we look at each other seriously, with respect, recognising that this is a stage, a point, that we are about to move on.

When I got back, he was gone.

In a bedroom in East Anglia, the sound of pigeons' wings is so close that I think they are in the room with us, hanging above the mantelpiece, the constant movement of their wings keeping them poised in space. Dawn is beyond the uncurtained windows, the bed we have borrowed for the night has no sheets, only blankets, and they are rough enough to make my whole body itch. The first of sleepless nights, white nights, exactly a year ago in June. Outside the day is already preparing its narcotic heat. Here he turns to me twice in the night and burrows deep and comes with an explosion of tension. Fear moves in with us. I believe at first that it is a fear of me, of women, and grow protective as we have been taught to do, denying ourselves; but the fear comes for me too, it is something that we generate together. At this time I believe that it is my fault, that my consciousness, my will must be subjugated, that I must be all passive, all giving, that what he needs is the earth, that stability. The birds are always there, purring about the room, the sun always rises here, promising a burning day in the long Suffolk grasses, there is always a man there in the bed, needing something; I begin to distrust the particular. This is how, lacking confidence in ourselves, we begin to destroy.

'I'm sorry, Francis.' There is still as much aggression as contrition. He pretends not to hear, breathes like a man at peace. I hide beneath the blankets, an earth mother in no sense at all, my mind wandering to other things, with an attendant yet ever fainter sense of guilt. Sun begins to move across the floor; nearby a church clock strikes six. I watch the ruffled head beside me with apprehension. Our limbs grow clammy under the blankets, uncomfortably hot.

'I'm going to have a bath.' I mumble to him, unable to speak clearly, hoping that he will be too proud to relax his pretence, in case what I say may be disastrous. He breathes, his patrician profile lifted to show the open beauty of his lips. I could stay, I could ignore the rough hotness of blanket and my own anger, I could stay and be gentle and make it up. But I wind myself in a bath towel found upon the floor and open the door, knowing his eye furiously upon me. The passage is cool and dark and I feel the dust upon my feet. Somewhere near, according to my memory of the party last night, there is a bathroom. Doors, doors, the sealed entrances of a stranger's house; I pass them, my fingers feeling the wall for some familiarity. There is a chink of light, widening into a rose pink glow as I push the door wider; and there is the bath, central, its great clawed feet freestanding, its taps a curl of brass. The pink curtains are open to the morning, a tangle of tree tops and sun, the floor is warmed, the bath deep and long, made for a giant. I drop my towel and turn those great brass handles into action and watch the water spurt and steam, a solid fall, making the scarred white surface sing. The plug, a polished stopper, ringed like a bull's nose. The long dark streaks of discolouration, operation scars, islands. The sill at nose level a chemist's shop of bath oils, foaming lotions. I pick a bottle, pour drops, watch my Niagara turn bright green. In this I shall be purged, changed, from this I shall emerge green as an elf. I slip down the steep shore, splash into the heat, lie half submerged, a pink archipelago, watching the growth of day upon the pitted wall. There is no such pleasure, anywhere. And around me, knowing nothing about it, the house sleeps on, the guests all piled haphazardly into beds, assorted couples waking with a moan of pain, hosts regretting it all, children grizzling uncomforted, sleeping again; downstairs there is all the mess, the stained glasses and overflowing rubbish from ashtrays, the hard gnawed ends of bread, the antique furniture ringed with sticky marks, littered with salami rind and cigarette ends and burnt-out matches, exactly the same as ever. And here am I, scrubbed, floating in my green water, clean of the old clothes I wore, the old skin that smelt of sweat and perfume and cigarettes and sperm, that was rough as an oyster shell compared to this new tenderness; free, waterborne, myself again.

When I got back, he was gone.

I see it in the paper two days later, with only a faint shock, dulled by expectation; as old people, scanning the deaths column at breakfast, notice only faintly the announced departure of a contemporary, hardly remembered; with these old, I become a survivor through another's failure to survive. 'Old Arthur's gone at last, and poor Mrs Murgatroyd too.' For most of those who die here, in this country that is not at war, are old. The dimmed shock, the second-hand information processed kindly by the newspaper column, is reserved for the old; and I, like the old, have in my deepest mind expected it. The sharp, periodic attacks of guilt begin at once, every ten minutes like a muscular pain; it takes another day for me to understand any more, to realise that this is a road with no end, a story with no explanation. I will never find out any more. By killing himself he has made years of my life meaningless, devoid of any conclusion. A shutter comes down and all the rest of what would have happened is on its further side. There is nothing spectacular, nothing tragic, but a gap. Nothing. Nothing in any of the rooms of that deserted darkened house, so painfully explored. Nothing around any corner.

Dr Vidler is the only person apart from me whom he has seen regularly. The announcement in the paper '. . . suddenly, at his parents' house in Oxfordshire' is baffling. If they exist, why have they not been different, changed something; helped me? I hate them as one hates the thought of executioners, masked, blindfold, helplessly lifting the axe. And Vidler, the professional, why has he not acted? Why may I not have been warned? There is only an address to which flowers may be sent. I telephone, am told nothing, forget to arrange for any flowers. But scrawled on the front cover of the telephone directory is another number, Vidler's.

'Hallo? Could I speak to Dr Vidler, please?'

'I'm sorry, he's with a client at the moment. Who is it speaking, please?'

'He won't know me. I'm speaking on behalf of a patient – a client – of his. Somebody who was his client. Mr Allard. Could I make an appointment to see him, please?'

'Well, I'm afraid he's fully booked this week. Next Tuesday at ten-fifteen?'

'It's urgent. I must see him before that. Could you tell him I rang? Sometime today, I could come. Just for a few minutes.'

'I'm sorry, but you haven't told me your name.' I imagine a girl of my own age, sympathetic enough but with a large book before her, in which everything is urgent.

'It's Catterall. Miss Catterall.'

'I'll see what I can do.'

It is a tall white house in St John's Wood, a white-painted front door with a bay tree standing in a pot on each side of it, a wide clean rise of steps. A bell rings deep inside the house, disturbing the calm behind those drawn Venetian blinds. The girl is blond, in a short white overall with bare brown legs and sandals. The hall is cool, with ribbed grey paper, white dado and ceiling, the closed points of tulips again straight, in a vase. The waiting-room, striped with filtered sunlight, ruffled by the purring of a cat crouched upon the sill. The magazines are all new, the ones I can never afford, with models in lawn dresses riding camels across the

Sahara. The cat stretches and comes towards me and its fur is warm; otherwise, the room is like a dentist's or a gynaecologist's, empty and tidy, for paying patients only, an ante-chamber in which fear must be contained.

'Miss Catterall? Would you like to come this way?'

Allan, Asfordby, Barker, Bond, Byford, Cass, Catterall; a name in a string of names, before one, after another one in a line to be counted exactly like the rest. There is no Francis Allard any more.

'Won't you sit down?'

The room has that expanse of carpet, that air of awaiting confession. From somewhere else I remember two feet planted aggressively apart, two polished shoes. Here are the framed prints, the untouched furniture, the tray of coffee things, here the intruding sunlight, the silence before accusation.

'Oh, yes. Thank you.' There is a couch, of course, black leather, but the man himself stretches out on it, propped on one elbow so that it is I who sit upright and awkward on a chair, looking down on him. The cat begins to scratch at the door, its claws hooking the paintwork in a sound that grates.

'I suppose she'd better come in. Come on, Susie.' He has sprung up again and passed me to open the door, a slight, spare man, hair growing in long tufts behind his ears, his head poked forward like a bird's. Scooping up the little cat, he goes back to settle again, and the purring once again reverberates. The uncomfortable sensation persists, of reversed roles. In a minute he will lie back and close his eyes and begin to confess to me why he let Francis die. But his eyes remain bright, and open, and he says nothing.

'I haven't come for psycho-therapy.' My voice sounds thick, catarrhal.

'No?'

'No. I came because I'm a friend of Mr Allard's. Because he's dead.'

'I know.'

'I just wanted to talk to you about it. I thought you might know—'

'Why? Don't you?'

'Not really. Not completely.'

'You lived with him, didn't you?'

'Did he talk about me, then?'

'He has mentioned you, naturally.'

'Oh, yes, of course.'

'You blame me for it, then.'

'What? I don't know.'

'But you came to see me.' The cat, restless, shifts and kneads her claws, ripping the chair arm. His hand moves and soothes.

'Well, I suppose I do, partly. He was seeing you, after all.'

'Because I'm a psychiatrist? I should have stopped him?'

'Well, yes.'

'Somebody should have stopped him? But you didn't, and you lived with him.'

Tears pour down my face unexpectedly, I am sobbing with exhaustion. 'I'm sorry, I never cry usually, I'll be all right in a minute I expect.'

'That's all right. Lots of people do cry here. It's nothing to apologise for, is it?'

'No. No, I suppose not. But how could I have? You blame me for it, don't you? He sat here and talked about me and you think it was all my fault.' In this conversation there are no personalities. It is a play for voices. All the emotions, anger, mistrust, affection, hatred, seem to come to the surface one by one, erupting; and to die down again. The tone becomes level, like walking in the desert.

'Why must we blame each other? I blamed you, and you blamed me. But what is there to blame for? Did we misuse our power over him? Did we force him this way or that?'

'I don't know.'

'But you blamed yourself. When you said you blamed me, you meant you blamed yourself, didn't you?'

'Yes. I wasn't right for him. I was incredibly selfish about things. The day after he went away, I just went on going to work, correcting things and reading in the evening, making up games for the children. The ones I teach. I was just kind of relieved, to have a bit of peace.'

I begin to know that face so well, as Francis knew it, the wide open dark eyes, raised eyebrows, head poking eagerly, hands spread open before it in a fan shape, as if in self-defence, when I say something with which he cannot agree; against the light I see his thinning scalp, sun shining through the sparse black hairs. I know the hands, that always move slowly, gracefully, and the clothes he wears, and the smell in the room, of furniture polish and coffee and the scent that could belong to a woman who always sits here before I do, who may move in a cloud of it out down the hall, as I wait to be shown up the stairs. I know that his wife is dead, that the receptionist is his daughter, only pretending to be a receptionist, that the waiting-room where I sit and thumb magazines is his sitting-room, only he never has time to sit. I know that there is a dog locked in the back kitchen, that when he has seen me, late in the evening he lets himself and the dog out, and walks away, head jutting in the air, down the twilit, lamplit street, while the dog gallops, panting its relief.

'You say you weren't right for him. Was that your fault?'

'I don't know.'

'Or was it your parents' fault, or your education's fault, or the fault of the place where you were born, or of all the things that have happened to you, or of all the people who have affected you during your life?'

'All those things just go to make up what one is. It

could only be my fault, how I behave now. I'm responsible for myself.' The individual child, cut away from its mother at birth, through upbringing and education made more separate, more sharply defined. Unlike, in competition with, challenging others. Everywhere, the nurturing of the individual will; I will live, I will fulfil myself, I will make money, I will be famous; I am unique, and others less than I. Childhood, growing up, school. 'We like to think we cater for the individual. Knowledge no longer a common pool, but aggressively acquired. The common good, the shared objective, these are rejected, and once rejected only at a price regained. The journey alone, the return alone; the return to carve a life, "I am responsible for myself".

'Look at it this way. I was the wrong psychiatrist for him. If he'd seen a colleague of mine, X or Y, he might still have been alive. X might have sent him to a mental hospital and prescribed shock treatment or drugs which would have kept him quiet, Y might have asked him into his own home and spent every waking minute with him and held his hand and pretended to be his mother. Either way, he might still have been alive. I played it the way he wanted, which was to have a verbal fencing match with him once a week. So, you can say it is my fault.'

I stare at him, following the thread. 'It might be true, but one can't know. It can hardly be your fault.'

'So can we establish that the idea of blame is irrelevant?'

'Oh. I see. Yes.' I rub my eyes so that the air is patterned with red, and wonder what he feels, underneath the structure of his talk.

'You wanted to stop him doing it. You minded that he did not want to live. It hurt your pride. You wanted to have that power over him, to say, live; when he wanted to die.'

'I didn't want any power. I just believe life is better

than death, that it's a waste to die young. But you're right about the pride, yes, of course.' That one day somebody might say, as I had said in my mind to Zvi, through you I have seen life anew.

'If you believed that being a vegetarian is better than eating meat, would you have blamed yourself if he had eaten meat?'

'No, of course not.'

'Only if you believed that you had the right to order him, the power to force him to give up meat. But you didn't. You believe in the individual's right to choice, in his responsibility to himself. You don't subscribe to the notion that the group, or society, has the right to determine an individual's behaviour?'

I am silent, collecting the strands of my thoughts, the little haywire ends, the woolgatherings.

'You agree that we have moved beyond the coercive power of the group? In this country, after all, suicide is no longer a crime or a sin. The guilt we feel for a suicide is an archaism, a left-over from a previous age.'

I am thinking of marching men, their bronzed faces turning to smile over their shoulders, swinging, one-two, one-two, in brilliant sunlight.

'Jo?'

I face him, dazed. I tell him, 'You believed he shouldn't commit suicide, didn't you? You must have, or you couldn't be a doctor.'

'There was only one way I could have made sure of it. That would have been by force. As I say, I could have forced shocks or chemicals on him, I could have had him locked up where he had no weapons to hand. But he came here of his own choice. He was a rational man. He was sick, in a way, yes. But many people are sick in more destructive ways. He came to me because the process of psycho-therapy interested him, I think. He was interested in outwitting it. As a patient, he was hopeless. As a client, I mean.' He smiles as my eyes catch him out. 'I knew I could no more change his attitudes than I could the colour of his eyes. He had simply chosen death, as an alternative.'

Hundreds of younger men have died this week, by accident, or because they believed they should. Somewhere I read of the strangely high incidence of kibbutzniks' deaths. Good officer material, the printed line says, high morale. The smiling brown faces move on and on, the marching comfortably booted feet, further down the road.

'And what did you do then?' I ask him. He is sitting up now, both elbows on his knees. The cat, removed, sits aloof and angry on the chair back. Outside it is nearly dark.

'I tried to help him to accept himself, as he was. It was all I could do. I didn't want to change him. Did you?'

All is in flux, so that I could say anything, and only hearing myself speak, find it true, or untrue. Francis died in Oxfordshire, he lay down quite comfortably and ate a bottle full of his mother's sleeping-pills and washed them down with whisky. I imagine him lying, his look of perfect health. 'Often I wished he would behave differently. But it was stupid, I suppose. I suppose he couldn't help it.'

'Yes, he could help it. But you couldn't.'

'I loved him, sometimes. I thought that—'

'Love is easily confused with the wish to change people. I am sorry, I do believe you. Why did you love him?'

I say calmly, 'He was lovable, at times.'

'So are we all.'

'But there was something particular about him.'

'Something that you wanted?'

'Yes.'

'But found you couldn't have?'

'Yes. Yes. Something elusive.'

'It is in you. If you want it. It is in you too.'

The dialogues go on, while the June weather blooms outside and the chill late spring turns into a heat-wave. Morning and evening, in the spare hours before and after work, we sit and face each other and the exchange continues, interspersed only by a drawing of curtains, an opening and closing of doors, a difficult early-morning awakening and a rush through the London tube train crowds, here, there, home, to work and back. Nothing really obtrudes. The arguments, the images, live in my head as I travel to and fro. For the first time in my life I am aware of change as internal, a moving and shifting of horizons within these streets, these houses, my own skin, my own mind. Everything external remains the same. The days dawn with the same intensity of blue, end with the same long twilight. I see no new places, no sights to astonish and overwhelm; all the enterprise of journeying takes place in a shaded room, within the small confines of my skull; rocks shift, rivers stream, the desert places are crossed; this is how it feels at the time. The man opposite me says very little, but listens. Sometimes he lies sprawled on the black leather couch, and the little cat walks about on his limbs, sometimes I am there and he neat, legs crossed, in the chair. He does not smoke, and to begin with the ashtray beside me fills with stubs, but after a day or two I forget about it and realise I have stopped. Between us there is a sense of lassitude, as we sink into silence and allow the gradual appearance of thoughts, the unplanned sentences, the remarks with no apparent connection. He is tired after the strain of seeing people all day, and I am dusty and hot from the tube journey, my throat aches after hours of teaching. The children at school, in between, are an organised chorus of clamour, I hear their voices rise at me as I grow tired, I carry them about with me still. At the beginning I tell him that I have not come for psycho-therapy, meaning that I do not want to be bullied; I arrive with my accusation and it is as if this lays some ground of equality between us. Nobody has yet said, you are the patient, I am the doctor, the consultation is so much, the diagnosis is this. A responsibility to each other now that Francis is dead seems to link us. It is as if we are drawn together, after hours, by a common need.

'Good evening, Miss Catterall.'

'Good evening, Dr Vidler.'

Outside the plane trees grow a darker green, their trunks stripped in patches, enclosed in iron. Heat upon metal throughout the day has made the street throb. Our palms involuntarily seek cool surfaces.

'You are confused about something this evening.'

'I've just heard the war is over. I had forgotten about it.'

'War? D'you mean in the Middle East?'

'It's less than a week since Francis died. I'd been thinking about the war.'

'Does it have some special significance for you, then?' There are wars, after all, everywhere.

'I was in Israel, five years ago. I thought I might stay there once. But what I was wondering was, what does one do if one wins? Everybody thought Israel was the underdog, everybody was all prepared to be sorry for the Israelis and say how ghastly it was for them and even intervene on their behalf. But they've won. And if you win, if you survive, there are more problems than ever.'

'There will be blame.'

'Yes. Nobody will say, it was self-defence. There'll be prisoners of war and occupied territory and martial law.'

'Who will be to blame?'

'I dreamed I was in Israel. I always dream this dream, and it has no ending. It is as if I don't dare to dream the ending, as if it is already censored. And yet I know too that it has already happened. That it is too late.'

Rain falls on the roof and this time I am alone. The steady patter through the small hours of a summer morning, once the heat-wave has broken. It rains, and the streets are sodden, the cars swish every now and again past my window. When the rain stops I shall be asleep again. Now it is the pattern behind which is silence, it is the rhythm of my breathing. I shut my eyes to re-create for myself the noise of the taftaffit, that other scene, the precious water dropping through the bone-dry night. Once it was there at the lightest tap of water on the tiles, behind the red of closed eyelids, in the tropic heat of the brain; there to be conjured as lightly as any reality and savoured and stored again. This time I see the grey tiles, the sliding drops from the grey sky; English summer rain at dawn, drawing in a long soft day. I am alone and in the present. That is the reality now.

7

This is the present, for it will not pass away, however much one longs for its passing. It is the present towards which I have been moving. But I am lying, of course. There is always a next day, another time.

'And so this is not your first time here?' I sense a curiosity, when I tell them. Yes, I am old enough. It is not the first time. Ten years have passed, in dream, in reality. I say casually, 'I was here ten years ago.' We are a long way along the road; he has been talking to me for hours.

And the landscape flowers around us, the continuous smooth curve of green, olive in the shadows of the hills, the roads white and rough edged, fringed with growing things; the sky of late afternoon is all pure, cloudless, darkening early in springtime; there is a cooler, evening wind, we are in the desert, in the south, where each separate plant lifts its head in the breeze; where the silence aches in the bones, in the base of the skull, making speech an effort.

'Some people', he is saying, 'like to use politics to change things. Some, guns and politics. Others, only guns.'

'And you used just guns.'

'I was young. There was no time to think. I was imprisoned twice by the British, then I had time. In Jerusalem and then in Akko. Oh, but they were great days, then, idealistic days.'

The song on the radio shouts between us, men's voices singing in rough unison, as if they worked as they sang. A crackle on the wires; it is an old recording, twenty-five years old; he turns up the volume and looks at me, I see him listen with a smile on his lips, pride, anger, nostalgia in the compressed curve; his breath is indrawn for him to hear the last words. Then there is the sudden ending, the announcer of 1972 introduces something else. His hand grips the knob of the gear lever and the engine is allowed its full power again, the van accelerates. Two hands, broad and brown and capable, immense hands, control the engine, the left lightly pushing the wheel, the right upon the gear handle as we turn and climb the faint incline, over the green furred breast of the hill. The shallow lands at last fall away before us like the sea.

'Was that when you learnt English? You speak very good English.'

'English and other things. I decided to leave, I wanted when I came out to be a soldier, just a soldier. I was always a fighter, I was born, I knew I would be a fighter. But it's not so easy, leaving the Irgun, you know. People said there was only one way out; death; they would always try to find you. But I managed, and I've been a soldier ever since. I've fought for my country in three wars.' He turns his hand over and shows me the clear white scar running across the palm and up the wrist, disappearing into the rolled shirt-cuff. 'Bayonet.'

On the back seat, rolling together as the van rocks over stones in the pitted road, the two children giggle and clutch their fingers to their mouths, bored with reverence, with the old stories. The mother, wrapped in black beside him, turns to frown, the corners of her mouth drawn down. She is all Russian, strong-boned, immovable. The children glance at me and giggle again and slide about on the seat, twitching their frail legs, flattening their slight thighs upon the plastic. Their bones show like birds' through the tan and the fine drawn skin, they are about eight and ten years old, a boy and a girl, garlanded in white dying flowers from the desert, their black hair tangled from the wind and dusted with pollen. Behind us the road stretches away between the endless hills to Eilat, before to Beersheva; there is only this road, the way through the flowering wilderness.

'Uri!' His wife shrieks, the van stops, a rattle of metal, the brakes noisy.

'What? What happened?' There is only the far black blur of a Bedouin shepherd and his flock upon the hill. But we are all out of the van, tumbled upon the roadside. 'The flowers,' she explains to me. 'Look.'

In the long flowering grasses, between poppy and yellow cactus, tall violet flowers are growing, their large heads drooping from the stem, the dark eye at the centre turned downwards.

'Do you have these in England?'

'No. No, we don't.'

'They are protected, here. Nobody must pick them. She drops upon her knees, heavy and yet graceful, her face turned delicately to the flowers to catch their scent.

'We learned it in school,' the girl says to me carefully, speaking English. 'Then we tell our parents.'

'They teach the children which flowers are protected by law,' her father says more fluently, at ease with me after the years in British jails, 'and then the children tell the parents. So gradually everybody gets to know. And that way the flowers are not picked.' He lies upon his stomach, a big man flattening the grasses, and holds a camera steady, the lens inches from the plant. The click moves the silence. The flowers shake in the wind and their shadows grow longer, striping the deep green. Already there is the yellow line of evening lying smooth along the hills; the shepherd, blackened, becomes one with the outline of rocks. And we clamber back into the hot petrol-smelling interior of the van and the engine churns between us, making our voices faint. I think of the flowers existing unseen, now that nobody wants to pull them out and break their roots open and leave them to die in jars.

'I was in the liberation, in forty-eight, and then in the Sinai campaign, and then in the Six Day War.'

The talk, like the engine, starts up easily again where it was left. 'Have you been in the Sinai yet? No?' The gears change, again his hand relaxes. 'As I said, I am an old fighter. But I want peace. Of course. That is true of our army, we fight well but we want peace.'

'Do you think you will ever have it?' I speak guardedly, saying this because his pause demands it, because he wants to be sure that I am listening. At the roadside young camels beside their mothers raise their heads and stare mildly; against the older camels' stark lines there is the baby woolliness still.

'Peace? With these Arabs? Impossible.'

And, 'Look! Abba!' The little girl, Shoshana, cries out again, and the van brakes, and we all peer. 'What is it? Do you see him?'

A great bird hangs in the sky, darkening the sun. His wings seem to shudder and yet he hardly moves. He is above us, poised and predatory, his shadow still upon the earth. And then he falls and is gone.'

'Was it an eagle?' Against the emptiness of clear sky and the wide land, it was so big a bird that I can only imagine.

'No, some kind of hawk. You saw how he fell. He's hunting his supper. They wait high up until they're sure of their mark, and then they dive.' Again the engine throbs louder and we rush along the deserted road, flying over the ruts.

'Why do you say it's impossible?' Hardened, now I will press him, force him back.

'Because of their morale. They want to fight. It is their religion. Revenge, bloodshed, it is all they know.'

'But surely it's their leaders. They're duped by their leaders. Manipulated. I'm sure no Arab soldiers really want war.' How the phrases sound, stale and colourless.

Five years, ten years gone. He looks at me sharply, with an assessing glance.

'You don't know. I say, it is their religion. There will be nothing good in those countries until the last bit, the last remains of Islam is taken away from them. Cut out, thrown away, finished. Until they lose this stupid religion, until they change their culture, their politics.'

'To what? Real socialism?'

'Communism. Of course, communism; what else can do it?'

There is silence. The children begin to yawn and moan quietly, and we will soon be in Beersheva. Hannah, their mother, settles as if to sleep and yet is listening, her black eyes half open. At our side on a stretch of young green grass stand two rusted tanks, their wheels sinking into the earth. Between and among them, the furry black goats of the Bedouin graze, their strong little legs strutting. A small boy scrambles down the slope towards the road, clutching in his arms a wet black kicking creature.

'Look, it's newborn. Do you see the kid?'

The boy in his tatters stands to stare after the car, his muscles clenched to hold the little goat. His hair is tinged reddish, his eyes are screwed up and his mouth gapes, to see more clearly. The goats behind him move in a rush, jostling each other.

'Whose are those?'

'The tanks? The goats? Russian tanks. From the last war.' Scrap metal, not yet worn away to dust by the passage of elements; I see them last as fingers against the sky.

'Where did you want to go, did you say? You want to go to Jerusalem tonight?'

'Yes. But I can get a bus from Beersheva.' The sun is setting, Shabbat and their holiday nearly over.

'You are sure? You are sure there is a bus from Beersheva tonight?' They are all solicitude for me, a stranger.

'Yes, yes, I think so.'

'Because we can take you up to the Tel Aviv road. We are going to Tel Aviv, you see, we could take you up and drop you where we join the road to Jerusalem, and you might get a bus from there more easily, or perhaps catch a tram.'

'Well, yes. If you're going that way. That's very kind of you. Thank you.' The children rock asleep against each other's shoulders after the long day, the sea air of Eilat, the hours' drive through the empty hills. I sit forward, shivering in my light clothes, watching the coming darkness and the road.

'What's that?' A grey fortress, square, windowless.

'The prison.'

'Oh.' My tone must have told him of my distaste.

'But that's what civilisation needs, isn't it? You can't have civilisation without these things. Prisons, rubbish tips. The more civilisation, the more rubbish.'

'It depends what you mean. . . .' The English argument, the scrupulous meaningless definitions; he is not interested, not listening. While we pause, sort, define and classify, the world looks away. On the darkening road a large group of Bedouin move aside in a flowing motion as we pass; they are going home, driving the goats and the compact little pale-brown sheep before them, they are boys with long sticks and women heavy with purple embroidery, and they all stare.

The driver says, 'Well, they don't need rubbish tips. They are rubbish.' He laughs noisily, but his children and his wife are dozing and so do not take their cue; I say nothing, nobody laughs with him, so he says it again. 'And they don't need lavatories, they are—'

I am silent, feeling a long needle enter under my skin, wondering how far it will go before anaesthesia begins. There is nothing to say. One must say something. There must be something to say. And either my silence makes him angry or some long buried spark in him ignites, spreading friction and fire through his whole being, for he begins to shout over his shoulder to me, ignoring his sleeping family, hardly watching the road; he shouts against my silence and my lack. 'You don't care about it, you don't care what happens to us. You will go home and write about it perhaps and say, what a pity, what a shame those people were wiped out; just as you said about the people in Bangladesh when the Pakistanis came and murdered them and left their children to starve. Send some blankets, send some tins. That's all you will say. Send some blankets to Israel. You don't care, you in England. What's your foreign secretary doing now but talking to that stupid Sadat? What did you do about Bangladesh? They were eating human flesh, those Pakistani soldiers, they were cannibals. What did you eat in England? Oh, it's nothing, it's just politics to you, foreign affairs, something happening in a backward little corner of the world. Do you know what they will do to us, these Arabs? I cannot tell you, you would be too afraid, you would not believe me. They are savages, they have a dirty army, they only know how to behave like animals. But you will not care. You will write about it. You will make a nice story, of how men died like dogs. Writing, what use is that? Who can you save? And what can you change? But you do not care, you are not interested.'

And now it is completely dark. We come to the outskirts of Beersheva and see the random dotted lights, closer, the lines of street lights yellow under the stars; the spiked leaves of the palm trees that go in an arid line down the middle of the road, growing in dust; the white outlines of houses, miles of them, built upon stilts, their shuttered windows and shallow balconies identical. Wind blows sheets of paper up against lamp posts and bus stops, orange peel and cellophane and old newspapers lie in the gutters, there are people strolling along slowly, going nowhere. We pass the green and red lights of the cinema and drive between flat spaces where there is only rubble, rocks, weeds, corrugated iron. There was once a small desert town out of a cowboy film, from where I took a bus to visit Gilbert. There was once Gilbert, who is dead. On the edges of the new estates that are eating patches out of the desert, houses of one storey stretch their reinforcement out of the concrete, waiting for the next floor; in silhouette, it is like a bone protruding. And then there are the sculptures, the hands that men have flung up against the sky, the exclamation points of progress. Beside them we are dwarfed and make no mark.

The silence that lasts for minutes is ended by our entry into the town. The needle has gone in, the numbness begins. He starts to talk again as if nothing has happened. 'I was one of the first here, in forty-eight. When we captured the town. I was one of the reconnaissance men. I had to come in and find out what it was like.'

'And what was it like?'

'A filthy little Arab town. There was nothing here. And now look at it.'

To eyes grown used over two days to the beauty of the Negev in spring there is a brutality, a shocking callousness of built form. And yet there are houses, schools, hospitals, clinics; this is what grows upon the razed earth, between the tin cans and the hoardings. Who can you save? And what can you change? The nerve begins to throb again.

'I'll get the bus to Jerusalem. I'm sure there is one, they said there'd be one tonight. Could you please drop me here after all?'

'Of course.' He turns the van towards the bus station and we pass the clutter of the market, now housed in concrete, where a man sells nuts and melon seeds in small paper bags, and a café or two are open, and a few Arabs in European dress, their white kefiyah alone marking them out, sit about at little tables drinking cheap brandy, count payment from rolls of notes, slip out again into the night. At the bus station the van waits, the engine running, as I ask about buses; in case I may return. The children are awake now and sit up, ruffled like young birds, watching me pick up my paper carriers. I take their hands, the warm slippery paws of the young. And as he says goodbye to me, and smiles between deep creases of good humour, bearing me no ill will, I take the calloused, capable and therefore reassuring hand of the man from the Irgun. For that is how I think of him, although times have changed.

Lightning Source UK Ltd.
Milton Keynes UK
UKHW042157130122
396988UK00006B/88